WILLIAM
THE OUTLAW

RICHMAL CROMPTON

FOREWORD BY FRANCESCA SIMON

ILLUSTRATED BY THOMAS HENRY

MACMILLAN CHILDREN'S BOOKS

First published 1927
This selection first published 1984 by Macmillan Children's Books

This edition published 2011 by Macmillan Children's Books
a division of Macmillan Publishers Limited
20 New Wharf Road, London N1 9RR
Basingstoke and Oxford
Associated companies throughout the world
www.panmacmillan.com

ISBN 978-0-330-54524-2

repr
transn
photo
permiss
ac

A CIP catalogue record for this book is available from the British Library.

Typeset by SX Composing DTP, Rayleigh, Essex
Printed and bound in the UK by CPI Mackays, Chatham ME5 8TD

CONTENTS

FOREWORD

William Brown terrified me. I'd never heard of him when I was growing up in America, but once I'd come to Britain and started writing *Horrid Henry* I couldn't escape him. Whenever I told anyone what Horrid Henry was like, they invariably said, 'Oh, he sounds exactly like a modern-day Just William.'

These are words guaranteed to horrify any writer. Who was this William anyway? Had I accidentally copied him? Was I doomed so early in my career? NOOOOOOOOOOOOOOO!!!

I didn't dare open a William book until I'd written four Horrid Henry's. Then I bravely thought it was time. I'd established Henry and his family, and was hopefully safe from being unduly influenced. So I borrowed a Martin Jarvis recording from the library, and one memorable day, travelling by car to France with my husband and young son, I pressed Play.

And what total joy awaited us. First that Horrid Henry was actually very different from William, who is so much kinder, and often well-intentioned, and not motivated at all by sibling rivalry. *That* was a great relief. Now I could just enjoy the sheer brilliance and humour of Richmal Crompton's iconic character.

Why is William so wonderful? First and foremost, he's hilarious. He is also indomitable, imaginative, fearless, spontaneous, resilient and constantly puncturing the pretensions of the rigid society he's trapped in. He is never defeated, never civilized into the proper, conforming little boy his parents long for. ('He's a bit – individualistic,' grimaces William's hapless father to a schoolteacher who promises – as if – to tame him.)

Instead William is in perpetual revolt against the conventional world his parents are trying to shove him into, sabotaging fetes, thwarting field trips, swapping Christmas gifts (why should the Infants get smaller gifts than the OAPs?). In the story 'Finding a School for William', Mrs Brown thinks wistfully about the bliss of a sedate, shiny-shoed boy with plastered down hair, instead of her own leaping, diving, tree-climbing, shouting, toe-dragging urchin.

We know better. Who wouldn't want to join the Outlaws 'on their paths of lawlessness and hazard' rather than sticking to the paved road?

But why do we all love mischievous, rebellious characters (at least safely tucked within the pages of a book)? Why didn't Richmal Crompton write about Hubert Lane and his followers? Or make Georgie Murdoch, from my favourite story 'Georgie and the Outlaws', with his impeccable manners and his hatred of mud and dirt and rough games, her hero?

Quite simply, I think William's imaginative engagement and delight in his world reconnect us all to the liberating energy of the child we once were. He's the person we wish we dared to be. We all enjoy reading about people who go against convention, and get a thrill from someone who acts on impulse and never worries about the consequences. In real life if you pass a door marked 'No Entry' you walk on by. William barges right through it. And – joy of joys – we get to enter with him.

Francesca Simon

CHAPTER 1

WILLIAM THE OUTLAW

WILLIAM and Ginger and Douglas and Henry (known as the Outlaws) walked slowly down the road to school.

It was a very fine afternoon – one of those afternoons which, one feels – certainly the Outlaws felt – it is base ingratitude to spend indoors. The sun was shining and the birds were singing in a particularly inviting way.

'G'omtry,' said William with scornful emphasis and repeated bitterly, '*G'omtry!*'

'Might be worse,' said Douglas, 'might be Latin.'

'Might be better,' said Henry, 'might be singin'.'

The Outlaws liked singing lessons not because they were musical, but because it involved no mental effort and because the master who taught singing was a poor disciplinarian.

'Might be better still,' said Ginger, 'might be nothin'.'

The Outlaws slackened their already very slack pace and their eyes wandered wistfully to the tree-covered hill-tops which lay so invitingly in the distance.

'Afternoon school's all *wrong*,' said William suddenly. 'Mornin's bad enough. But *afternoon*—!'

That morning certainly had been bad enough. It had been the sort of morning when everything goes wrong that can go wrong. The Outlaws had incurred the wrath of every master with whom they had come in contact.

'An' *this* afternoon!' said Ginger with infinite disgust. 'It'll be worse even than an ordinary afternoon with me havin' to stay in writin' lines for old Face.'

'An' me havin' to stay in doin' stuff all over again for ole Stinks.'

It turned out that each one of the four Outlaws would have to stay in after afternoon school as the victim of one or other of the masters whose wrath they had incurred that morning.

William heaved a deep sigh.

'Makes me feel *mad*,' he said. 'Miners havin' Trades Unions an' Strikes an' things to stop 'em doin' too much work an' *us* havin' to go on an' on an' *on* till we're wore out. You'd think Parliament'd stop it. People go on writin' in the papers about people needin' fresh air an' then 'stead of lettin' people *have* fresh air they shut 'em up in schools all day, mornin' *an'* afternoon, till – till they're all wore out.'

'Yes,' said Ginger in hearty agreement. 'I think that there oughter be a law stoppin' afternoon school. I think that we'd be much healthier in every way if someone made a law stoppin' afternoon school so's we could get a bit of fresh air. I think,' with an air of unctuous virtue, 'that it's our juty to tr'n get a bit of fresh air to keep us healthy so's to save our parents havin' to pay doctor's bills.'

Ginger ignored the fact that so far no one in all his healthy young life had ever paid a doctor's bill for him.

'I've a good mind to be a Member of Parliament when I grow up,' threatened Douglas, 'jus' to make all schools have a holiday in the afternoons.'

'*An*' the mornin',' added Henry dreamily.

But, attractive as this idea was, even the Outlaws felt it was going rather too far.

'No, we'll *have* to keep mornin' school,' said Douglas earnestly, ''cause of – 'cause of exams an' things. An' school-masters'd all starve if we didn't have *any* school.'

'Do 'em good,' said Ginger bitterly and added, darkly, 'I'd jolly well make some laws about school-masters if I was a Member of Parliament.'

'What I think'd be a good idea,' said William, 'would be jus' to have school on wet mornin's. Not if it's fine 'cause of gettin' a little fresh air jus' to keep us healthy.'

This was felt by them all to be an excellent idea.

'The rotten thing about it is,' went on William, 'that by the time we're in Parliament makin' the laws we'll be makin' it for *other* people an' too late to do *us* any good.'

'An' it seems hardly worth botherin' to get into Parliament jus' to do things for other people,' said Ginger the egoist.

They were very near the school now and instinctively had slowed down to a stop. The sun was shining more brightly than ever. The whole countryside looked more inviting than ever. There was a short silence. They gazed from the school building (grim and dark and uninviting) to the sunny hills and woods and fields that surrounded it. At last William spoke.

'Seems *ridic'lous* to go in,' he said slowly.

And Ginger said, still with his air of unctuous virtue, 'Seems sort of *wrong* to go when we reely don't believe that we oughter go. They're always tellin' us not to do things our conscience tells us not to do. Well, *my* conscience tells me not to go to school this afternoon. My conscience tells me that it's my *juty* to go out into the fresh air gettin' healthy. My conscience—'

Douglas interrupted gloomily: ''S all very well talkin' like that. You know what'll happen to us tomorrow morning.'

The soaring spirits of the Outlaws dropped

abruptly at this reminder. The general feeling was that it was rather tactless of Douglas to have introduced the subject. It was difficult after that to restore the attitude of reckless daring which had existed a few minutes before. It was William of course who restored it, swinging well to the other extreme in order to repair the balance.

'Well, we won't go tomorrow mornin' either,' he said. 'I'm jolly well sick of wastin' my time in a stuffy old school when I might be outside gettin' fresh air. Let's *be* Outlaws. Let's be *real* Outlaws. Let's go right away somewhere to a wood where no one'll find us an' live on blackberries an' roots an' things an' if they come out to fetch us we'll climb trees an' hide or run away or shoot at 'em with bows an' arrows. Let's go'n' live all the rest of our lives as Outlaws.'

And so infectious was William's spirit, so hypnotic was William's glorious optimism that the Outlaws cheered jubilantly and said, 'Yes, let's . . . *Hurrah!*'

'And never go to school no more,' said Douglas rapturously.

'No, never go to school no more,' chanted the Outlaws.

They decided not to go home for provisions because their unexpected presence there would be sure to raise comment and question.

And as William said, 'We don't *want* any food but

blackberries an' mushrooms an' roots an' things. People used to live on roots an' I bet we'll soon find some roots to live on. It'll be quite easy to find what sort to eat and what sort not to eat. An' we'll kill rabbits an' things an' make fires an' cook them. That's what real Outlaws did, an' we're real Outlaws now. An' we don't want any clothes but what we've got. When they fall to pieces we'll make some more out of the skins of rabbits we've killed to eat. That's what real Outlaws did, I bet.'

'Where'll we go to?' said Douglas. William considered.

'Well,' he said, 'we must be in a wood. Outlaws are always in woods 'cause of hiding an' eating the roots and things. And we oughter be on a hill 'cause of seeing people comin' when they come tryin' to catch us—'

'Ringers' Hill, then,' said Ginger blithely.

Ringers' Hill was both high and wooded.

The Outlaws cheered again. They were still drunk with the prospect of freedom, intoxicated by William's glorious optimism. They marched down the road that led away from the school singing lustily. The Outlaws were very fond of community singing. They liked to sing different songs simultaneously. William in sheer lightness of heart was singing – very unsuitably – 'Home Sweet Home', Ginger was singing, 'We won't go to school no more', to the tune of 'It ain't go'n rain no more', Douglas was singing 'Shepherd of the Hills', and Henry was singing 'Bye-bye, Blackbird'.

Suddenly two of their class-mates – Brown and Smith – came round the corner on their way to school. They looked at the Outlaws in surprise. Brown was deprived of the power of speech by a twopenny bull's eye of giant proportions which he had just purchased at the village shop, but Smith said, 'Hello! You're going the wrong way.'

'No, we aren't,' said William blithely, 'we're going the right way.'

Brown made an inarticulate sound through his bull's eye, meant to convey interest and interrogation, and Smith, interpreting it, said, 'Where are you going?'

'To Ringers' Hill,' said William defiantly and passed on, leaving Brown and Smith gazing after them amazedly.

'You di'n' ought to have told them,' said Ginger. But William was in a mood of joyous defiance.

'I don't care,' he said, 'I don't care who knows. I don't care who comes to fetch us home. We won't go. We'll climb trees an' shoot at 'em and throw stones at 'em. I bet no one in the whole world'll be able to catch us. I'm an Outlaw I am,' he chanted. 'I'm an Outlaw.'

Again his spirit infected his followers. They cheered lustily. 'We're Outlaws, we are,' they chanted, 'we're Outlaws.'

*

They sat under the largest tree on Ringers' Hill. They had been Outlaws now for half an hour and it somehow wasn't going as well as they'd thought it would. Douglas, wishing to test the food-producing properties of the place at once, had eaten so many unripe blackberries that he could for the time being take little interest in anything but his own feelings. Ginger had from purely altruistic motives begun to test the roots and was already regretting it.

'Well, I din' ask you to go about eatin' roots,' said William irritably. William had for the whole half hour been trying to light a fire and was by this time feeling thoroughly fed up with it. He had just used the last of a box of matches which he had abstracted from the lab that morning.

'I did it for *you*,' said Ginger indignantly, 'I did it to find the sort of roots that people eat, so you'd be able to eat 'em. Well, you can jolly well find your own roots now and I jolly well hope you find the one I did – the last one. It's the sort of taste that goes on for ever. I don' s'pose if I go on livin' for years an' years, I'll ever get the taste of it out of my mouth—'

'*Taste!*' said Douglas bitterly. 'I wun't mind a *taste* . . . it's *pain* I mind – *orful* pain – gnawin' at your inside.'

'I wish you'd shut up,' said William yet more

irritably, 'an' help me with this fire. All the wood seems to be damp or somethin'. I can't get anythin' to *happen*.'

'Blow it,' suggested Ginger, taking his mind temporarily from his taste.

Douglas, tearing himself metaphorically speaking from his pain, knelt down and blew it.

It went out.

William raised his blackened face.

'That's a nice thing to do,' he said bitterly. 'Blowin' it out. All the trouble I've had lightin' it an' then you jus' go an' *blow* it out. An' there isn't another match.'

'Well, it'd've *gone* out if we hadn't *blown* it out,' said Ginger optimistically, 'so it doesn't matter. Anyway, let's do somethin' int'restin'. We've not had much fun so far – eatin' roots an' things an' messin' about with fire. We don't want a fire yet. It's warm enough without a fire. Let's leave it till tonight when we need a fire, to sleep by and to keep the wild animals off. We'll light one with,' vaguely, 'flint an' steel lyin' about anywhere. But we won't light another now. We're all sick of it and if we go burnin' up all the firewood in the wood an'—'

'All right,' said William, impressed by the sound logic of the argument, 'I don't mind. I'm jus' about sick of it. I've simply wore myself out with it an' you've not been much help, I must say.'

'ALL THE TROUBLE I'VE HAD LIGHTIN' IT AN' THEN YOU
JUS' GO AN' BLOW IT OUT.'

'Well, I like *that*,' said Douglas, 'an' me nearly
dyin' of agony from blackberries.'

'An' me riskin' my life testin' roots,' said Ginger. 'I
can still taste it – strong as ever. It seems to be gettin'
stronger 'stead of weaker. It's a wonder I'm alive at all.
Not many people'd suffer like what I've suffered an'
still go on livin'. If I wasn't strong I'd be dead of it
now.'

Douglas, stung by Ginger's self-pity, again rose to the defence of his own martyrdom.

'A *taste*,' he said. 'I could stand any amount of tastes. I—'

At this moment a diversion was caused by the return of Henry. Henry had been out to catch rabbits to cook over the fire for supper. He looked hot and cross.

'Couldn't catch any,' he said shortly. 'I saw a lot on the other side of the hill. I hid behind a tree till they came out an' then I ran out after them, and I'm absolutely wore out with runnin' out after them an' I've not caught one.'

'Let's go down to the river,' said Ginger, 'I'm jus' about sick of messin' about here. There isn't anything to *do* here, 'cept eat roots, an' I've had enough of that.'

'No,' said William firmly, 'we've gotter stay up here. If we go down an' they start comin' out to fetch us home they'll overpower us easy. It's a – a sort of vantage ground up here. We can see 'em comin' up here an' escape or throw things down on 'em.'

'Well, I'm sick of stayin' up here,' said Ginger.

'Think of 'em,' said William tactfully, 'doin' *G'omtry* at school.'

At this the Outlaws' discontent faded and their spirits rose.

'Hurrah!' said Ginger, who now had completely forgotten his taste, 'and I bet we can easy make up a game to play here an'—'

'*Look!*' gasped Douglas suddenly, pointing down into the valley.

The Outlaws looked.

Then they stood motionless as if turned to stone.

There was no doubt about it.

Down in the valley coming along the path that led up to Ringers' Hill could be seen the figures of the headmaster and the second master.

For some moments horror and surprise robbed the Outlaws of the power of speech.

Then William said:

'*Crumbs!*' but no words could describe the tone in which he said it.

'They're – they're comin' after us,' gasped Ginger.

'Smith must have told him where we'd gone,' gasped Henry.

Ginger, recovering something of his self-possession, turned to William.

'I *said* you din' oughter've *told* him,' he said with spirit.

'B-but,' gasped William, still paralysed with amazement, 'how'd he know we're Outlaws an' never goin' back?'

'Prob'ly Smith heard us sayin' it,' said Ginger.

'Well, it's a nice set-out, isn't it? What we goin' to do? Fight him?'

Even William's proud spirit quailed at the thought of doing that.

'If – if only—' he began.

Then his speech died on his lips. His mouth dropped open again. His eyes dilated with horror and amazement. Behind the figure of the headmaster and second master came other figures – the mathematical master, the gym master, three or four prefects.

'They're all comin'!' gasped William, 'they're comin' to take us by force. They – they're goin' to surround the hill and take us by force.'

'Crumbs!' said Ginger again. '*Crumbs!*'

'What'll we do?' gasped Douglas.

They looked at William and into William's freckled face came a set look of purpose.

'Well, we've gotter do *something*,' he said. He scowled ferociously, then a light flashed over his face. 'I know what we'll do. Smith must jus' simply have told 'em "Ringers' Hill". That's what we told him, "Ringers' Hill". Well, you remember the signpost thing at the bottom of the hill with "Ringers' Hill" on it?'

Yes, they remembered it – a wobbly, decrepit affair at the bottom of the hill.

William's face was now fairly gleaming with his idea.

'Well,' he said, 'you remember it was all loose in its hole? I bet if we pushed hard we could push it right round so's the 'Ringers' Hill' pointed right on up the other hill. An' I bet they don' know this part 'cause they don't live here an' they never come here so I bet – well, let's try anyway, an' we'd better be jolly quick.'

Behind their leader they scrambled down the hillside to the signpost.

'Now *push*!' directed William.

The Outlaws pushed.

The signpost rocked in its hole and – joy! – slowly pivoted round in obedience to the Outlaws' straining weight. The solitary arm bearing the legend 'Ringers' Hill' now pointed to the hill in the opposite direction.

The Outlaws' spirits rose.

They gave a cautious muffled cheer.

'Now *quick*, back again to the top!' said William and they scrambled once more to the hilltop.

The procession led by the headmaster was approaching.

'Lie down under the bushes,' hissed William, 'so's they won't see you. An' watch what they do.'

Breathless with apprehension the Outlaws crouched under the bushes and watched. They could see the procession come up the road – nearer, nearer. Then – the headmaster paused under the signpost. The Outlaws held their breath. Did he know the lie of the land or would he be deceived? Evidently he didn't know the lie of the land.

'Here we are,' he called out. 'Here's the signpost – Ringers' Hill – up there.'

Slowly the procession passed on up the other hillside.

The Outlaws climbed out of their bushes. They still looked rather pale. 'That was a *jolly* narrow shave,' said Ginger.

'What we'd better do now,' said William grimly, 'is to look for a proper hidin' place case they find out an' come back.'

So intent had they been on looking down at the side of the hill where the dread procession was wending its way that they had not noticed an enormous man with bushy eyebrows and a generally ferocious aspect who was climbing up the hill from the other side. They did not in fact notice him until he had come up behind them and his gruff voice boomed:

'Well, is this all there is of you?'

The Outlaws turned round with a start.

There was a tense silence.

The Outlaws, having, as they thought, narrowly saved themselves from destruction on one side of the hill, were quite unprepared for this attack from the other. It unnerved them. It paralysed them. They had

BREATHLESS WITH APPREHENSION THE OUTLAWS
CROUCHED UNDER THE BUSHES AND WATCHED. THEY
COULD SEE THE PROCESSION COME UP THE ROAD –
NEARER, NEARER.

no reserve of ingenuity and aplomb with which to
meet it.

William gulped and blinked and said, 'Yes.'

'*All?*' boomed the ferocious man, 'well, all I can say
is that it's hardly worth my while to come all this way
for you. I'd understood that it was quite a different
sort of affair altogether. Do you mean to say that there
are only *four* of you?'

THEN – THE HEADMASTER PAUSED UNDER THE
SIGNPOST. 'HERE WE ARE,' HE CALLED OUT. 'HERE'S
THE SIGNPOST – RINGERS' HILL – UP THERE.'

William felt that he had done all that could be
expected of him and nudged Ginger.

'Er – yes,' quaked Ginger.

'Only *four* of you,' said the ferocious man
ferociously, 'and how old?'

Douglas and Henry had slunk behind William and
Ginger. Ginger nudged William to intimate that it was
his turn.

William swallowed and said feebly, 'Eleven – eleven and nearly three-quarters.'

'Pish!' said the man in a tone of fierce disgust. 'Eleven! As I say I'd never have agreed to come if I'd known it was this sort of an affair. I naturally imagined – however, now I'm here – and it's late to start with –' He looked at them and seemed to relent somewhat, 'I gathered that you know a fair amount about the subject and you must be keen. I suppose one should be thankful for four keen students even though they seem so very – however,' his irritability seemed to get the better of him again, 'let's get to business. We'll start over here . . . quickly please,' he snapped, 'or we'll never get through this afternoon—'

Dazedly, as if in a dream, the Outlaws went to where he pointed. They didn't know what else to do. The situation seemed to have got entirely out of hand. It seemed best to follow the line of least resistance and to give themselves away as little as possible. They stood in a dejected group in front of the ferocious man and the ferocious man began to talk. He talked about such things as strata and igneous rock and neolithic and eolithic and palaeolithic and stratigraphical and Pithecanthropus erectus and other things of which the Outlaws had never heard before and hoped never to hear again. He asked them questions and got angry because they didn't know the answers. He asked them

what he'd said about things and got angry because
they'd forgotten. He strode about the hilltop pointing
out rocks with his stick and talking about them in a
loud, ferocious voice. He made them follow him
wherever he went, and got angry because they didn't
follow nimbly enough. So terrifying was he that they
daren't even try to run away. It was like a nightmare.
It was far worse than Geometry. And it seemed to last
for hours and hours and hours. Actually it lasted an
hour. At the end the man became more angry than
ever, said that it was an insult to have asked him to
come over to address four half-witted guttersnipes and
muttering ferociously stalked off again down the
hillside.

The Outlaws sat down weakly on the ground
around the little heap of black twigs and dead leaves
which marked the scene of William's failure as a fire-
maker and held their heads.

'Crumbs!' moaned William, and Ginger mournfully echoed, 'Crumbs!'

'Well, anyway, he's gone,' said Henry trying to
look on the bright side.

But it wasn't really easy to look on the bright side.
The Outlaws were feeling very hungry and there
wasn't anything to eat. Ringers' Hill had lost its
charm. They'd had a rotten time there – not a bit the
sort of time they'd always imagined Outlaws having.

And the sun had suddenly gone behind a cloud. It was cold and dark. They were hungry and fed up.

'Wonder what time it is,' said Henry casually.

As if in answer the clock of the village church struck in the valley, One – Two – Three – Four – Five. Five o'clock. Tea-time. Into each mind flashed a picture of a cheerful dining-room with a table laid for tea.

'Well,' said William with an unconvincing attempt at cheerfulness, 'we'd better be getting something to eat. We might have had a rabbit if Henry'd caught one. Let's have a go at the blackberries.'

'There aren't any ripe ones,' said Douglas, 'and the others make you feel awful inside after you've eaten a few.'

Then suddenly to their secret relief Henry rose and said bluntly, 'I want my tea and I'm sick of being an Outlaw. I'm going home.'

On the road they met Brown and Smith. Brown and Smith were swinging happily along the road carrying fishing-rods and jars of minnows.

'I say, we've had a *topping* time,' they called. 'Have you? But you were rotters not to have told us.'

'Told you what?' said the Outlaws.

'That there was going to be a half-holiday.'

'*What?*' said the Outlaws.

'They sent us all away as soon as we got there. Said

they'd forgotten to give it out in the morning. We were
jolly surprised to meet you going away from school,
but when we got there we knew why but we thought
you jolly well might have told us.'

'Why was there a half-holiday?' gasped William.

'Oh, some old josser or something coming to give
some old jaw or other to some old society or other,'
said Smith vaguely, 'but we've had a *topping* afternoon, have you?'

In bitter silence the Outlaws walked on. They
hadn't had a topping afternoon. At the end of the road
a prefect was putting a letter into a pillar-box. Another
prefect stood by.

'What was it like?' said the one who stood by.

'He never turned up,' said the one who'd just
posted the letter. The Outlaws slowed their pace to
listen.

'We'd arranged to meet him on Ringers' Hill. The
Head and everyone was there. We'd never been to
Ringers' Hill before but there was a signpost up so we
couldn't have gone wrong. We waited three-quarters
of an hour and he never turned up. It's sickening. I've
just posted a letter from the Head telling him that we
went there and waited three-quarters of an hour. I
suppose he was kept somewhere. He might have let us
know, but some of those professors are beastly absent-
minded. We were looking forward to it awfully,

because it was Professor Fremlin, one of the greatest geologists in England, you know. Ringers' Hill's supposed to be an old volcano crater. It would have been awfully interesting. He was going to lecture on its formation and show us the strata and fossils there. We'd been reading it up for weeks so as to know something about it. A shame when we've got such a decent Geologist Society for the star turn show of the year to fall flat. Perhaps he was taken ill on the way.' He turned to the Outlaws. 'Now then, you kids, what are you hanging about for? Clear off.'

Blinking dazedly, walking very, very slowly, very, very thoughtfully, the Outlaws cleared off.

CHAPTER 2

THE TERRIBLE MAGICIAN

T HE advent of Mr Galileo Simpkins to the village would in normal times have roused little interest in William and his friends. But the summer holidays had already lasted six weeks and though the Outlaws were not tired of holidays (it was against the laws of nature for the Outlaws ever to tire of holidays), still they had run the gamut of almost every conceivable occupation both lawful and unlawful, and they were ready for a fresh sensation. They had been Pirates and Smugglers and Red Indians and Highwaymen *ad nauseam*. They had trespassed till every farmer in the neighbourhood saw red at the mere sight of them. They had made with much trouble a motor boat and an aeroplane, both of which had insisted on obeying the laws of gravity rather than fulfilling the functions of motor boats and aeroplanes. They had made a fire in Ginger's backyard and cooked over it a mixture of water from the stream and blackberries and Worcester Sauce and Turkish delight and sardines (these being all the edibles they could jointly produce), had pronounced the resultant concoction to be excellent and had spent the next day in bed. They had taken Jumble (William's mongrel) 'hunting' and had watched the ignominious spectacle of Jumble's being attacked by a cat half his size and pursued in a state of abject terror all the length of the village with a bleeding nose. They had discovered a wasps' nest and almost simultaneously its inhabitants had discovered them. They were only just leaving off their bandages. They had essayed tight-rope walking on Henry's mother's clothes line, but Henry's mother's clothes line had proved unexpectedly brittle and William still limped slightly. They had tried to teach tricks to Etheldrida, Douglas's aunt's parrot, and Douglas still bore the marks of her beak in several places on his face. Altogether they were, as I said, ripe for any fresh sensation when Mr Galileo Simpkins dawned upon their horizon.

Mr Galileo Simpkins had been thus christened by his parents in the hope that he would take to science. And Mr Galileo Simpkins, being by nature ready to follow the line of least resistance, had obligingly taken to science at their suggestion. Moreover, he quite enjoyed taking to science. He enjoyed pottering about with test tubes and he disliked being sociable. A scientist, as everyone knows, is immune from sociability. A scientist can retire to his lab as to a fortress and, if he likes, read detective novels there to his heart's content without being disturbed by anyone. Not that Mr Galileo Simpkins only read detective novels. He was genuinely interested in Science as Science (he put it that way) and though as yet he had made no startling contribution to Science as Science, still he enjoyed reading in his textbooks of experiments that other men had made and then doing the experiments to see if the same thing happened in his case. It didn't always ... Fortunately he was not dependent for his living on his scientific efforts. He had a nice little income of his own which enabled him to stage himself as a Scientist to his complete satisfaction. He took a great interest in the staging of himself as a Scientist. He liked to have an imposing array of test tubes and bottles and appliances of every sort – even those whose use he did not quite understand. He was very proud too of a skeleton which he had bought third-hand from a medical student and which he thought conferred great *éclat* on his position as a Scientist from its stronghold in the darkest corner. As you will gather from all this, Mr Galileo Simpkins was a very simple and inoffensive and well-meaning little man and before he came to the village where William lived, had not caused a moment's uneasiness to anyone since the time at three years old he had inadvertently fallen into the rain tub and been fished out half drowned by his nurse.

He had come to the village because the lease of the

house where he had lived previously had run out and the original owners were returning to it and he had seen the house in William's village advertised in the paper, and it seemed just what he wanted. He liked to live in the country because he was rather a nervous little man and was afraid of traffic.

The first sight of Mr Galileo Simpkins on his way from the station had not interested the Outlaws much except that as a stranger to the village he was naturally to be kept under observation and his possibilities in every direction explored at the earliest opportunity.

'He dun't look very *int*'restin',' said Ginger scornfully as, sitting in a row on a gate, the Outlaws stared in an unblinking manner quite incompatible with Good Manners at little Mr Galileo Simpkins driving by on his way from the station in the village cab. The driver of the village cab, who knew the Outlaws well, kept a wary eye upon them as he passed, and had his whip ready. The ancient quadruped who drew the village cab seemed to know them too, and turned his head to leer at them sardonically from behind his blinkers. But the attention of the Outlaws was all for the occupant of the village cab, who alone was quite unaware of them as the ancient equipage passed on its way. He was merely thinking what a fine day it was for his arrival at his new home and hoping that his skeleton (which he had packed most carefully) had travelled well.

William considered Ginger's comment for a moment in silence. Then he said meditatively: 'Oh . . . dunno. He looks sort of soft and 's if he couldn't run very fast. We c'n try playin' in his garden sometime. I bet he couldn't catch us.'

They then had a stone-throwing competition which lasted till one of William's stones went through General Moult's cucumber-frame.

When General Moult had finally given up the chase, the Outlaws threw themselves breathlessly (for General Moult, despite his size, was quite a good runner) on to the grass at the top of the hill and reviewed the further possibilities of amusement which the world held for them. They decided after a short discussion not to teach Etheldrida any more tricks, not so much because they were tired of teaching Etheldrida tricks as because Etheldrida seemed to be tired of learning them.

Douglas stroked his scars thoughtfully and said:

'Not that I'm *frightened* of her, but – but, well, let's try 'n think of somethin' a bit more *int'restin'*.'

No one had anything very original to suggest (they seemed to have exhausted the possibilities of the whole universe in those six weeks of holidays), so they made new bows and arrows and held a match which William won in that he made the finest long distance shot. He shot his arrow into the air and unfortunately it came to earth by way of Miss Miggs' scullery window. Miss Miggs happened to be in the scullery at the time and again the Outlaws, bitterly meditating on the over-population of the countryside, had to flee from the avenging wrath of an outraged householder. In the shelter of the woods they again drew breath.

'I say,' said Ginger, 'wun't it be nice to live in the middle of Central Africa or the North Pole or some-where where there isn't any houses for miles an' miles an' *miles*.'

'She runs,' commented Douglas patronisingly, 'faster'n what you'd think to look at her.'

'What'll we do *now*?' said Henry.

Dusk was falling, and ahead of them loomed the evil hour of bedtime which they were ever ready to postpone.

'I tell you what,' said William, his freckled face suddenly alight, 'let's go 'n see how *he's* gettin' on – you know, him what we saw ridin' up in the cab. We c'n go an' watch him through his window. It's quite dark.'

They watched him in petrified amazement. They watched him as, dressed in a black dressing-gown and a black skull-cap, he pottered about, laying out test tubes and pestles and mortars and crucibles and curious-looking instruments and bottles of strangely coloured liquids. Eyes and mouths opened still further when little Mr Galileo Simpkins brought in his skeleton and set it up with tender care and pride in its corner.

They crept away through the darkness in a stricken silence and did not speak till they reached the road. Then: '*Crumbs!*' said William, in a hoarse whisper. 'What *is* he? What's he *doin*'?'

'I think he's a sort of Bolsh'vist goin' to blow up all the world,' said Douglas with a burst of inspiration.

'An' a dead body an' all,' said Ginger, deeply awed by the memory of what they had seen.

'P'rhaps he's just doin' ordinary chemistry,' suggested Henry mildly.

This suggestion was indignantly scouted by the Outlaws.

''*Course* it's not jus' ordin'ry chemistry,' said William, 'not with all that set-out.'

'Dead bodies an' all,' murmured Ginger again in a sepulchral voice.

'An' dressed all funny,' said William, 'an' queer sorts of things all over the place. 'Sides, what'd he be doin' ordin'ry chemistry *for*, anyway? He's too old to be goin' in for exams.'

This was felt to be unanswerable.

'What I think is—' began William, but he never got as far as what he thought.

A plaintive voice came through the dusk – the voice of William's sister Ethel.

'William! Mother says it's long past your bedtime and *will* you come in and she says—'

The Outlaws crept off through the dusk.

The next day Joan came back from a visit to an aunt.

Joan was the only female member of the Outlaws. Though she did not accompany them on their more dangerous and manly exploits she was their unfailing confidante and sympathiser and could be always counted on to side with them against a hostile and unsympathetic world. She was small and dark and very pretty and she considered William the greatest hero the world has ever known.

She joined them the first morning of her return and they told her without any undue modesty of their exploits during her absence – of their heroic flights from irate farmers, of their miraculous creation of motor boats and aeroplanes (they omitted any reference to the over-officious law of gravity), of their glorious culinary operations (they omitted the sequel), their Herculean contest with the wasps, their tight-rope walking performance, their (partial) mastery over the brute creation as represented by Etheldrida, their glorious feats of stone throwing and arrow shooting.

'An' no one what's run after us has caught us – not

once,' ended William proudly and added, 'I bet we c'n run faster'n anyone else in the world.'

Joan smiled upon him fondly. She firmly believed that William could do anything in the world better than any one else in it.

'And what are you going to do today?' she said with interest.

That, the expressions of the Outlaws gave her to understand, was the question. The Outlaws had no idea what they were going to do today. They were obviously ready for any suggestion from the gentleman who, moralists inform us, specialises in providing occupation for the unoccupied.

'Let's make another motor boat,' said Henry feebly, but his suggestion was treated with well-deserved contempt. The Outlaws were not in the habit of repeating their effects. Moreover, the motor boat experiment had not been so successful as to warrant its repetition.

Suddenly Ginger's face lit up.

'I know!' he said, 'let's show Joan *him* . . . you know, him what we saw last night – with the dead body—'

Joan's eyes grew round with horror.

'It *wasn't* a dead body,' said Douglas impatiently, 'it was a skeleton.'

'That's the same as a dead body,' said Ginger

pugnaciously, 'it was a *body*, wasn't it? an' now it's dead.'

'Yes, but it's *bones*,' protested Douglas.

'Well, a body's bones, isn't it?' said Ginger.

But here Joan interrupted. 'Oh, what *is* it, *where* is it?' she said, clasping her hands, 'it sounds *awful*.'

Her horror satisfied them completely. With Joan you could always be so pleasantly sure that your effects would come off.

'Come on,' said William briskly assuming his air of Master of the Ceremonies, 'we'll show him you. We c'n get through the hole in the hedge 'n creep up to the window through the bushes without him seein' us at all.'

They got through the hole in the hedge and crept up to the window through the bushes. William, as Master of the Ceremonies, had an uneasy suspicion that in the cold morning light both man and room might look perfectly normal, that the ghostly effect of the night before might have vanished completely. But the suspicions proved to be groundless. The room looked, if possible, even more uncanny than it had done. And Mr Galileo Simpkins still pottered about it happily in his black dressing gown and skull cap (it was a costume in which he rather fancied himself). Mr Galileo Simpkins liked his nice large downstairs lab and felt very happy in it. As he stirred an experiment in a little crucible he sang softly to himself from sheer good spirits. He was quite unaware of the Outlaws watching his every movement with eager interest from the bushes outside the window. It was Ginger who saw and pointed out to the others the shelf at the back of the room on which stood a row of bottles containing wizened frogs in some sort of liquid.

Aghast, they crept away.

'Well, I'm *cert'n* that's what he's goin' to do,' said Douglas as soon as they reached the road, 'he's goin' to blow up all the world. He's jus' mixin' up the stuff to do it with.'

'Well, I *still* think he might be jus' an ornery sort of man doin' ornery chemistry,' said Henry.

'What about the dead body, then?' said Ginger.

'An' what about frogs an' things shut up in bottles an' things?' said William.

Then Joan spoke.

'He's a wizard,' she said, 'of *course* he's a wizard.'

William treated this suggestion with derision.

'A wizard,' he said contemptuously. 'Soppy fairy-tale stuff! *Course* he's not. There *aren't* any!'

But Joan was not crushed.

'There *are*, William,' she said solemnly, 'I *know* there are.'

'*How* d'you know there are?' said William incredulously.

'And what about the dead body?' said Ginger with the air of one bringing forward an unanswerable objection.

'The skeleton,' corrected Douglas.

'It's someone he's *turned* into a skeleton, of course,' said Joan firmly.

'Soppy fairy-tale stuff,' commented William again with scorn. Joan bore his reproof meekly but clung to her point with feminine pertinacity.

'It's *not*, William. It's *true*. I *know* it's true.'

There was certainly something convincing about her earnestness though the Outlaws were determined not to be convinced by it.

'No,' said Douglas very firmly. 'He's a blower up, that's what he is. He's goin' to blow up all the world.'

'What about the frogs in bottles?' said Henry.

'They're people he's *turned* into frogs,' said Joan.

The frogs certainly seemed to fit into Joan's theory better than they fitted into Douglas's. Joan pursued her advantage. 'And didn't you hear him sort of singing as he mixed the things? He was making spells over them.'

The Outlaws were, outwardly at least, still sceptical.

'Soppy fairy-tale stuff,' said William once more with masculine superiority. 'I tell you there *aren't* any.'

But there was a fascination about the sight and they were loth to go far from it.

'Let's go back an' see what he's doin' now,' said Ginger, and eagerly they accepted the proposal. The hole in the hedge was conveniently large, the bushes by the window afforded a convenient shelter and all would have gone well had not Mr Galileo Simpkins been engaged on the simple task of washing out some test tubes in a cupboard just outside the Outlaws' line of vision. This was more than they could endure.

'What's he *doin'*?' said William in a voice of agonised suspense.

But none of them could see what he was doing.

'I'll go out,' said Ginger with a heroic air. 'I bet he won't see me.'

So Ginger crept out of the shelter of the bushes and advanced boldly to the window. Too boldly – for Mr Galileo Simpkins, turning suddenly, saw, to his great surprise and indignation, a small boy with an exceedingly impertinent face standing in his garden and staring rudely at him through his window. Mr Galileo Simpkins hated small boys, especially small boys with impertinent faces. With an unexpected agility he leapt to the window and threw it open. Ginger fled in terror to the gate. Mr Galileo Simpkins shook his fist after him.

'All right, you *wait*, my boy, you *wait*!' he called.

By this time he wanted the boy with the impertinent face to understand that he was going to find out who he was and tell his father. He was going to put a stop to that sort of thing once and for all. He wasn't going to have boys with impertinent faces wandering about his garden and looking through his windows. He'd frighten them off now – at once. 'You *wait*!' he shouted again with vague but terrible menace in his voice.

Then he returned to his lab well pleased with himself.

The Outlaws crept back through the hole in the hedge and met Ginger in the road. They looked at Ginger as one might look at someone who has returned from the jaws of death. Ginger, now that the danger was over, rather enjoyed his position.

'*Well*,' he said with satisfaction, 'did you *see* him an' *hear* him? I bet he'd've *killed* me if he'd caught me.'

'Blown you up,' said Douglas.

'Turned you into something,' said Joan.

'Wonder what he meant by saying 'Wait' like that?' said William meditatively.

'He meant that he was goin' to put a spell on you,' said Joan composedly.

Ginger went rather pale.

'Soppy fairy-tale stuff,' said William.

'All right,' said Joan, 'just you wait and see.'

So they waited and they saw.

It was, of course, a coincidence that that night Ginger's mother's cook had made trifle for supper and that Ginger ate of this not wisely, but too well, and was the next morning confined to bed with what the doctor called 'slight gastric trouble'.

The Outlaws called for him the next morning and were curtly informed by the housemaid (who, like Mr Galileo Simpkins, hated all boys on principle) that Ginger was ill in bed and would not be getting up that day.

They walked away in silence.

'*Well*,' said Joan in triumph, 'what do you think about him being a magician *now*?'

This time William did not say 'Soppy fairy-tale stuff.'

Ginger returned to them, somewhat pale and wobbly, the next day. Like them he preferred to lay the blame of his enforced retirement on to Mr Galileo Simpkins, rather than upon the trifle.

'Yes, that's what he said,' agreed Ginger earnestly. 'He said, 'you wait,' an' then jus' about an hour after that I began to feel orful pains. An' I hadn't had hardly any of that ole trifle . . . well, not much, anyway; well, not *too* much . . . well, not as much as I often have of things . . . an' I had most *orful* pains an'—'

'He must have made a little image of you in wax, Ginger,' said Joan with an air of deep wisdom, 'and stuck pins into it. That's what they do . . . I expect he thinks you're dead now. That's why he said "You wait"!'

They did not scoff at her any longer.

'Well, I was nearly dead yesterday all right,' said Ginger. 'I've never had such *orful* pains. Jus' *like* pins running into me.'

'They *were* pins running into you, Ginger,' said Joan simply. 'We'd better keep *right* away from him now or he'll be turning us into something.'

'Like to turn *him* into something,' said Ginger who was still feeling vindictive towards the supposed author of his gastric trouble.

But Joan shook her head. 'No,' said Joan, 'we must keep *right* out of his way. You don't know what they can do – magicians and people like that.'

'*I* do,' groaned Ginger.

So they went for a walk and held races and played Red Indians and sailed boats on the pond and climbed trees – but there was little zest in any of these pursuits. Their thoughts were with Mr Galileo Simpkins the magician as he stirred his concoctions and uttered his spells and gazed upon his bottled victims and stuck pins into the waxen images of his foes.

'Let's jus' go 'n look at him again,' said William, when they met in the afternoon. 'We won't go near enough for him to *see* us but – but let's jus' go 'n see what he's *doin'*!'

'*You* can,' said Ginger bitterly. 'He's not stuck pins

into you an' given you *orful* pains. Why, I'm *still* feelin' ill with it. We had trifle again for lunch an' I can't eat more'n three helpin's of it.'

'No, we'd better not go near him again,' said Joan shaking her head, her eyes wide.

But William did not agree with them.

'I only want jus' to look at him again an' see what he's *doin'*. *I'm* goin', anyway.'

So they all went.

They had decided to creep down through the field behind the Red House to the road and thence through the hole in the hedge to the sheltering cluster of bushes that commanded the magician's room, but they had not so far to go before they saw him. It was a fine afternoon and Mr Galileo Simpkins had taken his detective novel and gone into the field just behind his house. And there he was when the Outlaws stopped at the gate of the field, lying on the bank in the shade, reading. He was feeling at peace with all the world. He did not see the five faces that gazed at him over the gate of the field and then disappeared. He went on dozing happily over his novel. He'd had a very happy morning. Though none of his experiments had come out still he'd much enjoyed doing them. He'd thought once of that boy with the impertinent face and felt glad that he'd frightened him away so successfully. He'd seen no signs

of him since. That was what you had to do with boys –
scare them off, or you got no peace at all . . . Very nice
warm sun . . . very exciting novel . . .

Meanwhile the Outlaws crept past the field and
were standing talking excitedly in the road.

'Did you *see*?' gasped Ginger, 'jus' sittin' an' readin'
ornery jus' as if he hadn't been stickin' pins into me all
last night.'

'Let's go home,' pleaded Joan. 'You – you don't
know *what* he'll do.'

'No,' said William, 'now he's all right readin' in
that field let's go into his room an' look at his things.'

There was a murmur of dissent.

'All right,' said William, 'you needn't. *I'm* jolly well
goin'.'

So they all went.

It was certainly thrilling to creep through the window
and stand in the terrible room with the knowledge that
at any minute the Magician might return, change them
into frogs and cork them up in bottles.

'Wonder if I can find the wax thing of me he was
sticking pins into last night,' said Ginger looking
round the bench.

'Let's make a wax thing of *him* 'n stick pins into it,'
suggested Henry.

'No, let's *turn* him into something,' said Douglas.

Joan clapped her hands.

'Oh *yes*,' she said, '*let's*! That *would* be fun! His spells and things must be all over the place.'

Ginger took up a pestle and mortar.

'This is what he was stirring today,' he said, 'wonder what this changes folks into.'

'Prob'ly depends what sort of a spell you say when you stir it,' said Joan.

'Well, let's try it,' said William.

'What'll we turn him into?' said Ginger.

'A donkey,' suggested William.

'Well, who'll do it?'

'Let me try,' said Joan who had a certain prestige as originator of the now generally accepted magician theory.

Ginger handed her the crucible. 'I think,' said Joan importantly, 'that I ought to have a circle of chalk drawn round me.'

They couldn't find any chalk so they made a little circle of test tubes around her and watched her with interest. Joan shut her eyes, stirred up the mixture in the crucible and chanted:

> 'Turn into a donkey,
> Turn into a donkey,
> Turn into a donkey,
> Mr Magician.'

Then she opened her eyes.

'It *may* be all wrong,' she admitted, 'I'm only guessing how to do it. But if it's a very good spell it *may* be all right.'

'Well, let's go and have a look at him,' said William, 'and if he's still there we'll come back and try again.'

So they went.

And now comes one of those coincidences without which both life and the art of the novelist would be so barren. Five minutes after the Outlaws had left Mr Galileo Simpkins peacefully reading his novel on a bank in the shade in the field, a boy crossed the field carrying a telegram. He came from the post office and the telegram was for Mr Galileo Simpkins, so, on seeing Mr Galileo Simpkins in the field, the boy took it up to him. Mr Simpkins opened it. It summoned him to the sick bed of a great-aunt from whom he had expectations. There was a train to town in ten minutes. Mr Simpkins had his hat and coat and plenty of money on him. He decided not to risk missing the train by going back to the house. He set off at once for the station, meaning to telegraph to his housekeeper from town (which he quite forgot to do). He left his book on the bank where he had laid it down on taking the telegram from the boy's hand.

Five minutes after he had gone Farmer Jenks, to whom the field belonged, brought to it a young donkey which he had just purchased, and departed. The young donkey had been christened 'Maria' by Mrs Jenks. Maria kicked her heels happily in the field for a few minutes, then realised that it was rather a hot afternoon. There was only one bit of shade in the field and that was the bank where but lately Mr Galileo Simpkins had reposed and where even now his book lay. Maria went over to this and lay down in it just by the book. In fact her attitude suggested that she was engaged in reading the book.

And so when five minutes later the Outlaws cautiously and fearfully peeped over the hedge, they saw what was apparently Mr Galileo Simpkins metamorphosed by their spell into a donkey lying where they had last seen him still reading his book. No words in the English language could quite describe the Outlaws' feelings. Not one of them had really expected Joan's spell to take effect. And here was the incredible spectacle before them – Mr Galileo Simpkins turned into a donkey before their very eyes by one of his own spells. They all went rather pale. William blinked. Ginger's jaw dropped open. Henry's eyes seemed on the point of falling out of his head. Douglas swallowed and held on to the gate for support and Joan gave a little scream. At the sound of the scream Maria turned her head and gave them a reproachful glance.

'*Well!*' said Joan.

'*Crumbs!*' said William.

'*Gosh!*' said Douglas.

'*Crikey!*' said Henry.

And '*Now* we've done it!' said Ginger.

Maria turned away her head and surveyed the distant landscape, drowsily. 'I wonder if he *knows*,' said William awefully, 'or if he thinks he's still a man.'

'He *must* know,' said Ginger. 'He's got eyes. He c'n see his legs 'n tail an' things.'

'*WELL!*' SAID JOAN. '*NOW* WE'VE DONE IT!' SAID GINGER.

'An' he was reading his book when we first came along,' said Douglas.

'P'raps,' suggested Henry, 'he's forgotten all about bein' a man an' only feels like a donkey now.'

'Well, he won't try stickin' pins into *me* again, *anyway*,' said Ginger.

HERE WAS THE INCREDIBLE BEFORE THEM – MR SIMPKINS
TURNED INTO A DONKEY BY ONE OF HIS OWN SPELLS!

But a new aspect of the affair had come to William.

'This is Farmer Jenks' field,' he said, 'he'll be mad findin' a donkey in it. He won't know it's reely Mr Simpkins.'

'Well, it won't matter,' said Ginger.

'Yes, I bet it will,' said William. 'P'raps it can talk still – the donkey, I mean – p'raps it'll tell people about us an' get us into trouble. I specks there's a law against turnin' people into things like what there is against murder – an' he's got a nasty look in his eyes. Look at him now. I bet he c'n still talk an' he'll go tellin' people an' we'll be put in prison or hanged or somethin'.'

'It's *your* fault,' said Ginger, 'why did you say a big thing like a donkey? If you'd said a little thing like a frog or somethin' we could've put him in a bottle, same as he did other folks, but what can you do with a big thing like a *donkey*?'

'Well, I never thought he'd *really* turn into one,' said William with spirit.

'Well, he *has* done,' said Ginger, 'an' we've gotter *do* something about it 'fore anyone comes along and he starts tellin' them about us.'

At this point Maria uttered a loud, 'Hee-haw!'

'There, you see,' said Henry relieved, 'he can only talk donkey talk.'

'I don' believe it,' said William doggedly. 'He's jus'

pretendin'. He was readin' his book when we came along an' I bet he can talk. He only wants to wait till someone comes along an' then get us into trouble . . . Look at him now eatin' grass . . . Well,' virtuously, 'he's got no *right* eatin' that grass. It's Farmer Jenks' grass . . . an' what're we goin' to do when they find out that the man's disappeared an' there's only a donkey left an' – they'll blame *us* . . . they always blame *us* for everything.'

'Let's turn him back now,' said Joan, 'we've prob'ly taught him a lesson. Now he knows what it feels like to be turned into something perhaps he'll stop turning other people into things.'

'And running pins into 'em,' said Ginger feelingly.

'Well, we'd better get him to his house, anyway,' said William, 'then he can turn himself back with his own things.'

Maria had arisen from the bank and was now munching grass a few yards away. Somewhat cautiously they approached her. William addressed her sternly.

'Now,' he said, 'we know that you're a magician an' that you turned people into frogs an' bones an' run pins into people so we turned you into a donkey, but we're goin' to let you turn yourself back if you *promise* never to be a magician any more. Will you *promise* never to be a magician any more?'

Maria opened her mouth to its fullest extent and emitted a 'hee-haw' that took William's breath away.

The Outlaws withdrew and held a hasty conclave.

'I think he meant to promise, William,' said Joan.

'Well, I don't,' said William, 'I don't. I think he meant he wun't promise.'

'Well, let's get him home, anyway,' said Douglas. 'Someone'll only be comin' along and findin' out all about it if we leave him here.'

Again William approached Maria and fixed her with a stern eye.

'You can come home an' turn yourself back now,' he said magnanimously, 'if you want to.'

For answer Maria turned her back on them, kicked her heels into the air, then leapt skittishly away.

It would take too long to describe in detail the struggle by which the Outlaws finally brought the recalcitrant Maria from the field into Mr Simpkins' garden and from Mr Simpkins' garden through the French window into Mr Simpkins' laboratory. Henry retired early from the contest after a kick on the shin.

'*Now* you know what he's like,' said Ginger bitterly, still obsessed by memories of his gastric trouble.

It was William who had the bright idea of running home for a bunch of carrots and by means of this they led the frisky Maria into the garden of Mr Simpkins'

home. There Maria for a time ran amok. She broke a
pane of glass in the greenhouse, she pranced about the
well rolled lawn, leaving innumerable hoof holes to
mark her progress. She trampled down a bed of
heliotrope. She completely demolished a bed of roses.
She bit William. She was finally brought through the
French window into the lab at the cost of all the glass
in the French window. The housekeeper, as it happened, was lying down and was a very sound sleeper.
A small child belonging to the jobbing gardener,
pressing its nose through the front gate, was the
amazed spectator of these proceedings.

Inside the lab Maria grew more frisky still. She
broke and ground into the carpet the test tubes that
had formed Joan's magic circle. She wrecked the bench
and everything upon it. She kicked over an entire shelf
of bottles.

'He's mad,' said William, 'he's mad at bein' a
donkey an' he doesn't know how to turn himself back.'

'Say somethin' to him,' urged Ginger.

William said something to him.

'If you can't turn yourself back,' said William,
'you'll have to stay like you are. We can't do anything
more for you.'

In answer to this Maria kicked over a small
cupboard and then put her head through a large glass
beaker.

'HE'S MAD AT BEIN' A DONKEY,' SAID WILLIAM, 'AN' HE
DOESN'T KNOW HOW TO TURN HIMSELF BACK.'

'Let's go,' said Ginger, 'let's go home. We've
brought him back to his own home. We can't do
anything more. And, anyway, it serves him right, him
and his dead bodies an' sticking pins into people.'

The Outlaws were just going to take his advice and

return home as unostentatiously as possible, when they discovered that their line of retreat was cut off. A small band of women headed by the Vicar's wife was coming up the drive towards the front door. Like five streaks of lightning the Outlaws disappeared behind a screen which Maria amid the general chaos had considerately left standing.

The small band of women headed by the Vicar's wife were the members of a local Anti-vivisection Society which had been formed in the village by the Vicar's wife a year ago. Up to now there had been little scope in the village for their activities, though they had all much enjoyed the monthly meetings at which they had had tea and cakes and discussed the various village scandals. But now, as the Vicar's wife said, was the Time to Act. They had heard of Mr Galileo Simpkins' skeleton and bottled frogs and they thought that the local Anti-vivisection Society should approach him and demand from him a guarantee that he would not in his researches touch the hair of the head of any living animal. Also they wanted an opportunity of inspecting the mysterious lab of which they had heard so much. Things in the village had been rather dull lately and like the Outlaws they welcomed any fresh diversion. . . .

They were approaching the front door, meaning to ring and ask to see Mr Simpkins in the normal fashion of callers. But to reach the front door they had to pass the window of the lab and it proved far too thrilling to be passed. The Outlaws, neatly hidden behind the screen, were invisible. Maria stood in the middle of the room, her head drooping in an utterly deceptive attitude of patient meekness. All around was wreckage. The visitors stood and gazed at the scene open-mouthed. Tacitly they abandoned their intention of knocking at the front door and being admitted as callers. Led by the Vicar's wife, they entered by the French windows.

'A *donkey*!' said Mrs Hopkins, Treasurer of the Anti-vivisection Society (that is to say, she collected their sixpences and bought the cakes for tea). 'I thought they used monkeys or rabbits.'

'They use different animals for different experiments,' said the Vicar's wife with an air of deep knowledge. 'I expect that a donkey is the most suitable animal for some experiments.'

'How *terrible*!' said Mrs Gerald Fitzgerald, covering her face with her hands. 'How truly terrible . . . Poor, patient, suffering, dumb beast.'

Maria laid back her ears and rolled her wicked eyes at them.

Mrs Hopkins and the Vicar's wife began to wander about the room.

They stopped simultaneously before the row of bottled frogs.

'Poor creatures!' said Mrs Hopkins unsteadily. 'Poor, patient, suffering creatures – once so beautiful and lovable and free.'

(It was only the week before that Mrs Hopkins had screamed for help on meeting a frog in her larder.)

Mrs Gerald Fitzgerald had by this time discovered the skeleton. She adjusted her glasses and looked slowly and closely up and down it several times. Then she pronounced in a sepulchral whisper: 'Human remains!'

The Outlaws held their breath in their retreat, but a resonant 'Hee-haw!' from Maria drew the members of the local Anti-vivisection Society from any further exploring.

'The patient creature,' said the Vicar's wife brokenly, 'seems to be asking for our help.'

Maria assumed again her attitude of deceptive meekness.

'We certainly must *do* something,' said Mrs Gerald Fitzgerald, 'we can't leave our dear dumb friend to torture. Look at the signs of struggle all around us. Look at its air of suffering. The foul work has evidently already begun. Let's – let's take it away with us.'

'On the other hand,' said the Vicar's wife slowly, 'there are the laws of private property to be considered. Mr Simpkins doubtless purchased this creature and the law will hold it to belong to him.'

'We can *buy* it from him then,' said Mrs Gerald Fitzgerald brightly. 'That would be a noble work indeed. How much money have we in hand, Mrs Hopkins?'

'Only threepence-halfpenny,' said Mrs Hopkins gloomily, 'we've been having iced cakes lately, you know. They're more expensive.'

'They cost more than that,' said the Vicar's wife, 'donkeys, I mean. But,' with a flash of inspiration, 'we can get up a bazaar for it or a concert for it.'

Their spirits rose at the prospect.

'Yes,' said Mrs Hopkins. 'Why, it's nearly a month since we had a bazaar. And *such* a good cause. Rescuing the poor dumb suffering creature from the hands of the torturer – How sad it looks and yet grateful as though it understood all that we were going to do for it.'

Maria rolled her eyes again and drooped her head still further.

'I'm going to take it *straight* home,' said the Vicar's wife, 'and give it a good meal and nurse it back to health and strength. I'll go to the police station and tell them that I have taken it and why. I'll just fix up something to lead it home by.'

She took down a picture and divested it of its picture cord, which she then tied round the neck of the still meekly unprotesting Maria. The others gazed at her in silent admiration. There was really no one like the Vicar's wife in a crisis.

Then, with the air of a general who has now marshalled her forces, she led out Maria, followed by her faithful band. The Outlaws, weakly wondering what was going to happen, crept out of their hiding place and followed at a distance.

'They don't know it's *him*,' said Joan in a thrilled whisper.

Maria behaved quite well till they got to the hill. Then her familiar devil returned to her. She did not kick or bite. She ran. She ran at top speed up the steep hill, dragging the panting, gasping Vicar's wife after her at the end of the cord. Maria's neck seemed to be made of iron. The weight of the Vicar's wife did not seem to trouble it at all. The picture cord, too, must have been pretty strong. The Vicar's wife did not let go. With dogged British determination she clung to her end of the cord. She lost her footing, her hat came off, she gasped and panted and gurgled and choked and sputtered. She dropped her bag. But she did not let go her end of the picture cord. Behind her – far behind her – ran her little crowd of followers, clucking in dismayed horror. Mrs Hopkins picked up the Vicar's wife's hat and Mrs Gerald Fitzgerald her bag.

At the top of the hill Maria stopped abruptly and

reassumed her air of weary patience. The Vicar's wife sat down in the dust by her side, gasping but still undaunted, holding on to the end of the cord. The others arrived and the Vicar's wife, still sitting in the road, put on her hat and wiped the dust out of her eyes.

'What happened?' panted Mrs Hopkins. 'Did it – bolt or something?'

But the Vicar's wife was past speech.

'Poor creature!' said Mrs Gerald Fitzgerald in an effort to restore the atmosphere, 'poor dumb creature.'

She put out her hand to stroke Maria and Maria very neatly bit her elbow.

The Vicar's wife arose from the dust and wearily but determinedly led Maria through the gate on to the Vicarage lawn. The Outlaws came cautiously up the hill and watched proceedings through the Vicarage gate.

The members of the local Anti-vivisection Society stood round Maria and gazed at her. A close observer might have noticed that their glances held less affection and pity than they had held a short time before.

'It doesn't seem at all – er – *cowed*,' said Mrs Hopkins at last. 'It seems quite – er as – *fresh*. . . . And it hasn't any *wounds* or anything.'

'Sometimes,' said Mrs Gerald Fitzgerald, 'they just use them for diseases. They just inject disease germs into them.'

'Do you mean,' said Mrs Hopkins, turning pale, 'that it may be infected with a deadly disease?'

'*Quite* possibly,' said Mrs Gerald Fitzgerald.

They looked at the Vicar's wife for advice and help. And again the Vicar's wife showed her capacities for dealing with a crisis. Though still dusty and shaken from her inglorious career up the hill at Maria's heels she took command of affairs once more.

'One minute,' she said, and disappeared into the house.

The members of the Anti-vivisection Society stood timorously in the porch, eyes fixed apprehensively upon Maria who stood motionless in the middle of the lawn looking as if butter would not melt in her mouth.

And the Outlaws still watched proceedings with interest through the Vicarage gate.

Then the Vicar's wife came out staggering beneath the weight of a large pail.

'Disinfectant,' she explained shortly to her audience.

She approached Maria who was still standing in maiden meditation fancy free on the lawn, and with a sudden swift movement threw over her the entire pail of carbolic solution, soaking her from head to foot. Then Maria went mad. She leapt, she kicked, she reared. Dripping with carbolic she dashed round the lawn. She trampled over the flower beds. She broke two dozen flower pots and destroyed their contents. She kicked the greenhouse door in. She put her back hoof through the Vicar's study window. She tried to climb an apple tree. She wrecked the summer-house. . . .

The members of the local Anti-vivisection Society withdrew into the Vicarage and bolted all the doors. Mrs Gerald Fitzgerald, after explaining that she wasn't used to this sort of thing, went into hysterics that rivalled Maria's outburst in intensity.

And still the Outlaws watched spellbound through the gate.

It was the Outlaws who first saw Mr Simpkins' housekeeper coming up the hill. She entered the Vicarage gate without looking at them. To her they were merely four inoffensive small boys and one inoffensive small girl looking through a gate. She little knew that they held the key to a situation that was becoming more complicated every minute. Mr Simpkins' housekeeper looked upset. She rang at the Vicarage front door and demanded to see the Vicar. The Vicar was out, but the Vicar's wife, looking very pale and keeping well within the doorway and casting apprehensive glances round the garden, where Maria, temporarily breathless and exhausted, was standing motionless – the picture of mute patience – on the lawn, interviewed her. From within the house came the unmelodious strains of Mrs Gerald Fitzgerald's hysterics. Mr Simpkins' housekeeper said that Mr Simpkins had vanished. He was nowhere to be found. The book he had been reading had been discovered in the field near the garden and his lab was in such a state as to suggest a violent struggle, and Mr Simpkins' housekeeper suspected foul play of which Mr Simpkins was the victim.

The Vicar's wife, who was a woman of one idea, only pointed sternly to Maria and said:

'What do you know about *that*, my good woman?'

Her good woman looked, saw a mournful-looking and very wet donkey and shook her head.

'Nothing 'm,' she said primly. 'But what I want to know is, where is Mr Simpkins? I thought the Vicar might advise me what to do, but as he's not in, 'm, p'raps I'd better go to the police straight.'

The Outlaws, who felt that with the advent of Mr Simpkins' housekeeper the plot was thickening, and who were consumed with curiosity as to why Mr Simpkins' housekeeper had followed the metamorphosed Mr Simpkins, crept up to the Vicarage door and listened. The mention of 'police' made them rather uncomfortable. The Vicar's wife saw them and frowned.

The Vicar's wife was a good Christian woman, but she could never learn to like the Outlaws.

'Go away, little boys,' she said tartly, 'how dare you come up to the door listening to conversation that is not meant for you? Go away at once. Or, wait one minute . . . Have any of you seen Mr Simpkins this afternoon?'

It was Joan who answered. She pointed across the lawn to Maria who was now placidly nibbling the Vicar's hedge and said:

'That's Mr Simpkins.'

There was a moment's tense silence. Then the Vicar's wife said sternly:

'Do you imagine that to be funny, you impertinent little girl?'

'No,' said Joan.

There was an innocence in Joan's face that convinced even the Vicar's wife.

'Perhaps,' she said more kindly, 'you are short-sighted, little girl. That,' pointing to Maria, 'is a donkey.'

'It's Mr Simpkins really,' said Joan earnestly, 'we turned him into a donkey and we can't turn him back.'

The Vicar's wife gasped, Mr Simpkins' housekeeper gasped, the other members of the Anti-vivisection Society came out to see what it was all about and all gasped. Mrs Gerald Fitzgerald for the time being abandoned her hysterics to gasp with them.

'PERHAPS,' SAID THE VICAR'S WIFE, 'YOU ARE SHORT-
SIGHTED, LITTLE GIRL. THAT IS A DONKEY.'
'IT'S MR SIMPKINS, REALLY,' SAID JOAN EARNESTLY.

'*What?*' said the Vicar's wife.

'*What?*' said all the rest of them.

'It's true,' affirmed William, 'we've turned him into a donkey and we can't turn him back again.'

At that moment there was a sound of great commotion outside and in at the gate rushed Mr Simpkins, followed by Farmer Jenks.

Farmer Jenks was not pursuing Mr Simpkins. Farmer Jenks and Mr Simpkins were coming on independent missions. Farmer Jenks had come to his field for Maria and found Maria gone. The jobbing gardener's youngest child had told him that four boys and a girl had taken the donkey out of the field. It took only a few words to make Farmer Jenks recognise his old enemies, the Outlaws, as the invaders of his domain and thieves of his donkey, and Farmer Jenks saw red. He had traced the donkey to the Vicarage garden. He didn't know how it had got there, but he knew how it had got out of his field, and he was out for his donkey and vengeance on the Outlaws. . . .

Mr Simpkins had reached town, to be met at the station by a telegram telling him that his great-aunt was better, so with feelings of deep disgust with life in general and great-aunts in particular, he had returned to his rural retreat – to find his housekeeper vanished and his laboratory wrecked. Again the jobbing gardener's youngest child had brightly come forward with all the information it could produce. It had seen four boys and a girl turn a donkey into his lab through the window and then let the donkey break things. Then more people had come and then they'd all gone up to the Vicarage. So Mr Galileo Simpkins had gone up to the Vicarage in search of more light on the situation, and in search of the Outlaws.

He and Farmer Jenks caught sight of the Outlaws simultaneously and neither could resist the temptation to make the most of the opportunity. Both flung themselves upon the Outlaws. The Outlaws fled round the lawn, pursued by Farmer Jenks and Mr Galileo Simpkins. Mrs Gerald Fitzgerald went back to the drawing-room to have a few more hysterics, the Vicar's wife dashed into the hall for the fire extinguisher and Maria watched proceedings with interest as she meditatively chewed the Vicar's hedge.

Farmer Jenks caught hold of William, lost his balance and fell with him to the ground. Mr Galileo Simpkins fell over Farmer Jenks and caught hold of Maria's tail as he fell. Maria, annoyed at this familiarity, went mad again. The Vicar's wife, with vague ideas of pouring oil on troubled waters, turned the fire extinguisher on to them all. Mrs Hopkins ran into the road shouting 'Murder' and Mr Simpkins' housekeeper went to fetch the police.

'I've got to draw the line somewhere,' said William's father to William's mother the next evening. 'I suppose I've got to pay my share for all the damage the quadruped did in the laboratory, but I don't see that I need re-stock the Vicar's garden. As far as I can make out his own wife took the creature there. Well, I've taken everything I can think of from William and done everything I can think of to him – it's against the law to drown him or I'd do that and be done with it—'

'Poor William,' murmured his wife, 'he *means* well – and such a lot of people say he's like you.'

'He *isn't*,' said his father indignantly, 'I'm more or less sane, and he's a raving lunatic. He can't possibly be like me. Do I go about turning donkeys into labs and for no reason at all? Do I – Nonsense!'

'Never mind, dear. He goes to school tomorrow,' said his wife soothingly.

'Thank Heaven!' said Mr Brown quite reverently.

Outside in the summer-house sat the Outlaws.

'It's simply no *use* explainin' to them,' William was saying. 'They sort of won't listen to you. They go on as if we'd *meant* to break all his ole glass things. Well, how were we to *know* his aunt was ill? I said that to them but they wun't take any notice. 'S almost funny,' he ended bitterly, 'the way they blame us for *every-thing* – took my bow an' arrow an' airgun an' money an' *everythin'* off me just as if we hadn't been tryin' to do *good* all the time. An' no one does anythin' to that old *donkey*. Oh, no! It was all its fault but no one does anything to it. Oh, no.

'An' we go to school tomorrow,' added Ginger, gloomily.

'Never mind,' said William with rising spirits, 'we've done all the sorts of things you can do in holidays an' – an' after all there's quite a lot of excitin' things you can do in school.'

CHAPTER 3

GEORGIE AND THE OUTLAWS

IT seemed to the Outlaws that before Georgie Murdoch came to live at the Laurels they had led comparatively peaceful lives. They had not at any rate been subjected to relentless and unceasing persecution as they were now. It was not Georgie who persecuted them. It was their own parents. But I will explain the connection between the advent of Georgie Murdoch and the persecution of the Outlaws. Before Georgie came to the Laurels the Outlaws' parents had realised that the Outlaws were characterised chiefly by rough-ness, untidiness, unpunctuality, lack of cleanliness and various kindred vices. They mentioned these faults to their possessors in a manner expressive of a resigned disgust several times a day. But they always said to each other, 'Well, boys will be boys,' or, 'They're all as bad as each other,' or, 'I've never known a boy who wasn't like that.' They were in fact consoled by the reflection that the Perfect Boy did not exist.

And then Georgie Murdoch came to live at the Laurels and Georgie Murdoch was the Perfect Boy.

The effect upon the Outlaws' parents was dynamic.
No longer did they view their offspring with
resigned disgust and tell themselves and each other
that boys would be boys, for was not Georgie
Murdoch a walking refutation of the theory?
Georgie Murdoch's whole existence proved con-
clusively that boys needn't be boys. So with renewed
vigour and a perseverance that was worthy of a better
cause the Outlaws' parents set to work to uproot those
vices of roughness, untidiness, unpunctuality and lack
of cleanliness that hitherto they had treated, not indeed
with encouragement, but with a certain resignation.
Day after day the Outlaws heard the never-ceasing
refrain, 'Georgie Murdoch doesn't behave like that,'
'You never see Georgie Murdoch looking like
that,' 'Nonsense, Georgie Murdoch can make his hair
stay tidy and his face stay clean, so why can't you?' or,
'Watch the way Georgie Murdoch eats'. . . .

But the time has come to describe Georgie Murdoch
in more detail. Georgie Murdoch was ten years of age.
He was neat and tidy and methodical and clean and
only spoke when he was spoken to and always did what
he was told. He hated messy things like mud and water
and clay and sand and he disliked rough games. He had
very beautiful manners and was much in request at
afternoon teas. He never forgot to say, 'How do you
do?' and 'Yes, please,' and 'No, thank you,' and 'How

very kind of you,' and he never had been known to drop a cup or knock over a cake stand. In summer he always dressed in white and could make one suit do for three days. That gives you a pretty good idea of Georgie Murdoch's personal habits. It is hardly necessary to add that he loved his lessons and thought that the holidays were far too long.

When first the Murdochs came to live in the village, the Outlaws were prepared to receive Georgie with friendliness. His fame as the World's Most Perfect Boy had not preceded him. All they knew was that he was about their own age and of their sex and they were ready to make the best of him.

Mrs Brown met him first when she went to call on his mother.

'He's *such* a nice little boy, William,' was her verdict on her return, 'I've asked him to come to tea tomorrow because I'd like you to make friends with him. He's just about your age, and *so* well-mannered.'

This description was not encouraging, and whatever enthusiasm William may previously have felt for the newcomer waned.

'Can I have some of the others to tea as well, Mother?' he asked with an air of engaging innocence. But unfortunately William's mother remembered the last occasion when 'the others' had been asked to help William entertain a little stranger. William and 'the others', after a short test of the little stranger's capacities which the little stranger had failed to pass with credit, had gone off for the afternoon on their own devices, leaving the little stranger to his. After wandering round the garden once and finding in it few possibilities of amusement the little stranger had returned home – just half an hour after he had left it. Mrs Brown wasn't going to have any more *contre-temps* like that. So she said very firmly, 'No, William.'

'All right,' acquiesced William with an air of weary patience, 'I was only thinkin' of *him*. I was only thinkin' that p'raps he'd sort of enjoy it better if there was more of us to play with.'

But Mrs Brown again said, 'No, William,' meaningly, and William, who had a suspicion that she remembered their entertaining of the last little stranger, forebore to press the point. So William was the solitary host when Georgie arrived. The prospect of being the solitary host had depressed him all morning, and the sight of Georgie's trim little figure in its spotless white sailor suit threw him into a state of despair that was almost homicidal in its intensity. He'd had a horrible suspicion all along that Georgie would be like that. And a whole afternoon with him . . . a *whole* afternoon!

Mrs Brown, however, gave Georgie a kindly smile of welcome as she received him.

'How *nice* to see you, dear,' she said, 'I'm *so* glad you could come. This is my little boy, William. He's been *so* much looking forward to your visit. I hope you're going to be great friends. How nice you look, dear. I wish William could only keep as clean and tidy as that. He gets so untidy.'

Georgie moved so as to get a better view of William. He looked him up and down and finally said:

'Yes, he *does* look untidy, doesn't he?' To which momentous announcement he added complacently, 'I hardly ever seem to get untidy.'

'Well,' said Mrs Brown, temporarily taken aback, 'will you play with William till tea time, dear? . . . nothing *rough*, mind, William.'

'No,' agreed Georgie, 'I don't like rough games.'

William, who by this time hated Georgie with a hatred which was the more bitter because Georgie was robbing him of a whole afternoon which might have been spent with his beloved Outlaws, led Georgie into the garden. They walked down to the bottom of the garden. Then William said distantly:

'What would you like to play at?'

'Don't mind,' said Georgie.

'Hide an' Seek?' said William.

This puerile suggestion was intended as a subtle insult, but Georgie took it seriously. He considered it in silence and at last said, 'No, thank you. Hide and Seek generally ends in getting so rough.'

For a moment William had not believed his ears, but Georgie added calmly:

'It generally ends by being a *very* nasty rough game.'

William swallowed and gazed at him helplessly. Then he suggested, more out of curiosity than from any other reason:

'Like to play Red Indians?'

'Red Indians?' queried that astounding child as if he had not heard of the game before.

'Yes,' said William, almost speechless with amazement. 'Scoutin' each other through the bushes an' makin' a fire, an'—'

But an expression of horror had overspread Georgie's smug countenance.

'Oh, *no*,' he said firmly, 'I don't want to get my suit dirty.'

William recovered with an effort.

'Well,' he said at last, 'what *would* you like to do?'

'Let's go for a nice quiet walk, shall we?' said Georgie brightly.

So they went for a nice quiet walk – straight along the road to the village. William at first made an effort to fulfil his duties as host by pointing out the objects of interest of the neighbourhood.

'There's a robin's nest in that hedge,' he said.

'I know,' said Georgie.

'That's Bunker's Hill over there.'

'I know,' said Georgie.

'That was a Clouded Yellow,' as a butterfly flitted past.

'I know.'

'They've got sort of scent bags on their wings.'

'I know.'

'What sort of bird is that flying over there?' challenged William.

'Well, what sort is it?'

'A starling.'

'I knew it was.'

William then tired of the conversation and began to while away the tedium of the journey as best he could by more active measures. Georgie, however, refused to take part in them. Georgie refused to jump over the ditch with William because he said he might fall in. He refused to walk on the fence with William because he said that he might fall off. He refused to swing on the gate with William because he said it might dirty his suit. He refused to climb a tree for the same reason. He refused to race William to the end of the road because, he said, it was rough. William was only deterred by his position as host and by Georgie's protective one year's juniority from forcibly making Georgie acquainted with the contents of the ditch as the inner prompting of his heart bade him to. Instead he leapt to and fro across the ditch (falling in only twice), swung on the gate, walked on the fence (over-balancing once) and trailed his toes in the dust in solitary glory, ignoring his companion entirely.

'What *will* your mother say?' said his companion once disapprovingly.

William received the remark with scornful silence.

When they returned to the Brown homestead Georgie was as immaculate as when he had set out, while William bore many and visible marks of his fallings into the ditch and on to the road and swinging on gates and climbing trees.

'*William!*' said Mrs Brown, 'you look *awful* . . . and look at Georgie – how clean and neat he is still.'

'Yes,' said Georgie looking at William with marked distaste, 'I *told* him not to. I *said* you wouldn't like it, but he wouldn't take any notice of me.'

The next day William met the Outlaws by appointment and gloomily told them the worst.

'And he's come to *live* here,' he ended with passionate disgust, 'him and his white suits.'

'And we shall *all* have to have him to tea,' said Ginger.

'And our mothers'll *never* stop talkin' about him,' said Douglas.

'And he'll prob'ly get worse the more we know him,' said Henry.

'Him an' his white suits!' repeated William morosely.

All these fears proved to be well founded.

As Ginger had predicted, they all had to have him to tea, and on each occasion Georgie remained clean and tidy and immaculate in his white suit and said at the end to his host's mother, 'Yes, I told him not to. I *said* you wouldn't like it.' And when the guest had departed the host's mother said to the host:

'How I *wish* that you were a little more like Georgie Murdoch.'

Henry's prediction was also fulfilled. For Georgie did get worse the more they knew him. In addition to the vices of personal cleanliness and exquisite manners he possessed that of tale-bearing. He was a frequent visitor at the Outlaws' houses. He would gaze at William's mother with a wistful smile and say, 'Please, Mrs Brown, I'm so sorry to disturb you but I think I ought to tell you that William is paddling in the stream after you told him not to,' or 'Please, Mrs Flowerdew, I'm so sorry to disturb you, but Ginger 'n' Henry's throwing mud at each other down the road an' getting in *such* a mess. I thought you ought to know.'

And the Outlaws couldn't get their own back. Georgie would never fight because it might dirty his suit, and any personal attacks upon Georgie (however mild) were faithfully reported by the attacked in person to the parent of the attacker.

'Please, Mrs Brown, William's just pushed me over and hurt me.' 'Please, Mrs Flowerdew, Ginger's just banged into me and made quite a bruise on my arm.' Moreover the Outlaws seemed to have a strong fascination for Georgie. He followed them around, watching their pursuits from a safe and cleanly distance, generally eating chocolate creams which he never offered to the Outlaws, and which never seemed to leave any traces on his face. Whenever any elders were in hearing Georgie would raise his voice and say in a tone of horror, 'Oh, you *naughty* boy! What *will* your mother say?' and having attracted the elder's attention and interference he would say sorrowfully, 'I told him not to. I *knew* you wouldn't like it.'

Yet such was the power of his white suit, his clean face, his sweet smile, his beautiful manners that Georgie was always referred to by the grown-ups of the neighbourhood as '*Such* a dear little boy.'

The Outlaws bore it as long as they could, and then they held a meeting to decide what could be done about it. It was not on the whole a very successful meeting. William kept muttering, 'We've gotter *do* something . . . him and his white suits.'

But not one of the Outlaws, usually so prolific in ideas of every sort, could think of any sort of plan to meet the case.

''S no good doin' anythin' to *him*,' said Ginger bitterly, ''f you just *touch* him he goes an' tells your mother.'

'Oh, you naughty boys!' mimicked Henry shrilly. 'What will your mothers say? I told him not to, I said you wouldn't like it.'

As an imitation it was rather good, but the Outlaws were not in a mood to be entertained by imitations of Georgie.

'Oh, shut up!' said William. ''S bad enough hearin' *him* sayin' it.'

'Well, let's think of something to *do*,' said Ginger again.

'I wish you wun't keep sayin' that,' said William irritably.

'Well, I'll stop when you've *thought* of something,' said Ginger.

'Think of somethin' yourself,' snapped William.

As you will gather from this conversation the perfect little gentleman was having a wearing effect upon the Outlaws' nerves. Henry, with a sudden gleam of inspiration, suggested haunting the Murdoch homestead by night, robed in a sheet, till the Murdochs should depart in terror to some other part of England, taking the perfect little gentleman with them, but it was decided, after a brief and acrimonious discussion, that this was not feasible. It was more than likely that the Murdochs would investigate the alleged ghost and discover the concealed Outlaw, and also it might prove difficult to gain egress from the parental home and ingress into the Murdoch home at the rather awkward hours suitable for 'haunting'.

The only other suggestion came from Douglas who had got full marks for Scripture the week before.

'I think Joseph must have been a bit like Georgie,' he said. 'I – I s'pose we couldn't take him right away somewhere and leave him in a pit same as what they did – an' take his coat home an' say a wild animal ate him?'

The Outlaws considered this alluring suggestion, but feared that it would be impracticable.

'There aren't any pits or wild animals like that in England in these days,' said William mournfully.

The Outlaws sighed, thinking – not for the first time – that the vaunted benefits of civilisation were more than nullified by its hampering elements.

'Well, we aren't any nearer *doin'* anythin',' said Ginger.

'There dun't seem anythin' to do,' said William,

whose gloom had been deepened by the thought of the simplicity of Joseph's brethren's problem compared with theirs.

'An' he's gettin' worse an' *worse*,' groaned Douglas.

'They're havin' a garden party next week,' contributed Henry, 'an' we'll all have to go.'

'An' watch him in his white suit,' put in William bitterly.

'Handin' cakes an' tellin' tales,' put in Ginger to complete the picture.

'What do they want goin' havin' *garden* parties for?' said William fiercely.

Henry, who was rather 'up' in the Murdoch news owing to the fact that Mrs Murdoch had been to tea with his mother the day before, answered him.

'Well, they've got a sort of cousin what's famous comin' to stay with them an' they want to sort of show him off,' he said, translating freely from the conversation he had overheard the day before, 'so they're goin' to ask everyone to meet him at a garden party.'

'How'd he get famous?' said William with mournful interest.

'Writin' plays,' said Henry.

William groaned.

'He'll be worse than ever,' he said, referring not to the writer of plays but to the perfect little gentleman.

The meeting broke up without having arrived at

any satisfactory plan, though Henry still cherished the haunting idea and Douglas still considered that something might be done in the pit and wild beast line.

The next day the famous cousin arrived at the Murdochs' and was proudly paraded through the village by Georgie resplendent in a new white suit and a smile that was more smug and complacent than ever. Close observers might have noticed that the famous cousin looked bored.

The next few days, however, were – outside their homes – days of respite for the Outlaws. For Georgie was too busy with the famous cousin to be able to spare any time for the Outlaws, and the Outlaws could wallow in the mud, climb trees, and turn somersaults in the road to their hearts' content without hearing the shrill little refrain, 'Oh, you *naughty* boys! what *will* your mothers say . . . I *told* them not to do it . . . I *said* you wouldn't like it.'

I said 'outside their homes'. For inside their homes things were if possible worse. For the interest of the whole village was, thanks to the visit of the famous cousin, now concentrated upon the Murdochs.

'I met little Georgie Murdoch out with his cousin today. He introduced me *so* nicely. I only wish that I thought *you'd* ever be half so polite,' or, 'I met little Georgie Murdoch in the village this morning. He'd gone to post a letter for his cousin. He looked *so* nice and clean. How I wish *you* could keep like that.'

As the day of the garden party approached the gloom of the Outlaws deepened.

But they knew that no excuses would avail them. They would have to go there and watch Georgie being 'more sick'nin' than ever', as Henry put it, parading his famous cousin, showing off his beautiful manners and basking in the admiration of all the guests – And after that he'd be more unbearable even than he had been before.

Fate seemed to be on the side of the Murdochs. The day of the garden party was warm and sunny and cloudless so that the garden party (contrary to its English custom) really could be a garden party and little Georgie could wear one of his white suits.

William set off to the festivity with his mother, engulfed in gloom and his Sunday suit and looking more as if bound for a funeral than a garden party.

They found a large crowd already assembled and in the middle of it was Georgie wearing his newest and whitest suit and smiling his smuggest smile, and with his golden curls glinting in the sunshine. . . .

'Isn't he a dear little boy?' heard William on all sides, and 'He's *such* a little gentleman,' and then from his mother the inevitable, 'I wish *you* could behave like that, William.'

William looked about him and soon picked out

Ginger and Henry and Douglas all in similar plight. Their mothers too were gazing rapturously at Georgie and telling their sons how they wished that they could ever behave like that or ever look like that or ever speak like that or ever keep as clean and tidy as that. And the Outlaws (who were quite used to it by this time) bore it in scornful silence.

Then William noticed the famous cousin. He was standing in the background watching Georgie, not with the radiant pleasure with which the mothers watched him, but with an expression more akin to that with which the Outlaws watched him. This caused William a passing interest which however he soon forgot in his deep passionate loathing of the perfect little gentleman.

Gradually the Outlaws eluded the maternal escorts and foregathered on the outskirts of the throng.

'Let's get out of this,' said Ginger gloomily.

They wandered down a small path that led off from the lawn and finally reached the rather muddy pond which the Murdochs dignified by the name of 'lake'. The Outlaws gazed at it gloomily. In ordinary circumstances it would have suggested a dozen enthralling games, but the Outlaws, encased in Sunday suits, and more or less clean and tidy, felt that any straying from the paths of strict decorum upon this occasion would be simply playing into the hands of the enemy. They wandered morosely into a small summer-house that stood near the banks of the pond, and there they held a further consultation. Feeling against William was running high. What after all was the use of a leader who could not cope with an emergency like this . . . ?

' 'Straordinary,' said Ginger aloofly, ' 'Straordinary that you can't think of anythin' to *do*.'

William glared at Ginger. He couldn't for the moment even fight old Ginger, which would have been something of a relief to his feelings. So he merely retorted coldly, ' 'Straordinary you can't think of anythin' to do yourself.'

And Henry said gloomily, 'And he gets sickniner an' sickniner.'

'He certainly does,' said a strange voice.

The Outlaws looked up to see the famous cousin lolling negligently against the side of the doorway of the summer-house.

'You are referring, I presume,' he said, 'to our little host, Georgie the Terrible.'

'Yes, we are,' said William belligerently, 'an' – an' I don't care if you *tellem*.'

'Oh, I shan't tell them,' said the famous cousin carelessly. 'I've thought far worse things about Georgie than you could ever put into words.'

'Uh?' said William, surprised.

'You only see him occasionally. For this week I've seen him every day.'

'Oh?' said William again.

'I've suffered,' went on the famous cousin, 'more deeply than you can ever have suffered. Georgie is, as it were, branded into my very soul. I have often wondered why – My hands, of course, are tied. I am the guest of Georgie's parents. Battery and assault upon Georgie would therefore ill become me. But *you*—' he looked at them scornfully – 'that one – two – three – four boys your size can continue to allow Georgie to exist as he is passes my comprehension.'

''S all very well talkin' like that,' said William indignantly, 'but he's such a little *sneak*! We can't do anythin' to him that he doesn't go an' tell our mothers an' then we get into trouble an' he gets more sickenin' than ever.'

'Sickniner an' *sickniner*,' murmured Henry again dejectedly.

'I see,' said the stranger judicially, 'I fully appreciate the difficulty. . . . Er – may I join the conference?'

He entered the summer-house and sat down next to William.

'Have you,' he said, 'discussed any plan of action?'

'Lots,' said William. 'Douglas wanted to put him in a pit an' say wild beasts had eaten him.'

'Same as they did Joseph in the Bible,' explained Douglas.

'Ingenious,' commented the stranger, 'but impracticable. . . . Now we want to approach the matter in a scientific frame of mind. Before fixing on a plan of action you should always study the enemy's weaknesses. Has the egregious Georgie any weaknesses?'

'*Has* he?' said William bitterly, 'he tells tales an' won't play games an'—'

The famous cousin raised his hand.

'Pardon me,' he said, 'those are vices, not weaknesses. In my sojourn with Georgie I have noticed two weaknesses. He will never own to ignorance even on the most abstruse subjects, and he is passionately fond of chocolate creams. Did you know that?'

'Y-yes. S'pose so,' said William, 'but I don't see how it will help.'

'Ah . . . you must somehow *make* it help. A good general always utilises his enemy's weak points. . . . I can't of course suggest or connive at any plan of action, but I'll help you. I'll tell you what I'll do. I'll offer a two pound box of chocolate creams as a prize for some competition. That brings in one weakness. I leave it to your ingenuity to make good use of the other. Georgie would, I believe, do anything for chocolate creams – I wish you good luck. Good day.'

The famous cousin disappeared leaving the

Outlaws gaping and mystified. But his visit had heartened them. The knowledge that one grown-up at least saw Georgie the Perfect Little Gentleman as he really was gave them a fresh confidence in the righteousness of their cause. Their despondency dropped from them.

'Let's go back to the others,' said William briskly, 'an' see what he's goin' to say about the chocolate creams.'

They emerged on the lawn and made their way to the group around Mrs Murdoch. Beside Mrs Murdoch stood Georgie still immaculately clean and smugly smiling, with curls that glinted in the sun.

'Isn't it *too* kind of my cousin,' Mrs Murdoch was saying. 'Yes, he loves children. He's *passionately* attached to Georgie. He wants the children to do a little *scene* – he's passionately interested in literature, of course, being one himself – a little scene from English history – any part of English history – my cousin's *passionately* fond of English history – and he's offered a two pound box of chocolate creams as a prize to the child who acts the best. . . . Collect your little friends, Georgie, darling.' Georgie's eyes were still gleaming from the mention of chocolate creams, 'and you might go down to the summer-house to talk things over and then come back and act your little scene to us here.'

THE OUTLAWS EMERGED ON THE LAWN AND MADE
THEIR WAY DISGUSTEDLY TOWARDS THE GROUP
AROUND MRS MURDOCH

'MY COUSIN'S OFFERED A BOX OF CHOCOLATE CREAMS
AS A PRIZE TO THE ONE WHO ACTS BEST,' MRS MURDOCH
WAS SAYING. GEORGIE'S EYES GLEAMED.

Georgie, the Outlaws and a few odds and ends of children who do not really come into the story, drifted down to the summer-house. The Outlaws looked at Georgie. Georgie's eyes still gleamed. Then they looked at William, and with a great relief at their hearts they read in William's sphinx-like face that at last he was justifying his position as leader.

He had a plan.

First of all William kindly but firmly gathered together the odds and ends and despatched them to the kitchen garden.

'There's too many of us for one scene,' he explained, 'so we'll do one scene and you do another scene. An' we'd better get right away from each other so's not to disturb each other . . . so you just go 'n make up your scene in the kitchen garden where nobody'll disturb you an' we'll stay an' make up ours here. Georgie'll show you the way to the kitchen garden.'

And while Georgie was showing them the way to the kitchen garden William unfolded his plan to the Outlaws. The odds and ends had fully intended to discuss the scenes from English history in the kitchen garden, but they discovered a bed of ripe strawberries, and considering a strawberry in the hand worth two scenes from English history in the bush, decided to leave the Past to its peaceful sleep and concentrate wholly upon the Present. . . . So they don't come into the story any more.

Georgie returned to the Outlaws in the summer-house. Upon his face was a resolute determination to win that box of chocolate creams at all costs.

'What'll we act?' he said eagerly.

'Well,' said William thoughtfully, 'he was down here talkin' to us a few minutes ago an' he said that his favourite period in English history was King John.'

'We'll do King John then,' said Georgie firmly.

'He said that his favourite part of King John was where he came back from losing his things in the Wash.'

'We'll do that then,' said Georgie hastily.

'Who'll be King John?' said William.

'*I'll* be King John,' said Georgie.

'All right,' said William with unexpected amenity, 'an' shall Ginger an' me be your two heralds an' Douglas and Henry your servants or somethin'?'

'Yes,' said Georgie, and added, 'You needn't *do* anythin' but jus' stand there – any of you. I'll do the actin'.'

'All right,' agreed William, still with disarming humility. 'You know all about the story, don't you?'

'Yes, of course I do.'

'About how King John went into the Wash tryin' to find his things—'

'Yes, I know all that.'

'An' the Wash was a kind of a bog—'

'Yes, I know.'

'An' he came out all muddy but couldn't find his things 'cause they'd sunk in the mud.'

'Yes, I know.'

'An' he came to his two servants called Dam an' Blarst—'

'Called—?'

'*Fancy* you not knowin' about King John's servants bein' called Dam an' Blarst!'

'I *did* know,' said Georgie, 'I've known it for *ever* so long . . . What did you say they were called?'

'Dam and Blarst.'

'Dam and Blarst. Of *course* I knew.'

'Well, let's get you ready for bein' King John . . . 'S no good goin' on as King John lookin' like that when you're s'posed to've just come out of a bog looking for your things . . . no one'd give anyone a prize for *that*.'

'I'm not going to get myself all muddy, so there!'

'All right,' said William, '*I'll* be King John. I don't care.'

'No, I'm going to be King John,' persisted Georgie.

'Well, you can't be King John,' said William firmly, 'if you don't get yourself a bit muddy like what he was when he come back from losin' his things in the Wash. It'll easy come off afterwards. Jus' take off your shoes an' stockings an' paddle about a bit at the edge of the pond. You needn't mess up anythin' but jus' your feet.'

There was a silence in which Georgie's love of chocolate creams fought with his instincts of cleanliness and put them to flight.

'All right,' he said, 'I don't mind muddying my feet just a *bit*.'

He took off his shoes and stockings. William and Ginger took off theirs too.

'Just to help you, Georgie,' they said, 'and to stop you fallin' in or anythin'.'

They held him firmly on either side, and walked him down to the pond. 'Jus' because we wun't like you to fall an' mess up your suit,' said William.

'Be careful, Georgie,' said Ginger, 'don' go too far.'

'Be careful, Georgie,' said William, 'mind you don't fall.'

At last they returned to the bank.

'Nice sort of *help* you were,' said Georgie indignantly, 'why, you made me go in *lots* further than I meant to and, look, you've got mud all over my trousers.'

'Sorry, Georgie,' said William meekly, 'that was where I splashed you by mistake, wasn't it? Shall I be King John if you don't like it?'

'No, I'm goin' to be King John,' said Georgie. 'Well, shall we go and do it now?'

William looked at him doubtfully. Georgie was gloriously muddy as far as his lower regions were concerned but his face and blouse were still spotlessly clean and his curls still glinted in the sun.

'It's not *quite* right yet, Georgie,' he said gently. 'Don' you remember how in History King John *dived* into the Wash after his things?'

'Yes, I know,' said Georgie, 'I know all about that.'

'Well, 's no good you goin' actin' King John an' not lookin' as if you'd jus' dived into a bog,' said William.

'I tell you,' said Georgie indignantly, 'I'm not goin' to put any more nasty mud on me.'

'All right,' said William kindly, 'let Ginger be King John . . . *he* won't mind.'

'No, *I'm* goin' to be King John,' said Georgie.

'We'll jus' put a bit of mud on your hair then,' said William persuasively, 'it'll soon wash off an' it would be awfully nice if you got the prize, Georgie.'

'All right,' said Georgie relenting, 'but only a *little*, mind.'

'Oh, yes, Georgie,' said William, 'only a *little* . . .'

They plastered his bead and face with mud from the pond and dropped a goodly portion of it upon his blouse. Fortunately Georgie could not see his upper half very well.

'You're only putting a *little* on, aren't you?' he asked anxiously.

'Oh, yes, Georgie,' William reassured him, 'only a little. Now you look *lovely*. You look jus' like King John after he'd been tryin' to find his things in the Wash – divin' in for 'em an' all . . .'

Certainly the perfect little gentleman was unrecognisable. His suit was covered with mud, his hair was caked with mud, his face was streaked with mud. He had waded in mud. His smile, though still there, was almost invisible. No longer did his curls glint in the sun.

'Now let's start, shall we?' said William, his spirits rising as he gazed at his handiwork. 'First of all I'll go on with Ginger – we're your heralds you know – and we'll say you're coming; "Make way for King John" or somethin' like that. Then you come on with Henry and Douglas and you speak to 'em. You know what King John said to 'em in History, don't you?'

'Yes, of course I do,' said Georgie. 'What did he say?'

'He just looked at 'em an' said, "Oh Dam and Blarst (their names, you know) I cannot find my things".'

'Of course I knew he said that.'

'Well, you jus' say that to 'em and – shall we start? I say, Georgie, you do make *a fine* King John.'

'Oh, I bet I'll win the prize all right,' said Georgie complacently from beneath his mud.

The grown-ups sat in an expectant semicircle, smiling indulgently.

'I do so *love* to see little children acting,' said one, 'They're always so sweet and natural.'

'I wish you'd seen Georgie last Christmas,' murmured Georgie's mother, 'as Prince Charming in a little children's pantomime we got up. I had his photograph taken. I'll show it to you afterwards.'

Just then William and Ginger appeared. They had replaced their stockings and shoes and looked for William and Ginger unusually neat and tidy.

'Well, dears,' said Mrs Murdoch smiling, 'have you chosen your little scene yet?'

'No,' said William, 'we can't get on with it with Georgie messin' about the pond all the time.'

At that moment Georgie, imagining that William and Ginger had heralded his approach with all ceremony, came proudly into view from behind the bushes, followed by Douglas and Henry. The mud from the pond was a peculiarly concentrated kind of mud and Georgie had wallowed in it from head to foot. One could only guess at his white suit and glinting curls. But through it shone Georgie's eyes in rapturous anticipation of a two pound box of chocolate creams.

William and Ginger gazed at him in well simulated horror.

'Oh, Georgie, you *naughty* boy!' said William.

'What *will* your mother say!' said Ginger.

Douglas and Henry stepped forward.

'We *told* him not to,' said Douglas.

'We *knew* you wouldn't like it,' said Henry to the speechless Mrs Murdoch.

Georgie felt that something had gone wrong somewhere but he was determined to do his part at any rate to win those chocolate creams.

He looked at Henry and Douglas. 'Oh, Dam and Blarst—' he began, but the uproar drowned the rest.

With a scream of horror audible a mile away Mrs Murdoch seized the perfect little gentleman by the arm and hurried him indoors.

Georgie explained as best he could. He explained that he was meant to be King John returning from the Wash and that Dam and Blarst were his two servants. But explanations were unavailing. No explanation could wipe out from the memories of those present that astounding picture of Georgie Murdoch standing in the middle of the lawn caked with black mud from head to foot and saying, 'Oh, damn and blast!'

The party broke up after that. No festive atmosphere could have survived that shock. The Outlaws, clean and neat and sphinx-like and silent, accompanied their parents home.

'*Well*,' said the parents, 'I'd never have believed *that* of Georgie Murdoch!'

'*Caked* with mud!'

'And such *language*!'

'It shows that you never can *tell*.'

A close observer might have gathered that at heart the Outlaws' parents were almost as jubilant over Georgie's downfall as were the Outlaws themselves.

The famous cousin, who was by the gate as William took his leave, managed to press a ten-shilling note into William's hand.

'To be divided amongst your accomplices,' he murmured. 'You surpassed my highest expectation. As artist to artist I tend you my congratulations.'

That, of course, is quite a good place to stop, but, there remains more to be said.

The next day Georgie appeared once more, cleaner and neater than ever and clad in a new white suit, walking decorously down the village street and smiling complacently. But it was no use. Georgie's reputation was gone. It had so to speak vanished in a night. Georgie might have paraded his clean white-clad figure and smug smile and golden curls before the eyes of the village for a hundred years and yet never wiped out the memory of that mud-caked little horror uttering horrible oaths before the assembled aristocrats of the village.

At the end of the month the Murdochs sold their house and removed. They told their new neighbours that there hadn't been a boy in the place fit for Georgie to associate with.

History does not relate what happened to the chocolate creams.

Perhaps the famous cousin ate them.

CHAPTER 4

WILLIAM PLAYS SANTA CLAUS

WILLIAM walked slowly and thoughtfully down the village street. It was the week after Christmas. Henry was still away. Douglas and Ginger were the only two of his friends left in the village. Henry's absence had its bright side because Henry's father had, in the excitement of the departure, forgotten to lock his garage and the Outlaws found Henry's father's garage a nice change from the old barn, their usual meeting place. William was glad that Christmas was over. He'd not done badly out of it on the whole, but Christmas was a season too sacred to the conventions and to uncongenial relatives to appeal to William.

Suddenly he saw someone coming down the village street towards him. It was Mr Solomon, the super-intendent of the Sunday School of which William was a reluctant and inglorious member. William had his reasons for not wishing to meet Mr Solomon. Mr Solomon had organised a party of waits for Christmas Eve from his Sunday School attendants and William had not only joined this party but had assumed leadership of it. They had managed to detach themselves from Mr Solomon quite early in the evening and had spent the night in glorious lawlessness. William had not seen Mr Solomon since that occasion because Mr Solomon had had a slight nervous breakdown and William was now torn between a desire to elude him and a desire to tackle him. The desire to elude him needs no explanation. The desire to tackle was equally simple. William had heard that Mr Solomon, who was ever prolific in fresh ideas, had decided to form a band from the elder boys of the Sunday School. It may be thought that Mr Solomon should have learnt wisdom from his experience on Christmas Eve but then Mr Solomon had decided to ensure success for his scheme by the simple process of debarring the Outlaws from it. William had heard of this and the news had filled him with such righteous indignation that it overcame even his natural reluctance to meet the organiser of the Christmas Eve carol party.

He confronted him squarely.

'Afternoon, Mr Solomon,' he said.

Mr Solomon looked him up and down with distaste.

'Good afternoon, my boy,' he said icily, 'I am on my way to pay a visit to your parents.'

This news was not encouraging. William turned to accompany him, consoled slightly by the knowledge that both his parents were out. Losing no time he boldly approached the subject of the band.

'Hear you're gettin' up a band, Mr Solomon,' he said casually.

'I am,' said Mr Solomon more icily than ever.

'I'd like to be a trumpeter,' said William, still casually.

'You have not been asked to join the band,' went on Mr Solomon with a firmness unusual in that mild young man, but his mind was still raw with the memories of Christmas Eve, 'and you will *not* be asked to join the band.'

'Oh,' said William politely.

'You may wonder,' went on Mr Solomon with deep emotion, 'why I am going to pay a visit to your parents.'

William didn't wonder at all, but he said nothing.

'I am going,' continued Mr Solomon 'to complain to your parents of your shameful behaviour on Christmas Eve.'

'Oh – that,' said William as though he remembered the incident with difficulty, 'I remember – we – sort of lost you, didn't we? It's easy losin' people in the pitch dark. It made it very awkward for us,' he went on complainingly, 'you gettin' lost like that.'

'You are at liberty, of course,' said Mr Solomon, 'to give your version of the affair to your parents. I shall give mine. I have little doubt which they will believe.'

William also had little, or rather no doubt at all, which they would believe. He was constantly being amazed and horrified by his parents' lack of credulity in his versions of affairs. He changed the subject hastily.

'I could easy learn a trumpet,' he volunteered, 'an' so c'd Ginger an' Douglas – an' Henry when he comes back an'   an' it won't be so easy to lose you with a band in daylight. It was with it bein' so dark that we sort of got lost Christmas Eve.'

Mr Solomon disdained to answer.

After a pause, William said solicitously:

'Sorry t'hear you've been ill.'

'My slight indisposition,' said Mr Solomon, 'was the result of our ill-fated expedition on Christmas Eve.'

'Yes,' said William who was determined to cover that ill-fated expedition as far as possible with the cloak of innocency, 'it was a nasty cold night. I was sneezin' a bit myself the next mornin'.'

Again Mr Solomon disdained to answer.

'Well, when I'm in your band,' said William with his irrepressible optimism, 'playin' a trumpet—'

'William,' said Mr Solomon patiently, 'you will *not* be in my band playing anything. If your parents continue to send you to Sunday School after receiving my complaint, I must – er – endure it, but you will *not* be in my band. Nor will any of your friends.'

At the suggestion that his parents might not continue to send him to Sunday School after receiving Mr Solomon's complaint, William's spirits had risen only to drop again immediately at the reflection that they would be all the more likely to insist upon it. Mr Solomon, of course, looked upon his Sunday School as a glorious privilege to its attendants. William's parents looked upon it more simply as their Sunday afternoon's rest. They would not be likely to put an end to William's attendance there on any consideration.

Mr Solomon turned in at the gate of William's home and William accompanied him with an air of courage that was, as I have said, derived solely from the knowledge that both his parents were out. Then taking a muttered farewell of his companion he went round to the side of the house. His companion went up the front steps and rang the front door ball.

William amused himself in the back garden for some time but keeping under strict observation the front drive where the baffled Mr Solomon must soon beat his retreat. But no baffled Mr Solomon appeared beating his retreat. Curiosity impelled William to creep cautiously up to the drawing-room window. There sat Mr Solomon, flushed and simpering, having tea with Ethel, William's grown-up sister. Of course – he'd forgotten that Ethel was at home. Ethel was evidently being very nice to Mr Solomon. Ethel happened to be in the temporary and, for her, very rare position of being without a male admirer on the spot. Everyone seemed to have gone away for Christmas. Her latest conquest, Rudolph Vernon, an exquisite young man quite worthy of his name, had left her almost in tears the week before to pay a Christmas visit to an aunt in the country from whom he had expectations. Mr Solomon was not of course a victim worthy of Ethel's bow and spear, but he was better than no one. She happened also to be suffering from a cold in her head which made any diversion welcome. Therefore she gave him tea and smiled upon him. He sat, blushing deeply and gazing in rapt adoration at her blue eyes and Titian red hair (for Ethel put every other girl for miles around in the 'also ran' class as far as looks were concerned). He had not even dared to tell her the real object of his visit lest it should prejudice her against him. William feasted his eyes upon the spectacle of the lately indignant Mr Solomon, now charmed and docile and, metaphorically speaking, eating out of Ethel's hand, then curiosity impelled him to come to yet closer quarters with the spectacle. He was anxious to ascertain whether the complaint had actually been lodged against him or whether Ethel's smiles had driven it completely out of Mr Solomon's mind. Though, generally speaking, he disapproved of Ethel as unduly exacting and trammelling to his free spirit, he was forced in justice to admit that there were times when she had her uses.

He went upstairs, performed a hasty and sketchy toilet, assumed his most guileless expression and entered the drawing-room. At his entrance Ethel's alluring smile gave way to an expression of annoyance and Mr Solomon's allured smile to one of sheepishness. But this reception had no effect upon William. William was not sensitive to shades of manner. He sat down upon a chair next to Mr Solomon with the expression of one who has every intention of remaining where he is for some time, and turned his guileless countenance from Ethel to Mr Solomon, from Mr Solomon to Ethel. Silence had fallen at his entrance but it was obvious that someone must say something soon.

'There you are, dear,' said Ethel without enthusiasm, 'would you like some tea?'

'No, thank you,' said William.

'Mr Solomon has very kindly come to make sure that you're none the worse after your little outing on Christmas Eve.'

William turned his guileless countenance upon Mr

Solomon. Mr Solomon went pink and nearly choked over his tea. Demoralised by Ethel's beauty and sweetness of manner he had indeed substituted for his intended complaint a kindly inquiry as to William's health after his exposure to the elements on Christmas Eve, but it was hard to have this repeated in William's hearing and beneath William's sardonic gaze. William made no comment on this statement.

'That's very kind of him, isn't it, William?' said Ethel rather sharply, 'you ought to thank him.'

William still eyed the embarrassed man unflinchingly.

'Thank you,' he said in a tone in which the embarrassed man perceived quite plainly mockery and scorn.

A silence fell. Ethel always found the presence of William disconcerting when she was engaged in charming an admirer. So did the admirer. But William sat on.

'Haven't you any homework to do, William?' said Ethel at last.

'No,' said William, 'it's holidays.'

'Wouldn't you like to go out and play then?'

'No, thank you,' said William.

Ethel wondered as she had wondered hundreds of times before why somebody didn't drown that boy. It was painful to have to conceal her natural

WILLIAM SAT ON AND ON. HE WAS NOT DISCONCERTED.

exasperation beneath a sweet smile for the benefit of the visitor.

'Aren't any of your friends expecting you, dear?' she said with overacted and unconvincing sweetness.

'HAVEN'T YOU ANY HOMEWORK TO DO, WILLIAM?' SAID
ETHEL AT LAST.

'No,' said William and continued to sit and stare in
front of him.

Suddenly the clock struck five and Mr Solomon
started up.

'Good heavens!' he said, 'I must go. I ought to have
gone some time ago.'

'Why?' said Ethel, 'it's very early.'

'B-but I ought to have been there by five.'

'Where?' said Ethel.

'It's the Old Folks' Christmas party. I was to give the presents – the Mixed Infants party too – I should have been at the Old Folks to give their presents at five and with the Mixed Infants at half-past five. I'm afraid I shall be terribly late.'

He looked about frantically.

'Oh, but,' said Ethel beseechingly, 'can't someone else do it for you? It seems such a shame for you to have to run off as soon as you've come.'

He was a most conscientious young man, but he looked into Ethel's blue, blue eyes and was lost. He didn't care who gave away the presents to the Old Folks and the Mixed Infants. He didn't care whether anyone gave them away. All he wanted to do was to sit in this room and be smiled upon by Ethel. It came to him suddenly that he'd met his soul's mate at last. He'd had no idea that the world contained anyone so wonderful and charming and kind and clever.

'Isn't there anyone who'd do it for you?' said Ethel again sweetly.

He thought for a minute.

'Well, I'm sure the curate wouldn't mind doing it,' he said at last. 'I'm sure he wouldn't, I've often taken his Boys' Club for him.'

'Well, William could take the message to him, couldn't he?' said Ethel.

Glorious idea! It would kill two birds with one stone. It would prolong this wonderful *tête-à-tête* and get rid of this objectionable boy. Mr Solomon's spirits rose. He smiled upon William almost benignly.

'Yes – you'll do that, won't you, William?'

'Yes,' said William obligingly, 'cert'nly.'

'Listen very carefully to me then, dear boy,' said Mr Solomon in his best Sunday School superintendent manner. 'Go to Mr Greene's house and ask him if he'd be kind enough – don't forget to put it like that – to take over my duties for this afternoon as I'm – er – unable to attend to them myself. Tell him that the two sacks containing the gifts for the Old Folks' party and the Mixed Infants' party are in my rooms. The bigger of the two is the Old Folks' party presents. He'll find in my rooms, too, a Father Christmas costume which he should wear for giving the Old Folks' presents and a Pied Piper costume for giving the Mixed Infants' presents. It's a pretty custom I've instituted – to wear the Pied Piper costume for the Mixed Infants. Then they form a procession and I lead them round the room and the mothers watch, before I give them the presents. Ask him if he can very kindly – *don't* forget to say that, dear boy – take over these two duties for me this afternoon and ask him if he can't to let me know at once by telephone. If I hear nothing more I'll take for granted that it's all right. Do you quite understand, dear boy?'

'Yes,' said William.

William walked slowly down the road to Mr Solomon's rooms. He had decided after all *not* to trouble to call upon the curate. He had decided very kindly to perform Mr Solomon's two little duties himself. He was most anxious to be admitted to Mr Solomon's band as a trumpeter, and he thought that if Mr Solomon found his two little duties correctly performed by William while he was pursuing his acquaintance with William's engaging sister, his heart might be melted and he might admit William as a trumpeter to his band despite his experience of Christmas Eve. Moreover there is no denying that the two little duties themselves strongly appealed to William. There is no denying that the thought of dressing up as Father Christmas and the Pied Piper and distributing gifts to Old Folks and Mixed Infants appealed very strongly indeed to William's highly developed dramatic instinct.

Mr Solomon's housekeeper admitted him without question. She was used to Mr Solomon's sending people of all ages and all classes to his rooms on various errands. She was annoyed at the marks

William's muddy boots made on the hall that she'd just cleaned, but beyond remarking bitterly that some people didn't seem to know what mats was made for, she took no further notice of him. A few minutes later William might have been observed staggering across from Mr Solomon's rooms to the School with two large sacks and two large bundles over his shoulders.

He found a small classroom to change in. It was intensely thrilling to put on Father Christmas's beard and wig and the trailing red cloak edged with cotton wool. He then carefully considered the two sacks. The larger of the two, Mr Solomon had said, was to be for the Old Folks, but William didn't approve of this at all. Why should the Old Folks have a larger sack than the Mixed Infants? William's sympathies were all on the side of the Mixed Infants. He shouldered the smaller sack therefore and set off to find the Old Folks' Party. As both parties were being held in the same building the corridors were freely adorned with placards pointing out the way by means of hands whose execution revealed much good intention, but little knowledge of anatomy. William easily tracked down the Old Folks' party. He listened for a moment outside the door to the confused murmur within, then flung open the door and entered dramatically. Old Folks in various stages of old age sat round the room talking to each other complainingly. A perspiring young man and woman were trying ineffectively to get them to join in a game. The guests were engaged in discussing among themselves the inadequacy of the tea and the uncomfortableness of the chairs and the piercingness of the draught and the general dullness of the party.

' 'Tisn't what it used to be in my young days,' one old man was saying loudly to his neighbours.

William entered with his sack.

At the sight of him they brightened.

The perspiring young man and woman hurried down to him eagerly.

'*So* glad to see you,' they gasped, 'you're awfully late – I suppose Mr Solomon sent you with the things?'

Not much of William's face could be seen through the all-enveloping beard and wig, but what could be seen signified assent.

'Well, do begin to give them out,' said the young man, 'it's simply ghastly! We can't get any *go* into it at all. They won't do anything but sit round and grumble. I hope you've got plenty of tea and 'baccy. That's what they like best. Are you going to make a speech?'

William hastily shook his head and lowered his sack from his shoulder.

'Well, begin at this end, will you? and let's hope to goodness that it'll cheer them up.'

William began and it was not until he had

presented an amazed and outraged old man with a toy engine that it occurred to him that it had been perhaps a mistake to exchange the two sacks. But having begun, he went doggedly on with his task. He presented to the old men and women around him dolls and small tin motor cars and miniature shops and little wooden boats and garish little picture books and pencil cases – all presents laboriously chosen by the worthy Mr Solomon for the Mixed Infants.

It was evident that the young man and woman helpers were restraining themselves with difficulty. The Old Folks were for the time being paralysed by amazement and indignation. Yet a close observer might have remarked that there was something of satisfaction in their indignation. They'd grumbled at the tea and room and chairs and draught till they were tired of grumbling at them. Something fresh to grumble at was almost in the nature of a godsend. Of course they'd have grumbled at their presents whatever they'd been, but anything so unusually and satisfactorily easy to grumble at as these unsuitable presents was almost exhilarating.

William gathered from the almost homicidal expressions with which the young man and woman helpers were watching him that it would be as well to retire as hastily as possible. He handed his last present, a child's paintbox, to a deaf and blind old woman by the door, and departed almost precipitately. Then the storm broke out and a torrent of shrill indignation pursued his retreating form.

He returned to the little classroom he had chosen as his dressing-room and stood contemplating his other costume and other sack. Yes, impersonally and impartially he could not help admitting that the changing of the sacks had been a mistake, but it was done now and he must just carry on as best as he could.

It took some time to change into the Pied Piper costume and he retained his beard and wig in order the better to conceal his identity. Then he shouldered his other sack and set off to follow the numerous placards whose hands crippled apparently by rheumatism or some other terrible complaint continued with dogged British determination to do their duty and point the way to the room where the Mixed Infants were assembled.

William had become very thoughtful. He was realising the fact that in all probability his fulfilment of Mr Solomon's rôles that afternoon would not be such as to melt Mr Solomon's heart towards him and make him admit him as trumpeter into his band. He doubted if even Ethel's charm would be strong enough to counter-balance the Old Folks' presents. And he did so dearly want to enter Mr Solomon's band as a trumpeter. He must try to think of some way.

He flung open the door of a room in which a few dozen Mixed Infants gambolled half-heartedly at the bidding of the conscientious 'helpers'. A little cluster of mothers sat at the end of the room and watched them proudly. The Mixed Infants, seeing him enter with his sack, brightened and instructed by the helpers, broke into a thin shrill cheer. A helper came down to greet him.

'How good of you to come,' she said gushingly. 'I suppose Mr Solomon couldn't get off himself. Such an indefatigable worker, isn't he? The procession first, of course – the children know just what to do – we've been rehearsing it.'

The Mixed Infants were already getting into line. The 'helper' motioned William to the head of it. William stepped into position.

'Twice round the room, you know,' said the helper, 'and then distribute the presents.'

William began very slowly to walk round the room, his sack on his shoulder, his train of Mixed Infants prancing joyously behind. William's brain was working quickly. He had not looked into the bag he was carrying, but he had a strong suspicion that he would soon be distributing packets of tea and tobacco to a gathering of outraged Mixed Infants. Surely the fury of the Old Folks presented with dolls and engines would be as nothing to the fury of Mixed Infants presented with packets of tea and tobacco. His hopes of being admitted into Mr Solomon's band faded into nothingness.

He began his second peregrination of the room. Fond mothers gazed in rapt admiration – each at her own particular Mixed Infant. William walked very slowly. He was trying to put off the evil hour when he must open the sack and take out the packets of tea and tobacco. Then suddenly he decided not to await meekly the blows of Fate. Instead he'd play a bold game. He'd carry the war into the enemy's country.

The mothers and helpers were surprised when suddenly William, followed by his faithful band (who would have died martyrs' deaths sooner than lose sight of that sack for one moment), walked out of the door and disappeared from view. But an intelligent helper smiled brightly and said:

'How thoughtful! He's just going to take them once round the School outside. I expect quite a lot of people are hanging about hoping for a glimpse of them.'

'Perhaps,' suggested a mother, 'he's taken them for a peep at the Old Folks' party.'

'Who is he?' said another. 'I thought Mr Solomon was to have come.'

'Oh, it's probably one of Mr Solomon's elder Sunday School boys. He told me once that he believed in training them up in habits of social service. He's a *wonderful* man, I think.'

'Isn't he?' sighed another, '*lives* for duty – I'm so sorry he couldn't come today.'

'Well, I'm sure,' said the first, 'he'd have come if some more pressing duty hadn't detained him. The dear man's probably reading to some poor invalid at this moment.'

At that moment as a matter of fact the dear man had got to the point where he was earnestly informing Ethel that no one had ever – ever – *ever* understood him in all his life before as she did.

'I don't think that Johnnie ought to have gone out of doors,' complained a mother, 'he hadn't got his chest protector on.'

'It's only for a second,' said a helper soothingly, 'it will air the room a bit.'

'But it won't put Johnnie's chest protector on,' said the mother pugnaciously. 'And what's the use of airing the room when we'd only just got it nice and warm for them.'

'I'll go out and see where they are,' said the helper obligingly. She went out and looked round the School playground. The School playground was empty. She walked round to the other side of the School. There was no one there. There was no sign of anyone anywhere. She returned to the mothers and other helpers.

'They must have gone to see the Old Folks' party,' she said.

'If they're not outside,' said Johnnie's mother, 'I don't mind. All I meant was that if he was outside he ought to be wearing his chest protector.'

'I think,' said another helper rather haughtily, 'that that boy ought to have *told* us that he was going to take them to see the Old Folks. When I offer to help at a party I like to be consulted about the arrangements.'

'Well, let's go and find them,' said Johnnie's mother. 'I don't want Johnnie wandering about these nasty draughty passages without it. I wish now that I'd never taken it off.'

They set off in a body to the room where the Old Folks' party was being held. The Old Folks, sitting round the room, still held their little dolls or engines and toy boats, and were grumbling to each other about them with morbid relish. One helper was at the piano singing a cheerful little song to which no one was listening. The other was bending over an octogenarian, who despite himself was becoming interested in the workings of his clockwork 'bus. This interest, however, was disapproved of by the rest.

'Disgustin', I call it!' an old man was saying to his neighbour holding out the toy train signal with which William had presented him.

The neighbour who was tired of talking about his toy mouse glared ferociously at the performer.

'Kickin' up such a din a body can't hear himself speak,' he muttered.

The mothers and helpers of the Mixed Infants looked around anxiously, then swept up to the helpers of the Old Folks. A hasty whispered consultation took place. No, the Pied Piper and Mixed Infants had not visited them at all. Probably they had returned to their own room by now. The mothers and helpers hurried back to the room. It was still empty. Talking excitedly they poured out into the playground. It was empty. They poured out into the street. It was empty. Part of them tore frenziedly up the street and part tore equally frenziedly to search the building again. Everything was empty. The old legend had come true. A Pied Piper followed by every Mixed Infant in the village had vanished completely from the face of the earth.

Ethel had just sneezed and Mr Solomon was just thinking how much more musically she sneezed than anyone else he had ever met, when the mothers and helpers burst in upon them. The helpers took in the situation at a glance, and never again did Mr Solomon recapture the pedestal from which that glance deposed him. But that is by the way. The immediate question was the Mixed Infants. The babel was so deafening that it took a long time before Mr Solomon grasped what it was all about. Johnnie's mother had a penetrating voice, and for a long time Mr Solomon thought that all they had come to say was that Johnnie had lost his chest protector. When the situation finally dawned on him he blinked with horror and amazement.

'B-b-but Mr Greene came to give the presents,' he gasped, 'it was Mr Greene.'

'It certainly wasn't Mr Greene,' said a helper tartly, 'it was a boy. We thought it must have been one of your Sunday School boys. We couldn't see his face plainly because of his beard.'

A feeling of horror stole over Mr Solomon.

'A b-b-boy?' he gasped.

'If I'd known he was going out like that,' wailed Johnnie's mother, 'I'd never have taken it off.'

'Wait a minute,' stammered Mr Solomon excitedly, 'I – I'll go and speak to Mr Greene.'

But the visit to Mr Greene was entirely fruitless of Mixed Infants. All it produced was the information that Mr Greene had been out all the afternoon and had received no message of any kind from Mr Solomon.

'They – they can't really have gone,' said Mr Solomon. 'Perhaps they are hiding in some other classroom for a joke.'

With a crowd of distracted mothers at his heels he returned to the School and conducted there a thorough and systematic search. Though thorough and systematic as a search could be, it revealed no Mixed Infants. The attitude of the mothers was growing hostile. They evidently looked upon Mr Solomon as solely responsible for the calamity.

'Sittin' there,' muttered a mother fiercely, 'sittin' there dallyin' with red haired females while our children was bein' stole – *Nero*!'

''*Erod*!' said another not to be outdone in general culture.

'*Crippen*!' said another showing herself more up-to-date.

The perspiration was pouring from Mr Solomon's brow. It was like a nightmare. He could not move anywhere without this crowd of hostile, muttering women. He had a horrible suspicion that they were going to lynch him, hang him from the nearest lamp-post. And what, oh what, in the name of St George's Hall, had happened to the Mixed Infants?

'Let us just look up and down the road again,' he said hoarsely. Still muttering darkly they followed him into the road. He looked up and down it wildly. There wasn't a Mixed Infant to be seen anywhere. The threatening murmurs behind him grew louder.

'Duck him,' he heard and 'Hangin's too good for him,' and 'Wring his neck with my own hands I will if he doesn't find 'em soon,' and from Johnnie's mother:

'Well, if I find him again it'll be a lesson to me never to take it off no more.'

'I – I'll go and look round the village,' said poor Mr Solomon desperately, 'I'll go to the police – I'll promise I'll find them.'

'You'd better,' said someone darkly.

He tore in panic down the road. He tore in panic up the nearest street. And then suddenly he saw William's face looking at him over a garden gate.

'Hello,' said William.

'Do you know anything about those children?' panted Mr Solomon.

'Yes,' said William calmly, 'if you'll promise to let me be a trumpeter in your band, you can have them. Will you?'

'Y-yes,' spluttered Mr Solomon.

'On your honour?' persisted William.

'HERE THEY ARE,' SAID WILLIAM. 'YOU CAN HAVE 'EM IF YOU LIKE.'

'Yes,' said Mr Solomon.

'An' Ginger an' Henry an' Douglas – all trumpeters?'

'Yes,' said Mr Solomon desperately. It was at that moment that Mr Solomon decided that not even Ethel's charm would compensate for having William for a brother-in-law.

'All right,' said William, 'come round here.'

THE GARAGE WAS FULL OF 'MIXED INFANTS' HAVING THE
TIME OF THEIR LIVES.

He led him round to a garage at the back of the house and opened the door. The garage was full of Mixed Infants having the time of their lives, engaged in mimic warfare under the leadership of Ginger and Douglas with ammunition of tea leaves and tobacco. Certainly the Mixed Infants were appreciating the Old Folks' presents far more than the Old Folks had appreciated the Mixed Infants'.

Johnnie, the largest and healthiest of the infants, was engaged in chewing tobacco and evidently enjoying it.

'Here they are,' said William carelessly, 'you can have 'em if you like. We're gettin' a bit tired of them.'

No words of mine could describe the touching reunion between the mothers of the Mixed Infants and the Mixed Infants, or between Johnnie and his chest protector.

Neither could any words of mine describe the first practice of Mr Solomon's Sunday School band with William, Ginger and Douglas and Henry as trumpeters.

There was, however, only one practice, as after that Mr Solomon wisely decided to go away for a very long holiday.

CHAPTER 5

WILLIAM AND THE WHITE ELEPHANTS

'WILLIAM,' said Mrs Brown to her younger son, 'as Robert will be away, I think it would be rather nice if you helped me at my stall at the Fête.'

William's father at the head of the table groaned aloud.

'*Another* Fête,' he said.

'My dear, it's *centuries* . . . *weeks* since we had one last,' said his wife, 'and this is the Conservative Fête – and quite different from all the others.'

'What sort 'f a stall you goin' to have?' said William, who had received her invitation to help without enthusiasm.

'A White Elephant stall,' said Mrs Brown.

William showed signs of animation.

'And where you goin' to gettem?' he said with interest.

'Oh, people will give them,' said Mrs Brown vaguely.

'*Crumbs!*' said William, impressed.

'You must be very careful with them, William,' said

his father gravely, 'they're delicate animals and must be given only the very best buns. Don't allow the people to feed them indiscriminately.'

'Oh, no,' said William with a swagger, 'I bet I'll stop 'em doin' it that way if *I'm* lookin' after 'em.'

'And be very careful when you're in charge of them. They're difficult beasts to handle.'

'Oh, I'm not scared of any ole elephant,' boasted William, then wonderingly after a minute's deep thought, '*white* 'uns, did you say?'

'Don't tease him, dear,' said Mrs Brown, to her husband, and to William, 'white elephants, dear, are things you don't need.'

'I know,' said William, 'I know I don't need 'em but I s'pose some people do or you wun't be sellin' 'em.'

With that he left the room.

He joined his friends the Outlaws in the old barn.

'There's goin' to be white elephants at the Fête,' he announced carelessly, 'an' I'm goin' to be lookin' after them.'

'*White elephants!*' said Ginger impressed, 'an' what they goin' to do?'

'Oh, walk about an' give people rides same as in the Zoo an' eat buns an' that sort of thing. I've gotter feed 'em.'

'Never seen *white* 'uns before,' said Henry.

'Haven't you?' said William airily. 'They're – they're same as black 'uns 'cept that they're white. They come from the cold places – same as polar bears. That's what turns 'em white – roamin' about in snow an' ice same as polar bears.'

The Outlaws were impressed.

'When are they comin'?' they demanded.

William hesitated. His pride would not allow him to admit that he did not know.

'Oh . . . comin' by train jus' a bit before the Sale of Work begins. I'm goin' to meet 'em an' bring 'em to the Sale of Work. They're s'posed to be savage but I bet they won't try on bein' savage with *me*,' he added meaningly. 'I bet I c'n manage any ole *elephant*.'

They gazed at him with deep respect.

'You'll let me *help* with 'em a bit, won't you?'

'William, can I help *feed* 'em?'

'William, can I have a ride free?'

'Well, I'll see,' promised William largely, and with odious imitation of grown-up phraseology, 'I'll see when the time comes.'

The subsequent discovery of the real meaning of the term White Elephant filled William with such disgust that he announced that nothing would now induce him to attend the Fête in any capacity whatsoever. The unconcern with which this announcement was received by his family further increased his disgust. The disappointment of the Outlaws at the disappearance of that glorious vision of William and themselves in sole charge of a herd of snowy mammals caused them to sympathise with William rather than jeer at him.

'If there isn't no white elephants,' said William bitterly, 'then why did they say there was goin' to be some?'

Ginger kindly attempted to explain.

'You see that's the point, William – there *isn't* white elephants.'

'Then why did they say there was?' persisted William. 'Fancy callin' *rubbish* white elephants. If you're goin' to have a stall of rubbish why don' they *say* they're goin' to have a stall of rubbish 'stead of callin' it White Elephants? Where's the *sense* of it? White elephants! An' all the time it's broken old pots an' dull ole books an' stuff like that. What's the *sense* of it . . . callin' it White Elephants!'

Ginger still tried to explain.

'You see there *isn't* any white elephants, William,' he said.

'Well, why do they say there is?' said William finally. 'Well, I'm jus' payin' 'em out by *not* helpin' – that's all.'

But when the day of the Fête arrived William had relented. After all there was something thrilling about serving at a stall. He could pretend that it was his shop. He could feel gloriously important for the time being at any rate, taking in money and handing out change. . . .

'I don't *mind* helpin' you a bit this afternoon, Mother,' he said at breakfast with the air of one who confers a great favour.

His mother considered.

'I almost think we have enough helpers, thank you, William,' she said, 'we don't want too many.'

'Oh, do let William feed the white elephants and take them out for a walk,' pleaded his father.

William glowered at him furiously.

'Of course,' said his mother, 'it's always useful to have someone to send on messages, so if you'll just *be* there, William, in case I need you . . . I daresay there'll be a few little odd jobs you could do.'

'I'll sell the things for you if you like,' said William graciously.

'Oh no,' said his mother hastily, 'I – I don't think you need do *that*, William, thank you.'

William emitted a meaning 'Huh!' – a mixture of contempt and mystery and superiority and sardonic amusement.

His father rose and folded up his newspaper. 'Take

plenty of buns, William, and mind they don't bite you,' he said kindly.

The White Elephant stall contained the usual medley of battered household goods, unwanted Christmas presents, old clothes and derelict sports apparatus.

Mrs Brown stood, placid and serene, behind it. William stood at the side of it surveying it scornfully.

The other Outlaws who had no official positions were watching him from a distance. He had an uncomfortable suspicion that they were jeering at him, that they were comparing his insignificant and servile position as potential errand-goer at the corner of a stall of uninspiring oddments with his glorious dream of tending a flock of snow-white elephants. Pretending not to notice them he moved more to the centre of the stall, and placing one hand on his hip assumed an attitude of proprietorship and importance. . . . They came nearer. Still pretending not to notice them he began to make a pretence of arranging the things on the stall. . . .

His mother turned to him and said, 'I won't be a second away, William, just keep an eye on things,' and departed.

That was splendid. Beneath the (he hoped) admiring gaze of his friends he moved right to the centre of the stall and seemed almost visibly to swell to larger proportions.

A woman came up to the stall and examined a black coat lying across the corner of it.

'You can have that for a shilling,' said William generously.

He looked at the Outlaws from the corner of his eye hoping that they noticed him left thus in sole charge, fixing prices, selling goods and generally directing affairs. The woman handed him a shilling and disappeared with the coat into the crowd.

William again struck the attitude of sole proprietor of the White Elephant stall.

Soon his mother returned and he moved to the side of the stall shedding something of his air of importance.

Then the Vicar's wife came up. She looked about the stall anxiously, then said to William's mother:

'I thought I'd put my coat down just here for a few minutes dear. You haven't seen it, have you? I put it just here.'

William's mother joined in the search.

Over William's face stole a look of blank horror.

'It – it can't have been *sold*, dear, can it?' said the Vicar's wife with a nervous laugh.

'Oh no,' said Mrs Brown, 'we've sold nothing. The sale's not really been opened yet. . . . What sort of a coat was it?'

'A black one.'

'Perhaps someone's just carried it in for you.'

'I'll go and see,' said the Vicar's wife.

William very quietly joined Ginger, Henry and Douglas who had watched the *dénouement* open-mouthed.

'*Well!*' said Ginger, '*now* you've been an' gone an' done it.'

'Sellin' her *coat*,' said Henry in a tone of shocked horror.

'An' she'll prob'ly wear it to church on Sunday an' she'll see it,' said Douglas.

'Oh, shut up about it,' said William who was feeling uneasy.

'IT – IT CAN'T HAVE BEEN SOLD, CAN IT?' SAID THE VICAR'S WIFE.

'Well I should think you oughter *do* something about it,' said Henry virtuously.

'Well, what c'n I do?' said William irritably.

'You won't half catch it,' contributed Douglas

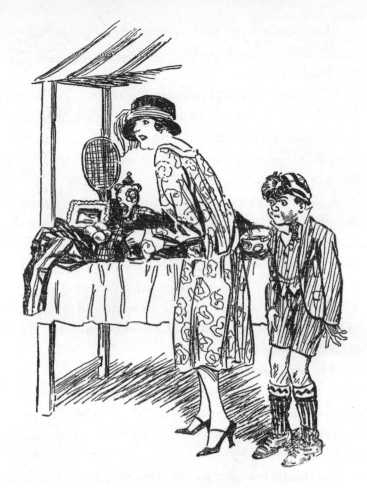

'OH, NO,' SAID MRS BROWN. 'THE SALE'S NOT REALLY
OPENED YET. WHAT SORT OF A COAT WAS IT?'

cheerfully, 'they'll be sure to find out who did it. You
won't half catch it.'

'Tell you what,' said Ginger, 'let's go an' get it back.' William brightened.

'How?' he said.

'Oh . . . sort of find out where she's took it an' get it back,' said Ginger vaguely, his spirits rising at the thought of possible adventure, 'ought to be quite easy . . . heaps more fun than hangin' round here anyway.'

A cursory examination of the crowd who thronged the Vicarage garden revealed no black coat to the anxious Outlaws. William had been so intent upon asserting his own importance and upon impressing his watching friends that he had not noticed his customer at all. She had merely been a woman and he had an uneasy feeling that he would not recognise her again even if he were to meet her.

'I bet she's not here,' said Ginger, ''course she's not here. She'll've taken her coat home jolly quick I bet. She'd be afraid of someone comin' an' sayin' it was a mistake. I bet she'll be clearin' off home pretty quick now – coat an' all.'

The Outlaws went to the gate and looked up and down the road. The rest of the company were clustered round the lawn where the Member, who was opening the Fête, had just got to the point where he was congratulating the stall holders on the beautiful and artistic appearance of the stalls, and wincing involuntarily whenever his gaze fell upon the bilious expanse of green and mauve bunting.

'*There* she is,' said Ginger suddenly, '*there* she is – walkin' down the road in it – *cheek*!'

The figure of a woman wearing a black coat could be seen a few hundred yards down the road. The Outlaws wasted no further time in conversation but set off in pursuit. It was only when they were practically upon her that they realised the difficulty of confronting her and demanding the return of the coat which she had, after all, acquired by the right of purchase.

They slowed down.

'We – we'd better think out a plan,' said William.

'We can watch where she lives anyway,' said Ginger.

They followed their quarry more cautiously.

She went in at the gate of a small house.

The Outlaws clustered round the gate gazing at the front door as it closed behind her.

'Well, we've got to get it back *some* way,' said William with an air of fierce determination.

'Let's jus' try askin' for it,' said Ginger hopefully.

'All right,' agreed William and added generously, '*you* can do it.'

'No,' said Ginger firmly, 'I've done my part *s'gestin'* it. Someone else's gotter *do* it.'

'Henry can do it,' said William, still with his air of lavish generosity.

'No,' said that young gentleman firmly, even pugnaciously, 'I'm jolly well *not* goin' to do it. You went an' sold it an' you can jolly well go an' ask for it back.'

William considered this in silence. They seemed quite firm on the point. He foresaw that argument with them would be useless.

He gave a scornful laugh.

'Huh!' he said. 'Afraid! *That's* what you are. *Afraid*. Huh. . . . Well, I c'n tell you *one* person what's not afraid of an' ole woman in an ole black coat an' that's me.'

With that he swaggered up the path to the front door and rang the bell violently. After that his courage failed, and but for the critical and admiring audience clustered round the gate he would certainly have turned to flee while yet there was time. . . . A maid opened the door. William cleared his throat nervously and tried to express by his back and shoulders (visible to the Outlaws) a proud and imperious defiance and by his face (visible to the maid) an ingratiating humility.

''Scuse me,' he said with a politeness that was rather overdone, ''Scuse me . . . if it's not troublin' you too much—'

'Now, then,' said the girl sharply, 'none of your sauce.'

William in his nervousness redoubled his already exaggerated courtesy. He bared his teeth in a smile.

'Scuse me,' he said, 'but a lady's jus' come into this house wearin' a white elephant—'

He was outraged to receive a sudden box on the ear accompanied by a 'Get out, you saucy little 'ound,' and the slamming of the front door in his face.

William rejoined his giggling friends, nursing his boxed ear. He felt an annoyance which was divided impartially between the girl who had boxed his ears and the Outlaws who had giggled at it.

'Oh yes,' he said aggrievedly, ''s easy to laugh, in't it. 'S nice an' easy to *laugh* . . . an' all of you afraid to go an' then *laughin'* at the only one what's brave enough. You'd laugh if it was *you*, wun't you? Oh yes!' He uttered his famous snort of bitter sarcasm and contempt. 'Oh yes. . . you'd laugh *then*, wun't you? You'd laugh if it was *your* ear what she'd nearly knocked off, *wun't* you? Lots of people 've *died* for less than that an' then I bet you'd get hung for murderers. Your brain's in the middle of your head joined on to your ear, an' she's nearly killed me shakin' my brain up like what she did. . . . Oh yes, 's easy to *laugh* an' me nearly dead an' my brains all shook up.'

'Did she hurt you *awful*, William?' said Ginger.

The sympathy in Ginger's voice mollified William.

'I sh'd jus' *think* so,' he said. 'Not that I *minded*,' he added hastily, 'I don' mind a little pain like that . . . I mean, I c'n stand any *amount* of pain – pain what would *kill* most folks . . . but,' he looked again towards the house and uttered again his short sarcastic laugh, 'p'raps she thinks she's got rid of me. Huh! P'raps she thinks they can go on stickin' to the ole black coat what they've stole. Well, they're not . . . let me kin'ly tell them . . . they're jolly well *not* . . . I – I bet I'm goin' right into the house to get it off them, so *there*!'

The physical attack perpetrated on William by the housemaid had stirred his blood and inspired him with a lust for revenge. He glared ferociously at the closed front door.

'I'll go 'n have a try, shall I?' said Ginger, who shared with William a love of danger and a dislike of any sort of monotony.

'All right,' said William, torn by a desire to see Ginger also fiercely assailed by the housemaid and a reluctance to having his glory as martyr shared by anyone else. 'What'll you say to 'em?'

'Oh, I've got an idea,' said Ginger with what William considered undue optimism and self-assurance, 'well, if she bought it for a shillin' I bet she'll be glad to sell it for *more'n* a shilling, won't she? Stands to reason, dun't it?'

Ginger, imitating William's swagger (for Ginger, despite almost daily conflicts with him, secretly admired William immensely), walked up to the front door and knocked with an imperious bravado, also copied from William. The haughty housemaid opened the door.

'G'd afternoon,' said Ginger with a courteous smile, 'Scuse me, but will you kin'ly tell the lady what's jus' come in here wearin' a black coat that I'll give her one an' six for it an'—'

Ginger also received a box on the ear that sent him rolling halfway down the drive, and the door was slammed in his face. It was opened again immediately and the red angry face of the housemaid again glared out.

'Any more of it, you saucy little 'ounds,' she said, 'an' I'll send for the police.'

Ginger rejoined the others nursing his ear and making what William thought was an altogether ridiculous fuss about it.

'She din't hit you *half* 's hard 's what she hit me,' said William.

'She did,' said the aggrieved Ginger, 'she hit harder . . . a jolly sight harder. She'd nachurally hit harder the second time. She'd be more in practice.'

'No, she wun't,' argued William, 'she'd be more tired the second time. She'd used up all her strength on me.'

'Well, anyway I saw yours an' I felt mine an' could

tell that mine was harder. Well, gettem to look at our ears. I bet mine's redder than what yours is.'

'P'raps it is,' said William, 'it nachurally would be because of mine bein' done first an' havin' time to get wore off. I bet mine's redder now than what yours will be when yours has had the same time to get wore off in as what mine has . . . an' let me kin'ly tell you I saw yours an' I felt mine an' I know that mine was a *jolly* sight harder 'n yours.'

After a spirited quarrel which culminated in a scuffle which culminated in an involuntary descent of both of them into the ditch, the matter was allowed to rest. Ginger had in secret been somewhat relieved at the housemaid's reception of his offer as he did not possess one-and-six and would have been at a loss had it been accepted.

An informal meeting was then held to consider their next step.

'I votes,' said Douglas who was the one of the Outlaws least addicted to dangerous exploits, 'I votes that we jus' go back to the Fête. We've done our best,' he added unctuously, 'an' if the ole coat's sold, well, it's jus' sold. P'raps she'll be able to get it back by goin' to a lawyer or to Parliament or somethin' like that.'

But William, having once formed a purpose, did not lightly relinquish it.

'*You* can go back,' he said scornfully, 'I'm jolly well

not goin' back without that ole coat.'

'All right,' said Douglas in a resigned tone of voice, 'I'll stay an' help.'

To Douglas's credit be it said that having uttered his exhortation to caution he was always content to follow the other Outlaws on their paths of lawlessness and hazard.

'Tell you what I'm goin' to do,' said William suddenly, 'I've *asked* for it polite an' if they won't give it me then it's *their* fault, in't it? Well I've *asked* for it polite an' they wun't give it me so now I'm jolly well goin' to *take* it.'

'I'll go with you, William,' volunteered Ginger.

'I think,' said William, frowning and assuming his Commander-in-Chief air, 'I'd better go on alone. But you jus' stay near an' then if I'm in *reel* danger – sort of danger of life or death – I'll shout an' you come in an' rescue me.'

This was such a situation as the Outlaws loved. They had by this time quite lost sight of what they were rescuing and why they were rescuing it. The thrill of the rescue itself filled their entire horizon. . . .

They went round to the side gate where they crouched in the bushes watching the redoubtable William as he crept Indian fashion with elaborate 'registration' of cunning and secrecy across a small lawn up to a small open window. Breathlessly they watched him hoist himself up and swing his legs over the window sill. They saw his freckled face still wearing its frown of determination as he disappeared inside the room.

He had meant to make his way through the room to the hall where he hoped to find the black coat hanging and to be able to abstract it without interference and return at once to his waiting comrades. But things are seldom as simple as we hope they are going to be. No sooner had he found himself in the room than he heard voices approaching the door and with admirable presence of mind dived beneath the round table in the middle of the room, whose cloth just – but only just – concealed him from view.

The lady whom the Outlaws had followed down the road – now divested of the fateful black coat – entered the room followed by another gayer and more highly-coloured lady.

'A *black* coat, did you say?' said the first lady.

William, beneath the table, pricked up his ears.

'Yes, if you *can*, dear,' said the highly-coloured lady, 'if you'd be so good, dear. I only want it for tomorrow for the funeral. I think I told you didn't I, dear? A removed cousin whom I hardly knew – a *very* removed cousin – but they've invited me and one likes to show oneself appreciative of these little attentions – not that I think he'll have left me a penny in his will and it certainly isn't worth while *buying* black but I *have* a black dress and if you *wouldn't* mind lending me a black coat.'

'Certainly,' said the first lady. 'I can let you have one with pleasure. It's in the hall. It's one I've only just bought . . .'

William ground his teeth . . . So it *was* in the hall! If he'd only been a few minutes earlier . . .

They went into the hall and William gathered that the black coat was being displayed.

'Quite a bargain, wasn't it?' he heard the first lady say.

It was all he could do to repress a bitter and scornful 'Huh!'

They returned – evidently with the coat.

'Thank you so much, dear,' said the highly-coloured lady, 'it's just what I wanted and *so* smart. What was it like at the Fête . . . ?' she was trying on the coat and examining herself smilingly in the overmantel mirror. 'I must say it *does* suit me.'

'Oh, very dull,' said the first lady. 'I really came away before it was actually opened. Just got what I wanted and then came away. It all looked as if it was going to be *most* dull.'

The highly-coloured lady sniffed and her com-placency gave way to aggrievement. 'I must say that I was a bit *hurt* that they didn't ask me to give an entertainment. I can't help feeling that it was a bit of a *slight*. People have so often told me that no function about here is complete without one of my entertainments and then not to ask me to entertain at the Conservative Fête . . . well, I call it *pointed*, and it points to one thing and one thing only in my eyes. It points to jealousy, and intrigue, and spitefulness, and underhandedness, and cunning, and deceit on the part of some person or persons unknown – but, believe *me*, Mrs Bute, quite easily guessed at!'

The highly-coloured lady was evidently in the state known as 'working herself up'. Suddenly William knew who she was. She must be Miss Poll. He remembered now hearing his mother say only yesterday, 'That dreadful Poll woman wants to give an entertainment at the Fête and we're *determined* not to have her. She's so *vulgar*. She'd cheapen the whole thing. . . .'

He peeped at her anxiously from behind his concealing tablecloth, then hastily withdrew.

'Of course,' said Mrs Bute, who sounded bored and as if she'd heard it many times before, 'of course, dear, but . . . the coat will do, will it?'

'Very nicely, thank you,' said Miss Poll rather stiffly because she thought that Mrs Bute really ought to have been more sympathetic. '*Good* afternoon, dear.'

'I'll wrap it up for you,' said Mrs Bute.

There was silence while she wrapped it up, then Miss Poll said, '*Good* afternoon, dear' again and went into the hall and there followed the sound of the closing of the front door, then sounds as of the mistress of the house going upstairs. William retreated through his open window and rejoined Douglas and Henry at the gate. Ginger had vanished.

'Quick,' he said, '*she's* got it.'

The figure of Miss Poll carrying a large paper parcel could be seen walking down the road. 'We've gotter follow *her*. She's got it now.'

At this minute Ginger reappeared.

'She's got it,' William explained to him.

'Yes, but there's another,' said Ginger, pointing, 'there's *another* black coat hangin' up in the hall. I've been round an' looked through a little window an' *seen* it . . . it's *there*.'

William was for a moment nonplussed. Then he said: 'Well, I bet the one she's took's the one, 'cause I heard her say wasn't it a bargain, an' it *was* a bargain too. Huh! I'm goin' after her.'

'Well, I'm *not*,' said Ginger. 'I'm goin' to stop here an' get the other one.'

'All right,' said William, 'you an' Douglas stay here an' Henry 'n me'll go after the other an' I *bet* you ours is the right one.'

So quite amicably the Outlaws divided forces. Ginger and Douglas remained concealed in the bushes by the gate of Mrs Bute's house, warily eyeing the windows, while William and Henry set off down the road after Miss Poll's rapidly vanishing figure.

William and Henry stood at Miss Poll's gate and held a hasty consultation. Their previous experience did not encourage them to go boldly to the front door and demand the black coat.

'Let's jus' go in an' steal it,' said Henry cheerfully. ''S not hers really.'

But William seemed averse to this.

'No,' he said, 'I bet that wouldn't come off. I bet she's the sort of woman that's always poppin' up jus' when you don' want her. No, I guess we've gotter think out a *plan*.'

He thought deeply for a few minutes, then his face cleared and over it broke a light that betokened inspiration.

'I *know* what we'll do. It's a *jolly* good idea. I bet . . . well, anyway, you come in with me an' see.'

Boldly William walked up to the front door and rang the bell. Apprehensively Henry followed him.

Miss Poll, wearing the black coat (for she had been trying it on and fancied herself in it so much that she had not been able to bring herself to take it off to answer the bell), opened the door.

William, his face devoid of any expression whatever, repeated monotonously as though it were a lesson:

'G'afternoon, Miss Poll, please will you come to the Fête to give an entertainment.'

Miss Poll went rather red and for one terrible minute William thought that she was going to attack him as the maid had done – but the moment passed. Miss Poll was simpering coyly.

'You – you've been sent on a message, I suppose, little boy?' Then, relieving William's conscience of the difficult task of answering this question, she went on, 'I *thought* there must be some mistake. . . . Of course,' she simpered again, then pouted, '*really* I'd be quite within my rights to refuse to go. It's most discourteous of them to send for me like this at such short notice but,' she gave a triumphant little giggle, 'I *knew* that *really* they couldn't get on without me. They didn't send a note by you, I suppose?'

'No,' said William quite truthfully.

She pouted again.

'Well, *that* I think is rather rude, don't you? However,' the pout merged again into the simper, 'I wouldn't be so *cruel* as to punish them for that by staying away. I *knew* they'd want me in the end. But these things are always so shamefully organised, don't you think so?'

William cleared his throat and said that he did. Henry, in response to a violent nudge from William, cleared his throat and said that he did too. Miss Poll, encouraged by their sympathy, warmed to her subject.

'Instead of writing to engage me *months* ago they send a message like this at the last minute. . . . What would they have done if I'd been out?'

Again William said he didn't know and again Henry, in response to a nudge from William, said he didn't know either.

'Well, I mustn't keep the poor dears waiting,' said Miss Poll brightly. 'I'll be ready in a second. I've only to put my hat on.'

Then Miss Poll underwent a short inward struggle which William watched breathlessly. Would she keep on the black coat or would she change it for another? Wild plans floated through William's head. He'd say would she please go in something black because the Vicar had died quite suddenly that morning or – or the Member had just been murdered or something like that. . . . It was obvious that Miss Poll was torn between the joy of wearing a coat in which she considered herself to look 'smarter' than in anything else she possessed and the impropriety of wearing for a festal occasion a garment borrowed for the obsequies of the very removed cousin. To William's relief the coat won the day and after buttoning up the collar to give it an even smarter appearance than it had before and putting on a smart hat with a very red feather, she joined them at the door.

'Now I'm ready, children,' she said, at which William scowled ferociously and Henry winced, 'they didn't say which of my repertoire' (Miss Poll pronounced it reppertwaw) 'I was to bring with me, did they?'

And again William said 'no' with a face devoid of expression and with perfect truth. And Henry said 'no,' too.

'As it's such short notice,' she went on, 'they really can't expect *anything* in the way of – well, of make-up or dress, can they?'

William said that they couldn't and Henry, being nudged again by William, confirmed the opinion. . . .

'Though I wish you children could see me in my charwoman skit. I'm an artist in make-up. . . . Now, can you imagine me looking *really* old and ugly?'

Henry quite innocently said 'yes,' and on being nudged by William, changed it to 'yes, please.' Miss Poll looked at Henry as if she quite definitely disliked him and turned her attentions to William.

'You know, dear . . . I can make myself up to look *really* old. You'd never believe it, would you? Now guess how old I am, really?'

Henry, not wishing to be left out of it, said with

perfect good faith, 'fifty' and William, with a vague idea of being tactful, said 'forty'. Miss Poll who looked, as a matter of fact, about forty-five, laughed shrilly.

'You children *will* have your joke,' she said, 'now I wonder what I'd better do for them to start with? You know, what makes me so *unique* as an entertainer, children – and if I'd wanted to be I'd be *famous* now on the London stage – is that I'm *entirely* independent of such artificial aids as mechanical musical instruments and books of words and such things. I depend upon the unaided efforts of my voice – and I've a perfect voice for humorous songs, you know, children – and my facial expression. Of course I've a *magnetic* personality . . . that's the secret of the whole thing . . .'

William was tense and stern and scowling. He wasn't thinking of Miss Poll's magnetic personality. He was thinking of Miss Poll's coat. The first step had been to lure Miss Poll to the Fête; the second and, he began to think, the harder, would be to detach the coat from Miss Poll's person.

'It's – it's sort of gettin' hot, i'n't it?' he said huskily.

'Yes, isn't it?' said Miss Poll pleasantly.

William's heart lightened. 'Wun't you like to take your coat off?' he said persuasively. 'I'll carry it for you.'

But Miss Poll who considered, quite erroneously,

that the coat made her look startlingly youthful and pretty, shook her head and clutched the coat tightly at her neck.

'No, certainly not,' she said firmly.

William pondered his next line of argument.

'I thought,' he suggested at last meekly, 'I thought p'raps you *sing* better without your coat.'

Henry, who felt that he was supporting William rather inadequately, said: 'Yes, you sort of look as if you'd sing better without a coat.'

'What nonsense!' said Miss Poll rather sharply, 'I sing *perfectly* well in a coat.'

Then William had an idea. He remembered an incident which had taken place about a month ago which had completely mystified him at the time, but which he had stored up for possible future use. Ethel had come home from a garden party in a state bordering on hysterics and had passionately destroyed a perfectly good hat which she had been wearing. The reason she gave for this extraordinary behaviour had been that Miss Weston had been wearing a hat *exactly* like it at the garden party ('*exactly* like it . . . I could have killed her and myself,' Ethel had said hysterically). The reason had seemed to William wholly inadequate. He met boys every day of his life wearing headgear which was exactly identical with his and the sight failed to rouse him to hysterical fury. It was one of the many mysteries in which the behaviour of grown-up sisters was shrouded – not to be understood but possible to be utilised. Now he looked Miss Poll up and down and said ruminatingly, 'Funny!'

'What's funny?' said Miss Poll sharply.

'Oh, nothin',' said William apologetically, knowing full well that Miss Poll would now know no peace till she'd discovered the reason for his ejaculation and steady contemplation of her.

'Nonsense!' she said sharply, 'you wouldn't say 'funny' like that unless there was some reason for it, I suppose. If I've got a smut on my nose or my hat's on crooked *say* so and don't stand there *looking* at me.'

William's steady gaze was evidently getting upon Miss Poll's nerves.

'Nothin',' said William again vaguely, 'only I've just remembered somethin'.'

'*What* have you remembered?' snapped Miss Poll.

'Nothin' much,' said William, 'only I've jus' remembered that I saw someone at the Fête jus' before I came out to you, in a coat *exactly* like that one what you've got on.'

There was a long silence and finally Miss Poll said: 'It *is* a little hot, *dear*. You were quite right. If you would be so kind as to carry my coat—'

She took it off, revealing a dress that was very short and very diaphanous and very, very pink, folded up the

152

coat so as to show only the lining and handed it to William. William, though retaining his sphinx-like expression, heaved a sigh of relief, and Henry dropped behind Miss Poll to turn a cartwheel expressive of triumph in the middle of the road. They had reached the gate of the Vicarage now. They were only just in time. . . .

'I'VE JUS' REMEMBERED,' SAID WILLIAM, 'THAT I SAW SOMEONE AT THE FÊTE IN A COAT EXACTLY LIKE THAT ONE WHAT YOU'VE GOT ON.'

William meant to thrust the coat into the arms of the Vicar's wife and escape as quickly as he could, leaving Miss Poll (for whom he had already conceived a deep dislike) to her fate.

It happened that the Member's agent had with difficulty and with the help of great persuasive power and a megaphone, collected the majority of the attendants at the Fête into a large tent where the Member was to 'say a few words' on the political situation. Many of those who had had experience of the Member's 'few words' on other occasions had tried to escape but the agent was a very determined young man with an Oxford manner and an eagle eye, and in the end he had hounded them all in. The Member was just buying a raffle ticket for a nightdress case and being particularly nice to the raffle ticket seller partly because she was pretty and partly because she might have a vote (one could never tell what age girls were nowadays). The agent was hovering in the background ready to tell him that his audience was awaiting him as soon as he'd finished being nice to the pretty girl, and at the same time keeping a wary eye on the door of the tent to see that no one escaped. . . . And then the *contretemps* happened. Miss Poll tripped airily up to the door of the tent in her pink, pink frock, peeped in, saw the serried ranks of an audience with a vacant place in front of them, presumably for the entertainer, and skipping lightly in with a 'So sorry to have kept you all waiting,' leapt at once into her first item – an imitation of a tipsy landlady, an item that Miss Poll herself considered the cream of her repertoire. The audience (a very heavy and respectable audience) gaped at her, dismayed and astounded. And when a few minutes later the Member, calm and dignified and full to overflowing of eloquence and statistics, having exchanged the smile he had assumed while being nice to the pretty raffle ticket seller for a look of responsibility and capability, and having exchanged his raffle ticket for a neat little sheaf of notes (typed and clipped together by the ubiquitous agent), appeared at the door of the tent he found Miss Gertie Poll prancing to and fro before his amazed audience, her pink, pink skirts held very high, announcing that she was Gilbert the filbert, the colonel of the nuts. The agent, looking over his shoulder, grew pale, and loose-jawed. The Member turned to him with dignity and a certain amount of restraint.

'What's all this?' he demanded sternly.

The agent mopped his brow with an orange silk handkerchief.

'I – I – I've no idea, sir,' he gasped weakly.

'Please put a stop to it,' said the Member and added hastily, remembering that the tent was packed full of votes, 'without any unpleasantness, of course.'

I have said that the agent was a capable young man with an Oxford manner, but it would have taken more than a dozen capable young men with Oxford manners to stop Miss Gertie Poll in full flow of her repertoire. She went on for over an hour. She merely smiled bewitchingly at the agent whenever he tried to stop her without any unpleasantness, and when the Member himself appeared like a *deux ex machina* to take command of the situation, she blew him a kiss and he hastily retired.

Meanwhile William, triumphantly bearing the black coat, made his way up to the Vicar's wife. He met Ginger and Douglas, also carrying a black coat and on the same mission.

'Bet you tuppence mine's the one,' said Ginger.

'Bet you tuppence mine is,' said William, 'where'd you get yours?'

'We got it out of her hall,' said Douglas cheerfully, 'we jus' walked in an' got it an' no one saw us . . . I bet *ours* is the one.'

'Well, come on an' see,' said William, pushing his way up to the stall presided over by the Vicar's wife.

'Here's your coat, Mrs Marks,' he said handing it to her, 'it was sold by mistake off the rubbish stall but we've got it back for you – me an' Henry.'

Before the Vicar's wife could answer, a frantic messenger came up to her.

'What *shall* we do?' she moaned. 'Miss Poll's enter-taining the tent and the Member can't speak.'

'Miss *Poll*!' gasped the Vicar's wife, 'we never asked her.'

'No, but she's *come* and she's singing all her *awful* songs and no one can stop her and the Member can't speak.'

The Vicar's wife, still absently nursing the coat that William had thrust into her arm, stared in front of her.

'But—but how awful!' she murmured, 'how *awful*!'

Then Ginger came up and thrust the second coat into her unprotesting arms.

'Your coat, Mrs Marks,' he said politely, 'what we sold by mistake off the rubbish stall. Me an' Douglas 'v got it back for you.'

He made a grimace at William which William returned with interest.

They waited breathlessly to see which coat the Vicar's wife should claim as her own.

She looked down at her armful of coats as if she saw them for the first time.

'B-but,' she said faintly, 'I got that coat back. The woman who bought it thought there must be some mistake and brought it to me. These aren't my coats . . . I don't know anything about these coats.'

Shrill strains of some strident music-hall ditty came from the tent. A second messenger came up.

'She won't stop,' she sobbed, 'and the Member's foaming at the mouth.'

'Oh, dear,' said the Vicar's wife, clutching her bundle of coats still more tightly to her. 'Oh, dear, oh, *dear*!'

At that moment a woman pushed her way through the crowds up to the Vicar's wife. It was Mrs Bute.

'Brought it here, they did,' she panted. 'Where is it? *Thieves!* Came into my hall bold as brass an' *took* it! . . . *There* it is!' she glared suspiciously at the Vicar's wife, 'what've *you* got it for . . . *my* coat . . . I'd like to know. I'd—' She tore it out of her arms and the other coat too fell to the ground. 'My *other* coat!' she screamed, '*both* my coats! *Thieves* – that's what you all are! *Thieves!*'

'Where are those boys?' said the Vicar's wife very faintly. But 'those boys' had gone. William, resisting the strong temptation to go and enjoy the spectacle of the Member foaming at the mouth, had hastily withdrawn his little band to a safe distance.

They were found, of course, and brought back. They were forced to give explanations. They were forced to apologise to all concerned, even to Miss Poll (who forgave them because she'd had such a perfectly *ripping* afternoon and her little show gone off so *sweetly* and everyone been so *adorable*). They were sent home in disgrace. . . . William was despatched to bed on dry bread and water, but being quite tired by the day's events and the bread happening to be new and unlimited in quantity, William's manly spirit survived the indignity.

And William's mother said the next day: 'I *knew* what would happen.' (William's mother always said that she knew it would happen after it had safely – or dangerously – happened.) 'I *knew* that if I let William come and help everything would go wrong. It always does. Selling people's coats and stealing people's coats and getting that awful woman to come that we'd *sworn* we'd never have again and stopping the Member speaking when he'd taken *ages* over preparing his speech, and upsetting the whole thing – well, if anyone had told me beforehand that one boy William's size could upset a whole afternoon like that I simply shouldn't have believed them.'

And William's father said: 'Well, I warned you, William. I told you they were difficult beasts to manage. Of course, if you lose control of a whole herd of white elephants like that they're bound to do some damage.'

And William said disgustedly: 'I'm just *sick* of white elephants and black coats. I'm going out to play Red Indians.'

CHAPTER 6

FINDING A SCHOOL FOR WILLIAM

WILLIAM'S suspicions were first aroused by the atmosphere of secrecy that enveloped the visit of Mr Cranthorpe-Cranborough. Mr Cranthorpe-Cranborough was a very distant cousin of William's father (so many times removed as to be almost out of sight) and was coming to stay for a weekend with the Browns. William gathered that his father had not met Mr Cranthorpe-Cranborough before in spite of the relationship, that the visitor was self-invited, and that the visit was in some way connected with himself. He gathered this last fact from whispered confabulations between his family during which they watched him in that way in which whispering confabulators always watch those who are the subject of the whispered confabulations.

William, while keeping eyes and ears alert, pretended to be sublimely unaware of all this. He went his way with an air of unsuspecting innocence that lured his family into a false security. 'Fortunately,' his mother whispered very audibly to Ethel once as he was just going out of the room, 'William hasn't the slightest idea what he's coming for.'

Meanwhile beneath William's exaggerated air of guilelessness William's mind worked fast. Whenever he came upon any scattered twos he put them together to make four. These fours he stored up in mind as he went his way, apparently absorbed in his games, the well-being of his mongrel Jumble, the progress of his tamed caterpillars and earwigs, the shooting properties of his new bow and arrows, and the activities of his friends the Outlaws. But there was no look or sign or whisper from the grown-up world around him that the seemingly unconscious William did not intercept and store up for future reference. William, as some people had been known to put it, was 'deep'.

'Yes, dear,' said Mrs Brown to Ethel, her nineteen-year-old daughter, 'he's going to arrive before tea and your father's going to try to get home for tea, and they're going to talk it over together quietly after tea in the morning-room.'

'Oh, well, I shall be busy,' said Ethel, 'I shall be helping Moyna Greene with her dress for the fancy dress ball, so I shan't be in their way. She's going as a lady of Elizabethan times and she's going to look *sweet*.'

'I expect they'd like to be left alone to talk things

over. . . . Sh!' as she perceived William who had heard every word lolling negligently in the doorway cracking nuts.

'Well, William,' brightly, 'had a nice afternoon?'

'Yes, thanks,' said William.

'We were just talking about Ethel's friend, Miss Greene, who's going to a fancy dress ball.'

'Yes, I heard you,' said William.

'She's going as a lady of the fourteenth century,' proceeded Mrs Brown still brightly.

'Uh-huh,' said William without interest as he cracked another nut.

Some of Mrs Brown's brightness faded.

'*William!*' she said indignantly, '*do* stop dropping shells on to the carpet.'

'A'right – sorry,' said William, stolidly turning to go away and cracking another nut.

'His *manners!*' said Ethel, elevating her small and pretty nose in disgust.

'Yes, dear,' said Mrs Brown soothingly, 'but *we* needn't bother about them *now*.'

William wandered out into the garden. Though he did not for a minute cease his consumption of nuts he grew yet more thoughtful. He was beginning to look forward to the projected visit of Mr Cranthorpe-Cranborough with distinct apprehension. Whatever it boded, William felt sure that it boded no good to him.

Still cracking nuts with undiminished energy and leaving a little trail of broken shells to mark his track over the immaculate lawn (and incidentally to make the gardener rise to dazzling heights of eloquence when he tried to mow it the next morning) William withdrew to the strip of untended shrubbery at the bottom of the garden, and, sitting down upon a laurel bush, began thoughtfully to throw pebbles at the next door cat who was its only other occupant. The next door cat, who looked upon William's pebble-throwing as a sign of his affection, began to purr loudly. . . .

William considered the situation. This Mr Cranthorpe-Cranborough was coming for some sinister purpose tomorrow. That sinister purpose must at all costs be frustrated. But first of all he must find out what that sinister purpose was. . . . He threw another handful of pebbles at the next door cat. The next door cat purred still more loudly. . . . The visitor was going to have a quiet little talk with his father after tea tomorrow. . . . By hook or by crook William decided to hear that quiet little talk. The only drawback to the plan was that the morning-room contained no possible place of concealment for eavesdroppers. . . .

'William dear, this is Mr Cranthorpe-Cranborough, a relation of ours who has come to pay us a little visit,' said Mrs Brown.

William looked up.

The first thing that struck you about Mr Cranthorpe-Cranborough was his bigness, and the second was his smile. Mr Cranthorpe-Cranborough's smile was as large and full as himself. His teeth were so over-crowded that when he smiled it almost seemed as if some were in danger of dropping out. He placed a large hand upon William's head.

'So *this* is the little man,' he said.

'Uh-huh?' said William.

'Oh, his *manners*,' groaned Ethel turning her eyes towards the sky.

'A-ha,' said Mr Cranthorpe-Cranborough, smiling like a playful ogre, 'you may safely leave his manners to *me*. I'm used to teaching little boys their manners.'

William took a nut out of his pocket and cracked it.

'William!' groaned Mrs Brown.

William took out a handful of nuts and handed it to Mr Cranthorpe-Cranborough.

'Have one?' he said politely.

'Er – no, I thank you,' said Mr Cranthorpe-Cranborough. Then he smiled the very full smile again, 'But I'd like a talk with you, my little man.'

His little man turned a sphinx-like countenance to him and cracked another nut.

'How far have you got in Arithmetic?' asked Mr Cranthorpe-Cranborough.

'Uh-huh?' said William.

Ethel groaned.

'Fractions?' suggested Mr Cranthorpe-Cran-borough.

William's whole attention was given to the inside of the nut that he had just cracked.

'Bad!' he said indignantly, 'an' I paid twopence for 'em. . . . I'll take it back to the shop.'

'Decimals?' said Mr Cranthorpe-Cranborough.

'No, Brazils,' said William succinctly.

'I think perhaps it would be better if we left them,' murmured Mrs Brown faintly, and she and Ethel departed, Ethel murmuring wildly, 'His *manners*!'

'And what about History?' said Mr Cranthorpe-Cranborough.

William, investigating another nut, seemed to have no views on history.

Mr Cranthorpe-Cranborough cleared his throat, smiled his large fat smile and said, 'Ha!' to attract William's attention. He failed, however. William's whole attention was given to throwing bits of his bad nut at the next door cat who had disappeared at the first intrusion of the grown-ups, but had now returned and was again purring loudly.

'What are the dates of Queen Elizabeth?' said Mr Cranthorpe-Cranborough.

'Uh?' said William absently, 'here's another of 'em bad an' chargin' *twopence* for 'em! Haven't they gotta *nerve!*'

Mr Cranthorpe-Cranborough gave up the attempt.

'I'm going to have a nice little talk with your father after tea, my little man,' he said.

William cracked a nut in (partial) silence and threw the shells at the cat. Then he said casually, 'I s'pose they've told you he's deaf? He gets awful mad if people don't shout loud enough. You've gotta shout *awful* loud to make him hear.'

'Er – your mother never mentioned it,' said Mr Cranthorpe-Cranborough taken aback.

'No,' said William mysteriously, 'an' don't say anythin' about it to her or to any of them. They don' like folks mentionin' it. They're – thcy're – sort of sens'tive about it.'

'Oh!' said Mr Cranthorpe-Cranborough still more taken aback. Then he recovered himself. 'Now let's have a few dates,' he said briskly.

'Yes, dates is more sense,' said William with interest, 'you can look at 'em before you buy 'em to see if they're bad. That's the worst of nuts. You can't see 'em through the shells.'

Viciously he threw the defaulting nut at the cat who remembered suddenly a previous engagement on the other side of the fence and disappeared.

While Mr Cranthorpe-Cranborough was engaged in recovering himself for a fresh assault upon William's ignorance Ethel appeared.

'Will you come in to tea now?' she said to the visitor with a sweet smile.

Mr Cranthorpe-Cranborough responded to the best of his ability with his fullest smile.

William, interested by the phenomenon, went up to his bedroom to practise, but found that he had not enough teeth to get the full effect.

When he descended he found his father in the hall hanging up his coat and hat.

'You're back early, Father, aren't you?' said William innocently.

'With your usual intelligence, my son,' said William's father, 'you have divined aright. . . . Where's Mr What's-his-name?'

'Having tea in the drawing-room, Father,' said William.

Mr Brown went into the morning-room. William followed him.

'Have you – met him?' said Mr Brown.

'Yes,' said William.

'Er – do you like him?'

'He's very deaf,' said William.

'Deaf?'

'Yes . . . you've gotta shout ever so hard to make him hear.'

'Good Heavens!' groaned Mr Brown.

'An' *he* shouts very hard, too, like what deaf people do, you know, with not hearin' themselves – but he dun't like you *sayin'* anythin' about him bein' deaf, but he likes you jus' shoutin'. They're havin' their tea now. He's given 'em quite sore throats already.'

Mr Brown groaned again but at that minute entered Mrs Brown and the guest. She performed a rapid introduction and departed. William had already disappeared. He had gone round to the front lawn and was sitting there leaning against the house cracking nuts. Just above his head was the open window of the morning-room. It was not possible from that position to overhear a conversation carried on in normal voices in the morning-room, but William hoped that he had assured that this conversation would be carried on in abnormal voices. His hopes were justified. His father's voice raised to a bellow reached him.

'Won't you sit down?'

And Mr Cranthorpe-Cranborough's in a hoarse shout:

'Thanks so much.'

'Now about this school—' yelled his father.

'Exactly,' bellowed Mr Cranthorpe-Cranborough. 'I hope to open it in the spring. I should like to include your son among the first numbers – special terms of course.'

There was a pause, then William's father spoke in a voice of thunder.

'Very good of you.'

'Not at all,' bellowed Mr Cranthorpe-Cranborough.

'He's – perhaps I'd better prepare you . . .' boomed Mr Brown's voice making the very window panes rattle in their frames, 'he – he doesn't quite conform to type. He's a bit – individualistic.'

Mr Cranthorpe-Cranborough drew in his breath, then with a mighty effort bellowed:

'But he ought to conform to type. It's only a matter of training – I'm most anxious to include your son on our roll when we open next spring.'

Purple in the face Mr Brown yelled:

'Very good of you.'

William, whose conscience never allowed him to do any more eavesdropping than was absolutely necessary to his plans, arose and thoughtfully cracking his last nut, walked round the house. At the side door he came across his mother and Ethel clinging together in terror.

'What *has* happened,' his mother was saying hysterically, 'why are they shouting at each other like that? What *has* happened?'

'They must be quarrelling!' groaned Ethel. A re-echoing bellow from Mr Brown (who was really only saying, 'Very good of you' again) made the house shake and Ethel screamed, 'They'll be *fighting* in a minute. . . . What *shall* we do?'

Mrs Brown noticed William and made an effort to control herself.

'Where are you going, William?'

William, his hands deep in his pockets, answered nonchalantly. 'Down to the village to buy a stick of liquorice,' he said.

He walked down to the village very thoughtfully.

So *that* was it. . . they were going to send him to that man's school, were they? Huh! . . . *were* they? William for one had made up his mind that they were not, but just for a minute he was not sure how he could prevent them. Silently he considered various plans. None seemed suitable. Open opposition was, he knew, useless. In open opposition he had no chance against his family. But there must surely be other ways. . . .

Mrs Brown had once stayed in Eastbourne where she had watched a neat little crocodile of neat little boys walking in a straight and tidy line past her house every day and the sight had impressed her. The thought of William walking like that – a neat and tidy component of a neat and tidy line talking politely to his partner, keeping just behind the boy in front, with plastered hair and shiny shoes, walking sedately – was an alluring and startling picture when compared with the William of the present, leaping over fences, diving into ditches, shinning up trees, dragging his toes in the dust, shouting . . . Mrs Brown had a vague idea that some mysterious change of spirit came over a boy on entering the portals of a boarding-school transforming him from a young savage to a perfect little gentleman, and she would have liked to see this change take place in William. Moreover Mr Cranthorpe-Cranborough had distinctly mentioned 'special fees'.

Mr Brown had no very strong feelings on the subject. He was prepared to leave it all to his wife. The only two people concerned who had any very strong feelings about it were Mr Cranthorpe-Cranborough and William. Mr Cranthorpe-Cranborough wanted to fill his new school. He did not consider William to be very promising material but he couldn't afford at the present juncture to be too particular about material. . . . And William had very strong feelings on the subject indeed. William could not even contemplate life divorced from the beloved fields and woods of his native village, his beloved Outlaws and Jumble his mongrel.

On returning home William found his father in the hall.

'What the dickens do you mean,' said his father irritably and hoarsely, 'by telling me the fellow was deaf? He's no more deaf than I am.'

William opened wide eyes of innocent surprise.

'Isn't he, Father?' he said, 'I'm awfully sorry.'

William's father, upon whom William's looks of innocence and surprise were always completely wasted, moved his hand to his throat with an involuntary spasm of pain.

'No, he isn't,' he said brokenly, 'and you knew perfectly well he wasn't. Your over-exuberant sense of humour needs a little pruning, my boy, and if I hadn't got the worst sore throat I've had in years I'd prune it for you here and now.'

William moved hastily out of the danger zone still murmuring apologies. He went to the morning-room where he found Mr Cranthorpe-Cranborough. Mr Cranthorpe-Cranborough addressed him, also brokenly.

'Your father doesn't seem to be very deaf, William,' he whispered hoarsely, 'I spoke to him in quite an ordinary tone of voice towards the end of our conversation and he seemed to hear all right.'

William fixed unfaltering eyes upon him.

'Yes, then your voice must be the kind he hears nat'rul. He does hear some sorts nat'rul. He hears all ours nat'rul.'

With this cryptic remark he withdrew leaving Mr Cranthorpe-Cranborough looking thoughtful.

The next morning Mr Cranthorpe-Cranborough asked William to go for a walk with him. 'William and I,' he said pleasantly to Mrs Brown, 'must get to know each other.'

William emerged from Mrs Brown's hands for the walk almost repellently clean and tidy. Mrs Brown was determined that William should make a good impression on Mr Cranthorpe-Cranborough.

For a time William walked in silence and Mr Cranthorpe-Cranborough talked. He talked about the glorious historical monuments of England and the joys of early rising and the fascination of decimals and H.C.F.'s and the beauty of all foreign languages. He warmed to William as he talked for William seemed to be drinking in his words almost avidly. William's solemn eyes never left his face. He could not know, of course, that William was not listening to a word he said but was engaged in trying to count his teeth. . . .

'Now which of our grand national buildings have you seen?' said Mr Cranthorpe-Cranborough, returning to his first theme.

'Uh-huh?' said William who thought he'd got to thirty, but kept having to start again because they moved about so.

'I say, which of our grand national buildings have you seen?' said Mr Cranthorpe-Cranborough more distinctly.

'Oh,' said William bringing his thoughts with an effort from Mr Cranthorpe-Cranborough's teeth to the less interesting one of our grand national buildings, 'I've never been to races,' said William sadly.

'Races?' said Mr Cranthorpe-Cranborough in surprise.

'Yes . . . you was talking about the Grand National, wasn't you?'

'Were, William, were,' corrected Mr Cranthorpe-Cranborough.

'I'm not quite sure where,' admitted William, 'but I know a man what won some money on it last year.'

'You misunderstand me, William,' said Mr Cranthorpe-Cranborough rather irritably, 'I'm referring to such places as Westminster Abbey and the Houses of Parliament.'

'Oh,' said William with waning interest, 'I thought you was goin' to talk about racin'.'

'Were, William, *were*.'

'At the Grand National.'

'No, William . . . no,' he was finding conversation with William rather difficult, 'have you never visited such places as Hampton Court?'

A gleam of interest came into William's face and he temporarily abandoned his self-imposed task of counting Mr Cranthorpe-Cranborough's teeth.

'Yes,' he said, 'I once went *there*. I remember 'cause there was a man there what told us it was haunted. Said a ghost of someone used to go downstairs there. Huh!'

William's final ejaculation was one of contemptuous amusement. But Mr Cranthorpe-Cranborough's face grew serious. His teeth receded from view almost entirely.

'No, no, William,' he said reprovingly, 'you must not make fun of such things. Indeed you must not. They are – they are not to be treated lightly. The fact that you have *seen* none is not proof that there *are* none . . . far from it. . . . Believe me, William – though I have seen none myself I have friends who have.'

'Didn't it scare 'em stiff?' said William with interest, and added dramatically, 'rattlin' an' groanin' an' suchlike.'

Mr Cranthorpe-Cranborough was too much absorbed in his subject to correct William's phraseology.

'It does not – er – rattle or groan, William. It is the figure of a lady of the fifteenth century, and everyone does not see it. It is indeed a sinister omen to see it. Some evil always befalls those who see it. Sinister, William, means on the left hand, and used in the sense in which we use it, is a reference to the omens of the days of the Romans.'

'Doesn't it *do* anythin' to 'em?' said William,

disappointed by the lack of enterprise betrayed by the ghost, and left completely cold by the derivation of the word sinister.

'No,' said Mr Cranthorpe-Cranborough, 'it just *appears* – but the one who sees it, and only one person sees it on each occasion, invariably suffers some catastrophe. It is not wise, of course, to allow one's thoughts to *dwell* upon such things but it is not wise either to treat them entirely with contempt. . . . Let us now turn our thoughts to brighter things. . . . Do you keep a collection of – the flora of the neighbourhood, William?'

'No,' admitted William, 'I've never caught any of *them*. Didn't know there was any about. But I've got some caterpillars.'

When William approached the morning-room just before lunch there were there his mother and Ethel and Robert, his grown-up brother. As William entered he heard his mother whisper:

'I think the time has come to tell him.'

William entered, negligently toying with a handful of marbles.

'William,' said his mother, 'we have something to tell you.'

'Uh-huh?' said William still apparently absorbed by his marbles.

'Oh, his *manners*!' groaned Ethel.

'This cousin of your father's,' said his mother, 'is really the headmaster of a boys' boarding-school and we *think* . . . though nothing's yet arranged . . . that we're going to send *you* to his school next spring. *Won't* it be nice?'

They all looked at William with interest to see how he should receive this startling news.

William received it as though it had been some casual comment on the weather.

'Uh-huh,' he said absently, as he continued to toy negligently with his marbles.

He had the satisfaction of seeing his family thoroughly taken aback by his reception of the news.

He was very silent during lunch. He had not yet formed any definite plan of action beyond the negative plan of pretending to acquiesce. He could see that his attitude mystified them and the knowledge was a great consolation to him.

After lunch Mr Cranthorpe-Cranborough, who by now looked upon the addition of William's name to his roll of members as a certainty, went into the garden and Mrs Brown went to lie down. William, after strolling aimlessly about the house, joined Ethel in the drawing-room. She was, however, not alone in the drawing-room. Moyna Greene in an elaborate fourteenth century dress of purple and silver was with her.

'You look perfectly sweet, Moyna,' Ethel was saying, 'but I think the ruffle *does* want altering just here.'

'I thought it did,' said Moyna, 'I'll do it now if I may. May I borrow your work basket? Thanks.' She slipped off her ruffle.

'Let me help said Ethel.

Just then the housemaid entered.

'Mrs Bott called to see you, Miss,' she said to Ethel.

Ethel groaned and turned to Moyna.

'Oh, my dear. . . . I'll be as quick as I can, but you know what she is. . . . She'll keep me ages. You *won't* run away, will you?'

'No,' promised the purple and silver vision.

'I'll tell you what you might do,' said Ethel. 'Go and let old Jenkins see you. I think he's in the greenhouse. I told him you were going as a fourteenth century lady and he said, 'Eh, her'll look rare prutty. I wish I could see her' – so he'd be so bucked if you would.'

'All right,' said Moyna, 'I'll just finish this ruffle and then I'll go out to him.'

'And I'll be as quick as I can,' said Ethel, 'but you know what she is.'

William went quietly out of doors. His face was bright with inspiration and stern with resolve. First of all he satisfied himself that old Jenkins really was in the greenhouse.

Jenkins turned upon him as soon as he saw him in the doorway. Between old Jenkins and young William no love was lost.

'You touch one of my grapes, Master William,' he said threateningly, 'an' I'll tell your pa the minute he comes home tonight, I will. I grow these grapes for your ma an' pa – not you.'

'I don' want any of your grapes, Jenkins,' said William with a short laugh expressive of amused surprise at the idea. 'Good gracious, what should *I* want with your ole grapes?'

Whereupon he departed with a swagger leaving old Jenkins muttering furiously, and went to join Mr Cranthorpe-Cranborough who was comfortably ensconced in a deck chair at the further end of the lawn wooing sleep. He had almost wooed it when William appeared and sat down noisily at his feet, and said in a tone that put any further wooing of sleep entirely out of the question:

'Hello, Mr Cranborough.'

Mr Cranthorpe-Cranborough greeted William shortly and without enthusiasm. He did not want William. He did not like William. His interest in William began and ended with the special fees which he hoped William's parents might be induced to pay him – 'special' in quite a different sense from the one in which Mrs Brown understood it. He had been quite happy without William and he meant his manner to convey this fact to William. But William was not sensitive to fine shades of manner.

'I've been thinkin',' he said slowly, ''bout what you said this mornin'.'

'Ah,' said Mr Cranthorpe-Cranborough, touched despite himself and thinking what a gift for dealing with the young he must possess to have made an impression upon such unpromising material as this boy's mind, and how one should never despair of material however unpromising.

'About what, my boy?' he said with interest, 'the History? the French? the Arithmetic?'

'No,' said William simply, 'the ghost.'

'Oh,' said Mr Cranthorpe-Cranborough, 'but – er – you should not allow your mind to *run* on such subjects, my boy.'

'No,' said William, 'it's not runnin' on 'em. But I've just remembered somethin' about this house.'

'What?' said Mr Cranthorpe-Cranborough.

William carefully selected a juicy blade of grass and began to chew it.

'Oh, it's prob'ly nothin',' he said carelessly, 'but what you said this mornin' made me think of it, that's all.'

William was adept at whetting people's curiosity.

'But what *was* it?' said Mr Cranthorpe-Cranborough irritably, 'what *was* it?'

'Well, p'raps I'd better not mention it,' said William, 'you said we oughtn't to let it run on our minds.'

'I insist on your telling me,' said Mr Cranthorpe-Cranborough.

'Oh, it's nothin' much,' said William again, 'only a sort of *story* about this house.'

'*What* sort of a story?' insisted Mr Cranthorpe-Cranborough.

'Well,' said William as though reluctantly, 'some folks say that an ole house use to be here jus' where this house is now an' that a lady of the fourteenth century was killed in it once an' some folks say they've seen her. I don' b'lieve it,' he ended carelessly, '*I've* never seen her.'

Mr Cranthorpe-Cranborough's interest was aroused.

'What is this – this lady supposed to look like, my boy?' he said.

'She's dressed in purple and silver,' said William, 'with a long train an' a ruffle thing round her neck an' very black hair, and she's s'posed to walk out of that window over there,' and he pointed to the drawing-room window, 'and then go across the lawn behind

181

those trees,' he pointed to the trees which hid the greenhouse from view.

'And you say that people profess to have *seen* her?' said Mr Cranthorpe-Cranborough.

'Oh, yes,' said William.'

'And what does her coming portend?'

'Uh?' said William.

'What – what *happens* to those who see her?' repeated Mr Cranthorpe-Cranborough impatiently.

At that moment Miss Moyna Greene, having finished and donned the ruffle, stepped out of the drawing-room window on to the lawn in all her glory of purple and silver. Mr Cranthorpe-Cranborough gazed at her and his jaws dropped open.

'Look!' he gasped to William, 'who's that?'

'Who's what?' said William gazing around innocently.

Miss Moyna Greene passed slowly to the middle of the lawn. Mr Cranthorpe-Cranborough's eyes, bulging with amazement, followed her. So did his trembling forefinger.

'There . . .' he hissed, 'just there.'

William stared straight at Miss Moyna Greene.

'I don't see anyone,' he said.

Drops of perspiration stood out on Mr Cranthorpe-Cranborough's brow. He took out a large silk handkerchief and mopped it. The figure of Miss Moyna Greene crossed the lawn and disappeared behind the trees. . . .

Mr Cranthorpe-Cranborough gave a gasp.

'Er – what did you say the – er – the sight of the vision is supposed to portend, William?' he said faintly. 'What – what *happens* to those who see it?'

'Oh, I don' suppose anyone's really seen it,' said William carelessly. 'I never have. I think they've simply made it up – purple dress an' ruffle an' all – but it's *s'posed* to mean very bad luck for the one who sees it.'

'W-w-what kind of bad luck?' stammered Mr Cranthorpe-Cranborough, whose ruddy countenance had faded to a dull grey.

'Well,' said William confidentially, 'it's s'posed to be seen by one of two people together an' the one what *sees* it is s'posed to be goin' to have some *very* bad luck *through* the other – the one what was with him when he saw it, but what didn't see it. The bad luck's s'posed always to come *through* the one what doesn't see it but what's *with* the one what *does*.'

Through the trees William spied the figure of Miss Moyna Greene who had evidently left Jenkins and was returning to the drawing-room.

'An' folks *say*,' added William carelessly, 'that it's worst of *all* if you see it twice – once going from the house and once comin' to it.'

The figure of Miss Moyna Greene emerged from the trees and passed slowly on to the lawn. Mr Cranthorpe-Cranborough watched it in stricken silence. Then he said to William with an unconvincing attempt at nonchalance:

MR CRANTHORPE-CRANBOROUGH GAZED ACROSS THE LAWN AND HIS JAW DROPPED. 'LOOK!' HE GASPED TO WILLIAM. 'WHO'S THAT?'

'You – you don't see anyone on the lawn, William, do you?' he said.

Again William looked straight at Miss Moyna Greene.

'No,' he said innocently. 'There ain't no one there.'

Miss Moyna Greene disappeared through the drawing-room window.

'All the bad luck,' repeated William artlessly, 's'posed to come *from the one* they're with when they see it, but I don' b'lieve anyone ever *has* seen it if you ask me.

He looked up at Mr Cranthorpe-Cranborough. Mr Cranthorpe-Cranborough was still yellow and still

THE FIGURE OF MISS GREENE CROSSED THE LAWN AND
DISAPPEARED BEHIND THE TREES.

perspiring. He took out his handkerchief and mopped his brow.

'You don' look very well,' said William kindly, 'can I do anythin' for you?'

Mr Cranthorpe-Cranborough brought his eyes with an effort from the direction in which Miss Moyna Greene had vanished to William. And his expression changed. He seemed to realise for the first time the full import of his vision.

'Yes, William,' he said with fear and shrinking in his manner. 'You can – er – you can fetch me a railway timetable, my dear boy, if you'll be so good.'

William and Ethel and Robert had gone to bed.

Mr and Mrs Brown sat in the drawing-room alone.

'He went very suddenly, didn't he?' said Mr Brown, 'I thought I'd find him here tonight.'

'I can't understand it,' said Mrs Brown, 'he behaved most *strangely*. *Suddenly* came in and said he was going. Gave no reason and was most *peculiar* in his manner.'

'And you didn't arrange anything about William going there?'

'I tried to. I said should we consider it settled, but he said he was afraid he'd have no room for William, after all. I suggested putting him on a waiting list, but he said he'd no room on his waiting list either. He wouldn't even stay to discuss it. He went off to the station at once though I told him he'd have to wait half an hour for a train. And the last thing he said was that he was sorry but he'd *no* room for William. He said it several times. So strange after his offering to take him at a special price.'

'Very strange,' said Mr Brown slowly. 'He was – all right at lunch you say?'

'Quite. He was talking then as if William were going.'

'And what did he do after lunch?'

'He went into the garden to rest. '

'And who was with him?'

'No one – Oh, except William for a few minutes.'

'Ah,' said Mr Brown, and remembered the sphinx-like look upon William's face when he said Good-night to him. 'I'd give a good deal to have been present at those few minutes – but the secret, whatever it was, will die with William, I suppose. William possesses the supreme gift of being able to keep his own counsel.'

'Are you sorry, dear, that William's not going to a boarding-school?'

'I don't think I am,' said Mr Brown.

'I should have thought you'd have found it so nice and quiet without him.'

'Doubtless I should. But it would also have been extremely dull.'

CHAPTER 7

THE STOLEN WHISTLE

WILLIAM had been to watch the sheep dog trials at a neighbouring Agricultural Show and had been much thrilled by the spectacle. It had seemed, moreover, perfectly simple. Just a dog and some sheep and anyone could do it. He had a dog, of course – Jumble, his beloved mongrel who had filled many and various rôles since he had joined William's *ménage*. He had been a walking dog and a dancing dog and a talking dog. He had even on one occasion represented a crowd in a play organised by William. It cannot be claimed that Jumble brought any great brilliance to bear on the fulfilment of these rôles. He was essentially passive, rather than active, in his representation of them. He walked and danced perforce, because William on these occasions held his front paws and he could do nothing else. His 'talking' was his natural reaction of excitement to William's softly whispered 'rats!' It did not really represent that almost superhuman intelligence that William claimed for it. Jumble himself took no pride in his accomplishments.

When he heard the word 'trick' he slunk off as quickly as he could, but if escape were impossible he yielded to the inevitable, and suffered the humiliation of walking or dancing with an air of supercilious boredom.

After breakfast on the morning after the sheep trials, William walked slowly and thoughtfully into the garden. There he was greeted effusively by Jumble who tried to convey to him by barks and leaps and whirlwind rushes that it was just the morning for a walk in the wood, where perhaps perhaps – with luck one might meet a rabbit or two. But William was not in a rabbit mood. He was in a sheep dog mood. He had definitely decided to train Jumble to be a sheep dog. It might be objected that with truth Jumble was not a sheep dog, to which objection it might with equal truth be replied that Jumble was as much a sheep dog as he was any other sort of dog. The sorts of dog in Jumble were so thoroughly mixed that there was no sort of dog you could definitely say he wasn't.

William had decided to use a whistle for giving his signals to Jumble chiefly because his newest and dearest treasure happened to be a whistle. It had been sent to him for his last birthday, by an uncle who, as William's father bitterly remarked, ought to have known better. It was not an ordinary whistle. It was the Platonic ideal of a whistle. It was very large and very ornate and emitted a sound rivalled only by a factory siren. William to the relief and surprise of his family had made little use of this since his reception of it. He had kept it in a box in a drawer in his bedroom. His family fondly imagined that he had forgotten about it and never allowed the conversation even remotely to approach the subject of musical instruments in general or whistles in particular, lest it should remind him of it. They could not know, of course, that William's whistle was his secret pride and joy and dearest treasure and that he did not use it simply because he considered it too precious to use till some great and worthy occasion presented itself. And here the great and worthy occasion had presented itself – the training of Jumble to be a sheep dog.

With Jumble bounding about in innocent glee and all unaware of his coming ordeal, he entered his bedroom and reverently took the whistle from its bed of cotton wool in the box in which he had received it. Then he placed it in his pocket and with Jumble still leaping exuberantly about him went out into the road.

He had now a dog and a whistle. The only thing that remained was to find some sheep. He swung down the road, one hand fingering lovingly the whistle that reposed in his pocket, his eyes fixed proudly on Jumble. Jumble, who fondly imagined that his hint about the walk in a rabbity wood had been taken, leapt ecstatically into the air at every passing fly or butterfly and as often as not overbalanced in the process. The very word 'trick' would have sent him slinking homeward, his tail between his legs, but no one uttered the fateful word so Jumble leapt and bounded in light-hearted glee with no thought in his mind but of scurrying white-tailed rabbits.

William was now walking along without paying much attention to his pet. His mind was set on other things. He was looking for sheep. Suddenly he saw them – a whole fieldful of sheep with no guardian or owner in sight. He brightened. The training of Jumble as a sheep dog could begin. With Jumble still at his heels he entered the field.

'Now, Jumble,' he said sternly, 'when I blow one blow on this whistle you drive 'em to the end of the field an' when I blow two you drive 'em back again.' Jumble gave a short sharp bark, which William, ever optimistic, took to be one of complete understanding.

William drew in his breath then blew a piercing blast on his whistle. The nightmare sound rent the air. A sheep who was cropping grass turned and gazed at him reproachfully. The others took no notice. Jumble continued to chase butterflies. William sighed and repeated his instructions.

'When I blow once on this whistle, Jumble, you drive 'em over there and when I blow twice you drive 'em back.' Jumble wagged his tail and William thought that he'd really tumbled to it at last.

He blew again – a mighty piercing blast. The sheep who had looked at him reproachfully turned and looked at him still more reproachfully. Jumble, upon whose mind the conviction was slowly forcing itself that something was being expected of him, sat up and begged.

William sighed.

'No, Jumble,' he said, 'jus' listen – when I blow *once*—'

He stopped. Jumble was off after another butterfly. It was simply no use talking to Jumble with all those butterflies about. He must make him understand by some other means. He pointed to the sheep.

'Hi, Jumble!' he urged, 'at 'em! Rats!'

Jumble looked from William to the sheep, head on one side, ears cocked. His master evidently wanted him to attack those big white things that inhabited the field. But why? They were doing no harm and there was a vein of caution in Jumble that objected to the unnecessary attacking of things three times his size. Still, he didn't mind showing willing and he needn't go too near.

With elaborate ostentation of ferocity he began to bark at the nearest sheep, making little leaps and rushes as if to attack it – but keeping all the time a respectful distance.

'Good old Jumble!' encouraged William, 'go on at them. Rats!'

Jumble, glad to learn from the tone of William's voice that he was doing the right thing, redoubled his pretence of fury and attack. The nearest sheep with a scared look on its face rose and moved farther away. Jumble's delight knew no bounds. He had frightened the thing. That big white animal three times his size was afraid of him. Some of his caution deserted him. He advanced again upon the sheep, his sound and fury redoubled. The sheep began to run. In a state of frenzied intoxication Jumble flung himself to the pursuit. Panic broke out among the flock. They rushed hither and thither bleating wildly, with Jumble, who imagined himself a Great Dane at least, pursuing them, barking loudly. William felt gratified. Things were getting a move on at last. Jumble was turning out a really fine sheep dog. Then he blew twice on his whistle.

'Now bring 'em back, Jumble,' he ordered.

But Jumble was deaf and blind to everything but the ecstasy of chasing these large foolish white creatures who did not seem to realise their size, who – joy of joys, miracle of miracles! were afraid of him – of *him*! The field was a medley of scurrying bleating sheep and leaping, barking, exulting, pursuing, ecstatic Jumble.

'Hi, Jumble!' called William again, 'stop it – bring 'em back now.'

But the sheep had found a way of escape and were streaming in a jostling panic-stricken crowd through the gate inadvertently left open by William on to the road where some streamed off in one direction, some in another, still bleating wildly.

Jumble surveyed the empty field. He'd cleared them out, which was evidently what William meant him to do. The place belonged to him and William now. He swaggered up to William and sat down sideways head in the air, mouth open, panting.

He fairly radiated conceit. He couldn't get over it – hundreds and hundreds of big white things each three times as big as himself flying in panic before him – before him – what a dog! *What* a dog! He gave William a glance that said:

'Well, what do you think of me, *now*?'

William could have told him quite adequately and eloquently what he thought of him but already sounds of commotion and shouting came from the direction of the farm whence the errant sheep had been sighted. Already men were running down the road to deal with the crisis. William, not wishing to be dealt with as part of the crisis, hastily picked up Jumble, scrambled through the hedge into a further field and thence by devious routes to the road and back to his home.

His first lesson to Jumble on sheep dogging had not

been altogether successful but William was not a boy lightly to abandon anything he had undertaken. Only he thought that perhaps it had been a mistake to begin on sheep. It would be best probably to work up to sheep gradually. Sitting on an upturned plant pot in his back yard, his chin on his hands, he frowningly considered the situation, while Jumble sat by him, leaning against the plant pot wearing a complacent simper, still seeing himself, alone and unaided, putting to flight vast hordes of large white animals. Yes, thought William, that had been the mistake – beginning with sheep instead of working up to them gradually. If he could begin on something small they could work up to sheep by degrees. His white mice – the very thing! He turned and gave Jumble a long and patient detailed account of what he wanted him to do.

'When I blow once, Jumble,' he said, 'you run 'em over to the end of the lawn and when I blow twice run 'em back to me again an' mind you don't let any of them escape.'

Jumble looked at him foolishly, obviously not even trying to understand and taking for granted that William was singing his praises, telling him that he could hardly believe his eyes when he saw him scattering them far and near. William went to fetch his white mice, leaving Jumble still simpering. He returned and knelt down with the box.

'Now run 'em *gentle*, Jumble,' he ordered as he released the flock.

But Jumble was in no mood for gentleness. Either he considered it an insult to try to make him a mouse dog instead of a sheep dog or he wished to show William that this was mere child's play after his late exploit. He'd killed two before William could rescue them. He listened to William's remarks with polite boredom and watched the subsequent obsequies with alert interest as though marking the spot for future investigation. He then watched the remnants of the flock being carried indoors with an air of wistfulness. He'd have quite liked to have gone on with them.

William was not really disheartened. He was sorry of course to lose two of his white mice, but his white mice themselves were capable of filling any gaps in their numbers with such speed and thoroughness that the shortage would not be of long duration. And he was still determined to teach Jumble to be a sheep dog. He ignored Jumble's attempts to suggest to him again the walk in the rabbity wood (Jumble felt that he'd have simply loved to have a go at rabbits now – he was just in the mood) and sat down again on the upturned plant pot to consider the matter. Perhaps the best thing to do was to train Jumble to be a sheep dog by himself without anything to represent the sheep, and then when Jumble was an expert sheep dog gradually intro-

duce sheep for him to work upon. He'd teach Jumble
to go to the other end of the lawn when he blew once
and return when he blew twice.

He did this by throwing a stone to the other end of
the lawn for Jumble to fetch and blowing once when
he threw it and twice when Jumble was ready to bring
it back. He hoped that if he did this often enough,
Jumble would begin to associate his departure and
return with the whistle instead of the stone. When he'd
been doing it for about half an hour his father came
out wearing an expression of mingled agony and fury.

'If I hear one more sound from that beastly
instrument of torture,' he said, 'I'll take it from you
and throw it into the fire. Do you know I've been
trying to sleep this last half hour? What the dickens are
you doing sitting there and blowing the thing like that,
to all eternity? Are you trying to play a tune?'

William did not explain that he was trying to teach
Jumble to be a sheep dog. He withdrew himself and
Jumble and the whistle out of harm's way as quickly as
possible.

He knew that it would be useless to continue the
training of Jumble within earshot of his father. It
would be safer to withdraw to the other end of the
village where there was no possibility of his father
hearing it. It was particularly annoying because he'd
thought that just before his father came out Jumble

really had begun to understand what he wanted him to do. He slipped the whistle into his pocket and set off down the road, Jumble following merrily at his heels. Jumble evidently thought that the walk through the rabbity wood was going to come off at last.

Right at the end of the village was a large brown house with a field behind it. The field was empty and well hidden from the road. Here William decided to complete the training of Jumble. Armed with a little pile of stones and his whistle he patiently threw stones and whistled his one blast then his two as Jumble departed and returned. Jumble was fetching the stones in a perfunctory fashion as one who does it merely to oblige. His considered opinion was that as a game it was going on a bit too long. It was in any case rather a puerile amusement for a dog who alone and unaided could put to flight great hordes of large white animals. And he wanted to have a go at those rabbits.

William really thought that Jumble knew what was expected of him at last. He decided to try without the stones. It was a great moment. He blew a single blast on his whistle and then waited to see if Jumble would fly at the note of command to the other end of the field. William never knew whether Jumble would have flown at the note of command to the other end of the field; it is a question that must remain to all eternity unanswered. For no sooner had William emitted the note of command than a furious tornado dressed in a mauve suit tore down upon him, revolving itself as it became calmer into an elderly gentleman who lived in the brown house.

'You wretched little mongrel,' he said addressing William not Jumble, 'you inhuman young torturer – you – you infant Nero! Do you know, I ask you, sir, that I've been trying to rest – to *rest* with this infernal row going on? What do you mean by it, you young scoundrel? What do you think you're doing with it – blowing it on and on and on like that? Are you trying to drive me *mad*?'

Before William could resist he had snatched the precious whistle from William and thrust it into his pocket. 'Now I've got it, my boy, and I'll *keep* it. And I'll take any other infernal instrument of torture you come around here with – and get out!'

Jumble growled and made ineffective darts towards the old gentleman but finding that the old gentleman did not obligingly turn and flee with bleats of terror like the sheep, he changed his tactics and wagged his tail propitiatingly. William, aghast and infuriated, tried to gather breath for a reply but before it came the old gentleman's roseate hue deepened to purple and he roared again:

'Get – OUT!'

William with one glance at the purple face threw

dignity to the winds and got out, closely followed by the incipient sheep dog. He was ablaze with righteous indignation. He felt that he'd rather have had anything stolen from him than the precious whistle, his glorious insignia as sheep dog trainer. Stolen – yes, that was it, stolen – *his* whistle *stolen*. The man in the mauve suit ought to be in prison – a robber, that was what he was – just an ordinary robber. He – he'd go and tell someone about it so that the man in the mauve suit could be put in prison.

He told his father first and his father said: 'Thank Heaven!'

Then he told the village policeman and the village policeman slapped his thigh and uttered a guffaw that sent Jumble flying down the road in panic.

After much silent cogitation William decided to approach the robber himself. He waylaid him on the road later in the day and said unctuously:

'Please, can I have my whistle back?'

The robber uttered a loud 'Ha!' and then said very firmly, 'No! you can*not* have your whistle back! On *no* account can you have your whistle back. You can *never* have your whistle back. Wild horses couldn't make me give your whistle back. You may look upon that whistle, my boy, as lost to you for ever and likewise every other fiendish contrivance you use to drive away my sleep. Ha!'

With that he passed on still snorting.

William stood motionless in the road gazing after him. Well, he'd tried every lawful means. He'd appealed to his father who ought to have protected his own son from these outrages. He'd appealed to the strong arm of the law who should have taken drastic steps against such lawless extortion of property, he'd appealed to the criminal's own better feelings – all to no avail.

The only thing that remained was to take matters into his own hands. For William felt that never could he hold up his head again while this blot upon his honour remained unavenged.

With no very clear plan of action in his mind, William progressed furtively up the drive of the big brown house. He had seen the old gentleman in the mauve suit drive down towards the station that morning in a cab with a suitcase, so that bold advance into the enemy's country was less heroic than at first it sounds.

For safety's sake William had left Jumble at home. Jumble was well meaning but could never understand the need for secrecy. Idly William thought that he'd train Jumble to be a police dog when he'd finished training him to be a sheep dog. He'd train him to hunt down robbers and bite them hard.

But he couldn't continue the sheep dog training till

he'd recovered his whistle – *his* whistle. Had you offered William then a hundred golden whistles set with gems in exchange for *his* whistle, he would have refused them with scorn. It was *his* whistle and he was going to have it or know the reason why.

He wandered round the front of the house with an elaborate display of secrecy that would have attracted anyone's attention from miles away had anyone been there to see. The front downstairs rooms were all empty with windows securely locked. The front and side doors also were locked. He had a wholesome awe of inhabitants of kitchen regions. They had such effective weapons to hand in the way of rolling pins and saucepans. Even had the doors and windows been open it would have been difficult to know where to begin looking for his whistle. There was moreover a horrible possibility that the man in the mauve suit might have taken it with him. His voyage of investigation round the house, though fruitless, gave him a certain amount of satisfaction by its vague element of heroism and danger. Having finished it he decided to go home and think out some more definite plan of campaign.

He set off still with a melodramatically conspiratorial air down the drive, and suddenly when he'd almost reached the gates he heard the sound of a motor car in the road outside. It was coming in. He looked about wildly for some place of hiding. There was none. With admirable presence of mind he stretched himself out by the edge of the drive and lay there with closed eyes. The car turned in at the gate – passed him, stopped, backed.

'Good Heavens,' said a girl's voice, 'it's a boy.'

'Is he dead?' said another.

Without opening his eyes William perceived that four people were getting out of the car. He remained motionless with closed eyes. He felt that as long as he remained in that position no one could call upon him to account for his presence in their private ground.

'See if he's breathing,' said someone.

A firm hand was laid on his chest. William was very ticklish and it needed all his self-control not to wriggle. But he remained stark and motionless.

'Yes, he's alive,' said the voice with a note of relief in it, 'he's breathing.'

'Let's take him into the house,' said someone else, 'and Freddie can see what's the matter with him.'

A youth's voice spoke.

'Well,' it said rather uncertainly, 'I've only been doing medicine a month, you know.'

'But, my dear, surely you can diagnose a little thing like this when you've been doing it a whole *month*,' said the voice.

'Oh yes,' said Freddie, 'I – I daresay I can. It – it's probably something quite simple.'

William, who was beginning to enjoy the situation, felt himself lifted up and placed in a car, taken up to the front door of the brown house, lifted out, carried in and laid upon a sofa.

'What is it, Freddie?' said a girl's voice, 'what's the matter with him? Perhaps he's been run over. He's breathing. See – put your hand over his heart, you'll feel its beating.'

But at this point, partly because he could contain his curiosity no longer and partly because his ticklishness could not endure the thought of a hand being placed again upon his chest, William opened his eyes and sat up. He saw three girls, one with red hair, one with black hair, one with fair hair and a very young man. The very young man looked relieved by William's return to consciousness.

'Better, dear?' said the girl with red hair.

'Yes, thank you,' said William.

'What do you think it was, Freddie?' said the girl with dark hair.

'Oh – er – j'st a slight er – vertigo, said Freddie.

'Well, you'd better stay there and rest a little, dear, hadn't you?' said the girl, 'just till you feel well enough to go home.'

'Yes,' said William speaking faintly and trying to assume the expression of one suffering from vertigo, whatever vertigo might be. He was much interested by

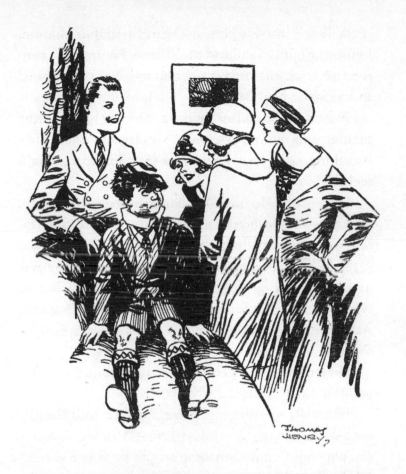

WILLIAM OPENED HIS EYES AND SAT UP. 'BETTER, DEAR?'
SAID THE GIRL WITH RED HAIR.

his present position and did not want to abandon it.
Moreover he was within the building that presumably
held his precious whistle and he hoped that Fate might

yet deliver it into his hands. The girl with fair hair put a cushion under his head and the girl with dark hair went to fetch the motor rug and spread it over him, and Freddie held his wrist and took out his watch hoping that the action would add to his medical prestige and that no one would notice that the watch was not going. The others gazed at him in an awed silence.

'Is he – all right now?' said one of them.

'Oh yes,' said Freddie putting away his watch, 'he ought to rest a little before he goes out, though.'

'Shut your eyes, dear,' said the girl with the red hair, 'and try to get a little sleep before you go home. Count sheep going through a gate.' William closed his eyes obediently, forebearing to remark that he'd had quite enough of sheep going through gates.

Then they all sat down in the window alcove and began to talk.

'It's really quite a jolly place, isn't it?' said the girl with the dark hair. 'Awfully decent of Uncle Charles to say we could come out here to picnic whenever we like.'

'Only while he's away,' said the girl with fair hair.

'I know. He's not exactly sociable but we can have some quite jolly times driving down here from Town while he's away. I think it would be an awfully good plan to have the dress rehearsal here on Thursday, don't you? All come down in cars and picnic and then have dinner here. He's got an angelic cook and he said we could feed here whenever we like and then drive back to Town by moonlight.'

'Don't you think we ought to mention it to him – the rehearsal, I mean?'

'Well, we might if it were anyone else but you know what he is. If it were any other play, too, we might, but a play about the Russian Revolution – well, it's like a red rag to a bull to him. He's scared stiff of a revolution, you know. It's a regular bee in his bonnet.'

'He said to me only last week that he never went away from home without being quite prepared to find the communists in possession of his home when he returned. So the poor old thing wouldn't be able to sleep o' nights if he thought we were rehearsing a play like that in his house. He won't be back till the day after so he won't know. In any case he doesn't know any of the people who're acting except us so it's just as well the old boy shouldn't know anything about it.'

'Right! And it would be fun to come down here and make a real excursion of it. This room is a bit too small, isn't it? Freddie, go and see whether the library would be better.'

Freddie departed and they turned to William again.

'Better, dear?' they said again.

'Yes, thank you,' said William.

'What is this vert whatever it is that Freddie says he's got?' said the dark-haired girl to the red-haired girl.

'Something to do with the backbone, I think,' said the red-haired girl vaguely. 'You know they call things that haven't any backbone invert something or other.'

'I suppose,' said the fair-haired girl to William, 'that you were walking down the road and the attack came on suddenly and you came in here for help and succumbed before you could get help.'

'Well,' said William with a burst of inspiration, 'I was coming in here for my whistle when this vert thing came over me sudden and I fell down.'

'For your whistle, dear?' said the fair-haired girl in a puzzled voice.

'Yes,' said William brazenly, 'Mr what's his name? The man what lives here?'

'Oh, Uncle Charles, Mr Morgan.'

'Yes – well, this Mr Morgan came out to me the other day to borrow my whistle an' he said he'd give it me back if I called for it today. He asked if I'd just lend it him till today and said that it would be all ready for me to take back today if I called for it.'

'But – why did he want to borrow your whistle?' said the fair-haired girl, still puzzled.

'Jus' to blow on. He liked it,' said William casually.

They looked at each other meaningly.

'Poor Uncle Charles,' said the dark-haired girl, 'I'm afraid he's – well, it *sounds* as if he were getting a little childish.'

'An' please,' said William firmly, 'I'd like to take it home now.'

'But, where is it? Did he say where it would be?'

'No, he didn't,' said William and added hopefully, 'but I speck it's somewhere about.'

'Well, we'll try to find it for you,' said the dark-haired girl doubtfully, 'but – don't lend him anything else, will you?'

'No,' said William fervently.

Making a complete and rapid recovery from his recent attack of vertigo, William arose from his couch and joined in the search. They looked round the drawing-room, dining-room and library without finding the whistle.

'Well, we'll remind him the very first time we see him,' said the red-haired girl obligingly.

'Thanks,' said William without enthusiasm.

'And now you feel well enough to go home, don't you? This gentleman who is a doctor – well, *almost* a doctor, will drive you home in the car and explain to your mother exactly what's wrong with you.'

But William and Freddie seemed equally anxious to avoid this anti-climax so they finally yielded to William's assertion that he felt *quite* all right now and

would *much* rather walk home, and to Freddie's assertion that probably the family already had a doctor, and
it would be against medical etiquette for him to go
butting into someone else's patient and it would do the
kid good to walk – get the circulation going again after
the vertigo. So Freddie returned to the library and the
three girls walked down to the gate with William and
watched him depart down the road.

'Poor little child,' said the fair-haired girl with a
sigh.

'He doesn't *look* as if he had a diseased backbone,'
said the red-haired girl.

'No,' said the dark-haired girl, 'but some of these
internal things don't show.'

William walked jauntily. He hadn't got his whistle,
but he'd had quite an interesting morning.

It was Thursday evening. William crept up the drive
again and walked round to the brown house.

The windows of the library and drawing-room
were lit up. The drawing-room was apparently being
used as a green room. Actors in various stages sat on
chairs or sofa, or 'made up' in front of the Venetian
mirror. In the library the play was just beginning. An
inhuman-looking bearded gentleman of obviously
Communist persuasions, his face deeply – perhaps too
deeply – scored by lines of cruelty and ill-temper, was

sitting on the armchair, his boots on the table. A large
red flag was planted beside him and the table was
covered with a red flag. Brutal-looking soldiers held a
shrinking prisoner in front of him. Other brutal-
looking soldiers lounged about the room. The play
was evidently just beginning. Neither Freddie nor any
of the three girls were in this scene. William, who had
only a faint hope of recovering his whistle, but a very
real curiosity as to the dress rehearsal, stood outside in
the darkness, flattening his nose against the window.
The brutal man in the chair was overacting – banging
the table and shaking his fist and snarling and shouting
– but this made it all the more thrilling to William.
Then suddenly he heard the sound of wheels coming
up the drive. Still impelled by curiosity, he crept round
the house to see who it was. Then he stood amazed. It
was the man in the mauve suit. He was descending
from a taxi with his suitcase, and preparing to enter his
front door. Then a glorious inspiration came to
William. The taxi drove off, but before the owner of
the house could enter his door, a small boy whom he
could not see distinctly in the darkness darted forward
and seized his arm.

'Don't go in,' he whispered, 'there's danger.'

Mr Morgan's jaw dropped.

'What?' he gasped.

'I say there's *danger*,' said the boy again rather

irritably, 'if you go in that house you'll never come out alive.'

'B-but it's *my* house,' said Mr Morgan, 'I've *often* been in and come out alive.'

'Come here and I'll show you,' whispered William. 'Come round here.'

He led the amazed but unprotesting householder round to the lighted window of the library.

'There!' he said, 'look at that.'

Mr Morgan looked at it while his mouth and eyes slowly opened to an almost incredible extent and his cheeks grew paler and paler. There in his library with feet on his writing table, sat a brutal communist commander beneath the red flag. Brutal communist soldiers lounged in all his best chairs and some poor unhappy prisoner stood trembling before the brutal communist commander.

'W-what is it?' he gasped.

'It's broke out,' said William succinctly, 'the revolution – it's broke out.'

'B-but I heard nothing on the way,' gasped the poor man again, drops of perspiration standing out on his brow.

'No, it's been very sudden,' explained William unabashed, 'quite a lot of people don't know anything about it yet.'

'What I always said would happen,' groaned Mr

Morgan. 'On us before we know where we are! The first blaze kindled in this very village and my home – my *own* house – taken for headquarters. I've always feared it – always.'

'They're having the people from the village in one by one,' said William cheerfully. 'They've got 'em all locked in the cellars. They're killin' most of them.'

'And – and all my valuables there,' groaned Mr Morgan, 'all my money and everything. If only I could collect some of it I could make good my escape.'

He shuddered as the brutal communist commander within shook his fist with a particularly brutal gesture in the shrinking prisoner's face.

'Well,' said William slowly. 'When first I started watchin' through this window it was open an' they were alone – it was before they started havin' in the prisoner – an' I heard them saying that they were afraid the reg'lar army'd soon be upon them an' the signal that the reg'lar army was comin' upon 'em was three blows on a whistle from the road so as soon as they heard three blows on a whistle from the road it'd mean that the reg'lar army was comin' upon 'em an' they'd have to clear out quick – so if we could give three blows on a whistle from the road they'd clear out jolly quick an' you could nip in an' get your stuff before they come back. But – but, I've not got a whistle, have you?'

There was a tense silence during which William held his breath.

'I have, as it happens,' said the old gentleman excitedly, 'by a curious chance, one came into my possession the other day – but it's in my bedroom. How am I to get at it?'

'Where's your bedroom?' said William shortly.

'Just above us. The window, I see, is open.'

'Where's the whistle?' said William trying not to sound too eager.

'In the right-hand small drawer in my dressing-table. What are you doing?'

For William

'THERE!' SAID WILLIAM. 'LOOK AT THAT!' MR MORGAN LOOKED AT IT, WHILE HIS MOUTH AND EYES SLOWLY OPENED AND HIS CHEEKS GREW PALE.

with a speed and agility worthy of one of his remotest forebears was shinning up the tree, and swinging himself from the tree to the window sill of the room just above. He disappeared into the room. Soon he

THERE IN MR MORGAN'S LIBRARY, WITH HIS FEET ON
THE WRITING TABLE, SAT A BRUTAL COMMUNIST
COMMANDER, WITH A PRISONER TREMBLING BEFORE
HIM IN THE HANDS OF BRUTAL COMMUNIST SOLDIERS.

reappeared, swung himself on to the tree and came back as quickly as he had gone.

In his hand he held his beloved long-lost whistle.

'Brave boy!' said the old gentleman fervently, 'now go down to the road and blow three times.'

William crept away into the darkness with the whistle. He could not refrain from chuckling as he reached the road. The old gentleman waited and waited, but no blast came from the darkness into which William had disappeared.

William was creeping back. He knew that it was a dangerous proceeding, but curiosity triumphed over caution. He wanted to know what had happened to the old gentleman and the brutal communist commander and – everyone. Cautiously he approached the library window. The old gentleman was sitting in his chair and the brutal communist, the prisoner and a lot more people were sitting on other chairs and on the floor drinking lemonade and eating sandwiches. Someone had opened the window and William could hear what they were saying. The three girls and Freddie were there.

'You gave me quite a fright, Uncle,' the red-haired girl was saying, 'when I saw you out there in the dark. Whatever were you doing?'

'Oh – er – nothing much,' said Mr Morgan, who had evidently not given himself away, 'just having a look round – er – just having a look round at the garden before I came in.'

'We thought you weren't coming back till tomorrow.'

'I hadn't meant to.'

'You don't mind us having had the rehearsal here, do you?'

'Not a bit, my dear. Not a bit.'

'The real reason we didn't tell you was that we knew you were just a bit nervous of communists and things like that. I told the others so that day we arranged it – the day that boy was here.'

'What boy?' said Mr Morgan sharply.

'Oh, a poor boy we picked up on the road unconscious and nearly dead, and Freddie examined him and found that he was suffering from some terrible disease of the spine.'

Mr Morgan's sniff expressed no great respect for Freddie's diagnosis.

'The poor child had come for his whistle.'

'What whistle?' said Mr Morgan still more sharply.

'He said you'd borrowed a whistle from him and promised to give it back that day. We looked all over the place for it, but couldn't find it so he had to go away without it. . . . What's the matter, Uncle?'

Mr Morgan was staring into space, his complexion changing from pink to a dull red. He'd *thought* there was something familiar about that boy though he hadn't been able to see him plainly in the darkness. There came to him memories of that curious snigger he'd heard as the boy disappeared in the darkness with the whistle.

The red deepened to an apoplectic purple.

He gave a sudden furious bellow of rage.

William, chuckling to himself, crept away again through the night. . . .

CHAPTER 8

WILLIAM FINDS A JOB

PROBABLY if she hadn't been so pretty the Outlaws would not have noticed her at all. But as it was they not only noticed her but noticed also that she was crying. She was sitting on the doorstep of a small house and her hair was a mass of auburn curls, and her eyes were blue and her mouth – well, the Outlaws were not poetic but they dimly realised that her mouth was rather nice. They looked at her and passed on sheepishly, then they hesitated, and, still more sheepishly, returned. William was the spokesman.

'What's the matter?' he said gruffly.

She raised blue, tear-filled eyes.

'Wot?' she said.

'What's the matter?' repeated William still more gruffly.

She wiped away a tear with the corner of a pinafore.

'Wot?' she said again.

'Anyone been hurtin' you?' said William still

gruffly, but with the light of battle in his eye. She looked up at him.

'No,' she said, and returned to the corner of her pinafore.

The light of battle died away from William's eye. He looked disappointed.

'Lost anythin'?' he then asked, assuming the expression of one who is willing to search every corner of the globe for whatever she had lost. She looked up at him again.

'No,' she said listlessly.

'Well, what's the *matter*?' persisted William.

'My daddy's out of work,' said the little girl.

This nonplussed the Outlaws. They'd have fought anyone who'd hurt her, they'd have found anything she'd lost, but this seemed outside their sphere.

'What d'you mean?' said Douglas, 'd'you mean he's got nothin' to do?'

'Yes,' said the little girl, 'nobody'll give 'im any work to do, an' he's got to stop at home all day.'

'Coo!' said Ginger feelingly, 'I wish I was him.'

'Well,' said William, 'don' you worry, that's all. Don' you worry. We'll get him some work,' and added as an afterthought, 'What can he do?'

'He can do anythin',' said the little girl peeping at him from behind the corner of her pinafore. 'Wot can you do?'

Then someone called her in and the Outlaws found themselves standing around in a semicircle gazing with ardent sympathy and admiration at a closed door. They hastily assumed their normal manly expressions and went on down the road.

'Well,' said Ginger the optimist, 'he can do anythin', so it ought to be pretty easy to get him a job.'

'Yes,' said William, 'we'd better start on it at once, 'cause we want to go out shootin' tomorrow.'

'My bow's broke,' said Henry sadly.

'Lend you my pea shooter,' said Douglas.

'Let's think of the things he could be,' said William, 'there's lots of 'em.'

'A doctor or a lawyer or a clergyman,' said Henry dreamily. 'Let's make him a clergyman.'

'No, he couldn't be any of those,' said William irritably, 'those are special sorts of people. They start turnin' into those before they leave school. But he could be a gardener or a butler or – or a motor car driver—'

'Shuvver,' put in Ginger with an air of superiority.

'Motor car driver,' repeated William firmly, 'or – or a sort of man nurse. I read in a book once about a man what once had a sort of man nurse – he sort of went queer in his head – the man, not the man nurse – an' the man nurse looked after him – or he could be a sort of man what looks after people's clothes—'

'A valley,' put in Ginger.

'A man what looks after people's clothes,' repeated William firmly, 'or – or a fireman, or a policeman, or a postman, or servin' in a shop. Why,' with growing cheerfulness, 'we'll be able to find hundreds an' *hundreds* of things for him to do.'

'He only wants one,' said Douglas mildly.

'What'll we start on?' said Ginger.

William assumed his frown of generalship and mentally surveyed the field of operation.

'Well,' he said at last, 'I'll try'n get him a job as a man what drives a motor car, an' Ginger try'n get him one as a gardener, an' Henry try'n get him one as a man what looks after people's clothes, an' Douglas as a man what looks after people what aren't quite right in their head, an' we'll have a meetin' in the ole barn after tea an' tell how we've got on . . . an' if we've *all* got him work, of course,' he added with his unfailing optimism, 'we'll let him choose.'

William began to make tentative efforts at lunch.

'When are we goin' to have a car?' he demanded innocently.

'Not while I'm alive,' answered his father.

William considered this in silence for some minutes, then asked:

'How soon after you're dead?'

His father glared at him and William cautiously withdrew into silence. A few minutes later, however, he emerged from it.

'Seems sort of funny to me,' he remarked – meditatively, to no one in particular, 'that we don't have one. Neely everyone else I know's got a car. They're an awful savin' in bus tickets an' shoes an' things. Seems to me sort of wrong to keep spendin' money on bus tickets an' shoes when we could save it so easy by buyin' a car.'

No one was taking any notice of him. They were discussing an artist who had taken The Limes furnished for a month. Robert, William's seventeen-year-old brother, was saying, 'One daughter, I know, I saw her at the window.' William continued undaunted:

'We'd jus' want a man to look after it that's all an' I could easy get that for you. I know a man what's good at lookin' after 'em an' I could get him for you. An' they're cheap enough. Why, someone told me about someone who knew someone what got one for jus' a few pounds – an ole one, of course, but they're jus' as good as new ones – only a bit older, of course. The ones what were made when first they was invented must be goin' quite cheap now an' one of them'd do quite all right for us – jus' to save us bus tickets an' shoes – with a man to look after it. Ginger an' me'd paint it up an' it would be as good as new. Shouldn't be surprised,' with rising cheerfulness, 'if

you could get an ole one – a really ole one – for jus'
a few shillin's an' Ginger'n me'd paint it for you and
this man'd mend it up for you an' drive it for you
an—'

There was a sudden lull in the general conversation
and his mother said:

'Do get on with your lunch, William. What *are* you
talking about?'

'About this car,' said William doggedly.

'What car?'

'This car of ours. Well, this man—'

'*What* man?'

'This man what's goin' to drive it for us—'

But this touched Robert on a tender spot.

'Any car belonging to the house will be driven by
me,' he said firmly.

William was nonplussed for a minute. Then he said
gently, 'I don't think Robert ought to tire himself out
drivin' cars. I think Robert ought to be keepin' himself
fresh for his exams an' things, not tire himself out
drivin' cars. This man'd drive it an' save Robert the
trouble of tirin' himself out drivin' cars because
Robert's got his exams an' things to keep fresh for. An'
besides all these girls what Robert likes to take out
with him – he wun't talk to 'em prop'ly if he has to be
tirin' himself out drivin' the car all the time—'

'Shut up,' ordered Robert angrily.

Temporarily William shut up.

'Are you taking Gladys Oldham on the river this afternoon?' said his mother.

'Gladys Oldham?' said Robert coldly. 'Whatever made you think I'd be taking a girl like Gladys Oldham anywhere?'

His mother looked bewildered.

'My dear – only last week you said—'

Robert spoke with dignity and a certain embarrassment.

'Last week?' he said frowning, as if he had a difficulty in carrying his mind back as far as that . . . 'well, I remember I did once think her an entirely different sort of person to what she turned out to be. . . . He's called Groves, isn't he, mother?'

'Who, dear?' said his mother mildly.

'The artist who's taken The Limes.'

'I believe so, dear.'

'I've seen the daughter – she's – she's—'

He stopped confusedly, trying to hide his blushes.

'She's the most beautiful girl you've ever seen in your life,' put in his father sardonically.

'How did you know?' asked Robert. 'Have you seen her?'

'No, I didn't know – I guessed,' said his father.

Robert seemed about to launch into a fuller description of Miss Groves, then stopped, glancing suspiciously at William. But William was intent upon his own thoughts. Noticing a slight lull in the conversation he rose again hopefully to the attack.

'This man,' he said, 'you'd find him awful useful—'

'*What* man, William?' groaned his mother.

'This man what I keep tellin' you about,' said William patiently. 'It seems to me sort of silly to wait till you get a car to get a man to drive it. I think the best thing is to get this man at once an' then when we get the car there he is all ready to drive it for us at once 'stead of havin' to waste the car while we start lookin' round for a man to drive it and—'

'The lunatic asylums of the country,' remarked Mr Brown, 'must be full of men who've had sons like William.'

William looked at him hopefully.

'If you feel like that, father,' he said, 'I know that this man—'

'Oh, shut up,' said Robert again.

'Yes,' said William bitterly, 'what I'd like to know is why you can go on talkin' an' talkin' an' talkin' an' *talkin'* about girls an' the minute I start talkin' about this man—'

'What man?'

'This man I've been tellin' you about ever since I started talkin' only no one listens to me. What I say is that this man—'

'William,' said his mother, 'if you say one word more about that man whoever he is—'

'All right,' said William resignedly, and turned his whole attention to his pudding.

He renewed the attack, however, after lunch. The car prospects didn't seem very hopeful but it might be worth while to explore other avenues. He stood at the drawing-room window looking out at the garden where Jenkins, the gardener, was weeding the bed on the lawn.

'Poor ole man,' said William compassionately, 'I think he'd do with someone to help him, don't you, mother?'

His mother looked up from the sock she was darning.

'I think that's a very kind thought, dear,' she said, 'and I'm sure he'd appreciate it. Take one of the kneeling mats out because the grass is rather damp.'

William's face fell but after a moment's hesitation he took a kneeling mat and went out to help weed the bed. He returned a few minutes later pursued by an indignant Jenkins after having unwittingly uprooted all his pet seedlings.

'Finished, dear?' said his mother. 'You've not been long.'

'No,' said William, 'I kind of worked hard an' got

it finished quick. . . . Mother, don't you kind of think you'd like another gardener 'stead of Jenkins?'

'Why ever?' said his mother in surprise.

'Well, he always seems so sort of disagreeable an' this man—'

'What man?'

'This man I keep tellin' you about,' said William patiently, 'he's an abs'lutely *wonderful* man. He can do anythin'. He can drive a car. . . he's the one what's goin' to drive our car . . . an' – an' there's nothin' he *can't* do, look after clothes an' people what are queer in the head an' – an' – she was ever so nice an' cryin'.'

'William, dear,' said Mrs Brown, 'I really don't know what you're talking about, but before you do anything else go and wash your hands and brush your hair.'

William sighed as he went to obey. His family seemed to have no souls above hands and hair and that sort of thing.

The Outlaws met the next afternoon to report progress.

'I did all I could,' said William, 'I tried to make 'em get a car so's we could have him to drive it an' they jus' wun't. I tried makin' 'em have him as a gardener an' they wun't do that either.'

Ginger, looking melancholy, related his experiences.

'I thought we might have him as a gardener, too,' he said, 'an' so I tied a string across the doorway of the greenhouse 'cause I thought that if ours fell an' sprained his ankle I could tell 'em about this new one an' then they'd get him. I din't think it would do ours any harm to sprain his ankle – jus' give him a nice rest for one thing an' – an' he's such a crabby ole thing. It might make him kinder same as what they say sufferin' docs in books.'

'Did he fall?' said the Outlaws with interest.

'No,' said Ginger sadly, 'he saw me doin' it an' went an' told my father.'

'Was he mad?' said the Outlaws with interest.

'Yes,' said Ginger still more sadly, 'he was awful mad. Simply wouldn't listen to me tellin' him I'd tied it there to practise skippin'.'

The Outlaws murmured sympathy and then Henry spoke.

'Well, I tried to get 'em to have him as a man what looks after clothes—'

'Valley,' murmured Ginger.

'An' I kep' tellin' my father an' my brother that their clothes looked to me's if they wanted brushin' or cleanin' or pressin' or somethin' an' I was goin' to tell 'em about this man what'd come an' do it for them, but,' mournfully, 'they din't give me a chance to get's far as that. Seems to me that it's very funny that one can't try'n help a poor man what's out of work without bein' treated like that about it.'

Again the Outlaws murmured sympathy, then Douglas spoke up.

'I thought I'd try'n get him as a sort of man nurse so I acted like I was goin' queer in my head.'

'What did they do?' said William.

An expression of agony passed over Douglas's face.

'Gave me Gregory powder,' he said, 'an' I couldn't sort of seem to make 'em understand I was actin' queer in the head. They seemed to think I was actin' ordin'ry. Anyway when they got reely mad I had to stop it 'cause I was afraid they'd start on me with more Gregory powder, an' it's a wonder I'm not poisoned dead with the first lot. It's more diff'cult than you'd think,' he ended meditatively, 'to make folks think you're queer in the head.'

'So nobody's got nothing,' William summed up the situation sadly and ungrammatically.

But Ginger was more cheerful.

'Well, there's lots other houses in the village 'sides ours,' he said, 'an' there's lots other fam'lies in the village 'sides ours. I votes we start on them. Seems to me that people outside your own fam'ly always give you more 'f a chance to explain what you mean than people in your fam'ly. They don't start bein' mad at you before you've reely got to what you want to say like people in your own fam'ly do.'

The Outlaws considered the suggestion in silence. Then William pointed out its obvious disadvantage.

'Yes, but most of the people round here,' he said simply, 'know us, an' so it wun't be much use.'

'There's someone new come to The Limes,' said Henry, 'I heard my mother talkin' about them.'

'So did I mine,' said Douglas, 'he's an artist.'

'Oh, yes,' said William, 'so did I mine. An' he's got – a daughter what's the most beautiful girl what Robert's ever seen.'

'Well, let's try him,' said Ginger, 'he oughter want someone to look after his clothes or drive his car or nurse him when he's queer in the head or something. Who'll try him? I votes William does first.'

'All right,' said William who was always ready for any fresh adventure. 'I'll go straight off now 'fore he gets anyone else.'

William entered the garden gate of The Limes and looked cautiously around him. There was no one in sight. The building was a long, low one with French windows opening straight on to the garden.

William was furtively exploring this in order to see how the land lay before venturing up to the front door when a voice called out:

'Boy! Hi! Come here!'

A man had suddenly appeared at one of the down-stairs windows and was beckoning to him.

Warily William approached. The man had a pointed beard, and very bushy eyebrows.

'Boy!' he called again.

'Uh-huh?' said William non-committally, coming up to the window. The room inside was evidently a studio. Several easels stood about and the table was littered with tubes of paint and palettes.

'Just what I wanted,' said the man, 'a boy – a real human boy – of the ruffian type, too. Splendid! My boy, I've been longing for you all morning. I've tried to materialise you. You are probably at this moment nothing but the creature of my brain. I wished for a boy and a boy appeared. I was just thinking that I must go out into the highways and byways to search for one when lo! the boy my thoughts had conjured up stood before us. I'm a superman, a magician. I always had a suspicion that I might be. Come in, boy.'

Distrustfully William entered the studio. The man gazed at him rapturously.

'Just what I wanted,' he said, 'a dirty rapscallion of a boy with a crooked tie and a grimy collar.'

This insult stung William to retaliation. He gazed coldly at the artist who had a smear of yellow paint down one side of his face, and said:

'Bet I'm as clean as you are . . . an' as to *ties*—' his

gaze wandered down to the artist's flowing bow and stayed there meaningly.

'Spirited withal!' commented the artist, 'better and better. . . . Come in.'

William came in.

'Sit down.'

William sat down.

'Now I'm going to draw you,' went on the artist. 'I'm a genius whose immortal masterpieces are but inadequately recognised by his generation, therefore perforce I eke out a modest livelihood illustrating magazine stories, and some idiot here,' he touched a manuscript, 'has written one about a boy. Fancy writing a story about a boy. Now where shall I find a boy? thought I. I wish I had a boy, and lo! a boy appears. . . . Keep still, boy. Stand just so . . . look here . . . and keep quite still.'

William, his brain working quickly, stood just so, looked there and kept quite still.

The artist sketched in silence, putting William into various postures. At the end he passed him the sketches for his inspection. William gazed at them coldly.

'Not much like me,' he commented.

'Think not?' said the artist, 'probably you have an idealised conception of your appearance.'

William looked at him suspiciously.

'I've not got anythin' like what you said,' he remarked, 'never even heard of it so I can't have. Would you like a man to drive your motor-car?'

'I've not got a motor-car,' said the artist, busily engaged in putting finishing touches into his sketch.

'Well,' said William, 'what about someone to brush your clothes?'

'I prefer my clothes unbrushed,' said the artist; 'dust protects the material.'

William considered this point of view with interest, storing it up for future use, then returned to the point at issue.

'Wun't you like someone to look after you when you're queer in the head?'

'No,' said the artist, 'it's more fun not having any-one to look after you when you're queer in the head.'

He put the sketches on to one side and took up a manuscript from the table.

'Good Lord,' he groaned as he glanced through it, 'Charles the First's time. Why the dickens do they write stories about Charles the First's time? Where the deuce am I to get anyone to sit for me in the costume of Charles the First's time? Tell me that.'

William told him.

'I know a man what'd come to sit to you,' he said, promptly, 'he'd want payin'.'

'Oh, he would, would he? . . . All right, I'll pay him.

But the question is, has he got a costume of Charles the First's time?'

'I don't—' began William, then stopped. 'Oh, yes, I expect so. . . . Oh yes, he's sure to have. Oh, yes, we'll get him one anyway.'

'A protégé?' said the artist.

'Uh-huh?' said William. 'No. He's as nice as what you are. Nicer.'

'*Touché*,' said the artist. 'Well, bring him along in his Charles I costume and I'll pay him half a crown an hour.'

The remuneration seemed princely to William.

'A'right,' he said, impressed. 'A'right. I'll bring him along. An' if you find out you want any other sort of man he'll be that, too. He can do anythin'.'

With that he departed and joined the Outlaws who were still waiting for him in the road.

'Well, you *have* been a time,' said Ginger.

'Gottim a job,' swaggered William.

'What as?'

'Bein' drawed. He's got to have special clothes. Any of you gotta Charles the First dress? He's got to have one.'

'Crumbs, no!' said the Outlaws.

'Well,' said William, 'we've got to get him one. I've got him the job an' the rest of you got to get him the dress.'

'He might have one already,' said Ginger the optimist. 'He might've been to a fancy dress dance in one.'

The other Outlaws looked doubtful.

'No harm goin' to see anyway,' said William.

So they went to see.

The little girl with blue eyes and auburn curls was
sitting on the doorstep. She looked prettier than ever.
And she was still crying.

'Cheer up,' said William, 'we've got your father a
job.'

She continued to cry.

'Has he got a Charles the First dress?' asked William.
'If he has he can come to the job straight away.'

'He can't come to no job at all,' said the little girl
mopping her blue eyes languidly with the corner of her
pinafore, 'he's ill.'

The Outlaws stared at her.

'Crumbs!' said William appalled.

She stared at the Outlaws.

'Go away,' she said, 'I don't like you.'

The Outlaws went away, but despite her professed
dislike of them it never occurred to them to relax their
efforts on her behalf.

'We'll jus' have to get a Charles the First dress an'
do it for her an' take him the money,' said William.

'How'll we get a Charles the First dress?' said
Douglas.

'Oh, we will somehow,' said William, cheerfully, 'somehow we will. See if we don't.'

With this they separated and went to their respective homes for tea.

William was rather silent at tea. He was silent because he was thinking about the Charles the First costume. He was rather vague as to what a Charles the First costume was like, but he had a well-founded suspicion that the only fancy costume he possessed – a much-worn Red Indian costume – would not pass muster in its stead. He wondered whether they could transform it in some way to a Charles the First costume by adding an old lace curtain for instance, or wearing a waste-paper basket as a headdress instead of the feathered band. . . . His sister, he knew, had a fairy queen dress. Mentally he considered the picture of the fairy queen dress superimposed upon the Red Indian costume. It would look sort of queer and after all historical dresses had to look sort of queer – that was the most important thing about them – so it might do. Robert seemed to be talking a good deal. William began to listen idly.

'I've seen her again,' Robert was saying, 'she was looking out of a window upstairs. I heard him call to her. She's called Gloria. . . . Haven't you really seen her, mother?'

'No,' said Mrs Brown mildly, 'I've not seen either of them.'

A glorious blush overspread Robert's face.

'She's wonderful,' he said, 'marvellous. I simply can't describe her. But it seems so strange that one never sees her in the village. One just catches accidental glimpses of her as one passes the house by chance. . . . It seems so strange that one doesn't see her about . . . Gloria, that's her name. I heard him call her that. I think it's such a beautiful name, don't you?'

'Perhaps,' agreed Mrs Brown doubtfully; 'somehow it suggests to me the name of a gas cooker or a furniture polish, but I daresay that it is beautiful really.'

'She's beautiful anyway,' said Robert hotly.

William was listening intently. Mrs Brown, perceiving this, hastily changed the conversation. She was aware that William took an active and not always a kindly interest in his brother's frequently changing love affairs.

'You're going to the fancy dress dance tonight, aren't you, dear?' she said to Robert.

'Yes,' said Robert.

'Did you decide on the pierrot's costume, after all?'

'Oh, no,' said Robert, 'didn't I tell you? Victor's going to lend me his Charles the First costume. He'd meant to go in it but his cold's so bad that he can't go at all, so he's sending it over to me.'

'How kind,' said Mrs Brown. 'William, dear, do stop staring at your brother and get on with your tea.'

William obligingly began to demolish a slice of cake in a way that argued a rhinoceros's capacity of mouth and an ostrich's capacity for digestion. Having assuaged the pangs of hunger for the time being, he turned to Robert.

'You got that costume upstairs, Robert?' he said guilelessly.

'Perhaps I have and perhaps I haven't,' said Robert.

Thoughtfully William demolished another piece of cake.

Then he said, still thoughtfully, and to no one in particular:

'I'd sort of like to see a Charles the First dress. I sort of think it might be good for my history. I think,' with a burst of inspiration, 'that I'd sort of learn the dates of him better if I'd seen his clothes. It's history, an' my report said I din't take enough int'rest in history. Well, I'd sort've take a better int'rest in it if I'd seen his clothes. It'd sort of make it more int'resting. I bet I'd get an ever so much better hist'ry report next term if I could only see the Charles the First dress what Robert's got.'

'Well, you can't,' said Robert firmly.

'And you've had quite enough cake, dear,' said his mother.

William turned to the buns, picked out the largest he could see and returned to the attack.

'I'm not doin' anythin' particular this evenin', Robert,' he said, 'I'll help you dress if you like.'

'Thanks, I don't,' said Robert.

'And don't talk with your mouth full, William,' said his mother.

William finished the bun in silence, then returned yet again to the attack.

'I bet I could show you how to put it on, Robert. They're awful hard to put on are Charles the First dresses. I don't s'pose you could do it alone. I'd be able to show you the way the things went on. Prob'ly you'll have 'em all laughin' at you if you try to put 'em on alone. I'll go up now if you like an' put them out ready for you the way they ought to go on.'

'Well, I don't like,' said Robert, 'and you can shut up.'

William took another very large bun for consolation. Robert looked at him dispassionately.

'To watch him eating,' he remarked, 'you'd think he was something out of the Zoo.'

That remark destroyed any compunction that William might otherwise have had on Robert's behalf in the events that followed.

Robert, fully attired in his Charles the First costume discreetly covered by an overcoat, came downstairs. He wore a look of pleasure and triumph.

The pleasure was caused by his appearance which

he imagined to be slightly more romantic than it really was. The triumph was triumph over William. He knew that William had been anxious to see the costume, from what Robert took to be motives of idle curiosity with a not improbable view to jeering at him afterwards. Robert, who considered that he owed William a good deal for one thing and another (notably for a watch which William had dismembered in the interests of Science the week before), had determined to frustrate that object. Directly after tea he had locked his bedroom door and pocketed the key, and a few minutes later he had had the satisfaction of seeing William furtively trying the handle. William, however, was not about the hall as he descended the stairs.

The costume had proved satisfactorily magnificent, but the drawback to the whole affair was that SHE would not be there to see it. At that moment he would have given almost anything in exchange for the certainty that SHE would see him in his glory. For Robert considered that the costume made him look very handsome indeed. He did not see how any girl could look at him in it and remain completely heart whole. . . . If only SHE were to be there. . . .

He took down his hat, bade farewell to his mother and set off down the drive. A small boy whom he could not see, but who, he satisfied himself, was not William (it was Henry) stepped out of the bushes, handed him a note and disappeared. He went down to the end of the drive and, standing beneath the lamp-post in the road, read it. It was typewritten.

'Dear Mr Brown,' it read,

'I have seen you in the road passing by our house, and because you look good and kind, I turn to you for help. Will you please rescue me from my father? He keeps me a prisoner here. He is mad, but not mad enough to be put in an asylum. He thinks he's living in the reign of Charles the First and he won't let anyone into the house unless they're dressed in Charles the First clothes, so I don't know how you'll get in. If you can get in please humour him and let him draw you because he thinks that he is an artist, and when once he's drawn you he'll probably let you do what you like. Then please rescue me and take me to my aunt in Scotland and she will reward you.

'GLORIA GROVES.'

The letter was the result of arduous toil on the part of the Outlaws. Every word had been laboriously looked up in the dictionary and then laboriously typed in secret by Henry on his father's typewriter.

Robert stood reading it, his face paling, his mouth and eyes opening wide with astonishment. He looked down at the costume which was visible beneath his coat.

'Charles the First costume,' he gasped. '*Well . . .* By Jove . . . of all the *coincidences*!'

Then, with an air of courage and daring, he set off towards The Limes.

William entered the studio unannounced. The artist looked up from his easel.

'Hello,' he said, 'you back?'

'Yes,' said William, 'that man I told you about's comin'.'

'Costume and all?' said the man.

'Yes,' said William, 'but I'd better explain to you a bit about him first. He's queer in the head.'

'In other words you're bringing me the village idiot.'

'Yes,' said William relieved at having the matter put so succinctly.

'It's sort of like that. He's not dangerous, but he dresses up in Charles the First costume (that's why I thought he'd do for you) an' he thinks it *is* Charles the First time an' so you've got to talk to him as if it was Charles the First time jus' to keep him quiet. He'll get mad if you don't. He'll be drawed all right 'cause he likes bein' drawed but the minute he sees any girls he always wants to start rescuin' them an' takin' them up to their aunts in Scotland.'

'Why Scotland?' said the artist mildly.

' 'Cause that's part of his madness,' explained William.

'Well, there's only one girl on the premises,' said the artist, 'and that's my daughter . . . been in quarantine for mumps . . . just out of it today . . . and I don't suppose he'll see her . . . so that's all right.'

'You'll give me the money, won't you?' said William. ' 'Cause – 'cause I keep his money for him. . . . See?'

'We'll talk about that later,' said the man, 'if he comes and when he comes. Are you his keeper, by the way?'

'Well,' said William guardedly, 'I sort of am and I'm sort of not.'

But just then he heard the sound of the opening of the front gate and discreetly retired again through the open window.

Robert walked up the garden path, his face stern and set with resolve. Robert was a voracious reader of romantic fiction and had often longed for something like this to happen to him. Its only drawback in his eye was that he hadn't enough money to take the heroine of the drama to Scotland, but he could not imagine the hero of a story being baffled by a little thing like that. They always seemed to have enough money to take the heroine anywhere. But the first thing to do was to rescue her. Then he'd pawn something or other, pawn his Charles the First costume perhaps . . . but then he'd have nothing to go to Scotland in . . . though in any case one couldn't travel to Scotland wearing a Charles the First costume. It was all very baffling . . . but the first thing to do was to rescue her. She might have some jewels or heirlooms that they could pawn. Heroines in books always had jewels and heirlooms. . . .

'Oh, there you are. . . . Come in.'

The voice came from one of the open French windows. It was the madman standing at one end of the room at an easel. He evidently thought he was an artist just as the girl had warned him. Hastily Robert flung his overcoat over a garden seat and entered in all the glory of his Charles the First costume.

'Good evening,' said the artist. 'You've come to sit for me?'

Robert assumed the simpering expression of one who humours a madman.

'Oh, yes,' he said, 'I've come to sit for you.'

Certainly the effect of the simper superimposed upon the stern set expression of resolve would have justified anyone regarding Robert in his bizarre costume as mentally though not dangerously deranged. The artist posed him appropriately and then proceeded to test the sanity or insanity of his sitter.

'Well,' he said, 'how's Charles the First today?'

Robert went paler and gathered his forces together. At all costs he must humour him.

'His Majesty,' he said solemnly, 'seems of a truth well today.'

Rather good that, he thought.

The artist looked at him keenly . . . but the pallid earnestness of Robert's expression beneath the humouring simper convinced him . . . it was true . . . he *was* potty. Well, he must just humour him . . . he *had* to get those sketches off today . . . and he didn't look dangerous.

'I'm glad to hear that,' he said, and added with a burst of inspiration, 'gadzooks.'

For a minute or two he worked in silence. Then – he found the pose he had chosen rather difficult, and for a few seconds he stood frowning at Robert meditatively. The artist's bushy eyebrows made him look very ferocious when he frowned. Robert began to tremble. The man might fly at him or something. He must say something about Charles the First to soothe him . . . at once . . . What a pity he knew so little about Charles the First . . . except that he was executed . . . or was he executed? . . . Better avoid that part of it perhaps, especially as presumably he was supposed to be still alive. . . . He didn't even know whom Charles the First had married. He might, of course, have been a bachelor. . . . He must say something quickly. . . . The man's stare was growing positively murderous. . . . With a ghastly smile he said:

'King Charles's – er – wife – was looking well this morning.'

The man's ferocious stare vanished. Robert heaved a sigh of relief and furtively wiped his brow.

'Er – yes, wasn't she?' said the artist, who'd moved a little to one side and so got a better view of his sitter, 'do you mind turning a little more this way?' and added as an afterthought, 'prithee, gadzooks!'

Robert obediently turned a little that way and for a few minutes all was well. The artist sketched in silence. Robert was beginning to feel a little less nervous. He gazed round the studio. . . . Where was SHE, he wondered?. . . Perhaps already preparing to fly with him to her aunt's in Scotland. . . . He hoped that she'd remember to bring along a few heirlooms to pawn, but then he thought with dismay that he'd never pawned anything in his life and didn't know how one set about it. That was awful. He couldn't help admitting that he seemed rather inadequate for the glorious rôle which Fate had thrust upon him. Then he comforted himself by the thought that every hero had to start, had to do the thing for the first time. It would probably be all right.

The artist became suddenly doubtful about the

pose again. He didn't think it was quite natural. Once more he gazed frowningly at the sitter and once more the perspiration stood out on Robert's brow. He must say something else about Charles the First at once. He searched feverishly in his mind for something else to say about Charles the First. He wished he'd tried harder with his history when he was at school. It was awful knowing nothing, nothing about Charles the First. He couldn't even remember what he looked like though he knew that there'd been pictures of all the kings and queens in his history book. By Jove, that was an idea.

'King Charles,' he said, 'had his picture painted . . . the one in the history b— I mean just had his picture painted. It turned out quite a good likeness, I believe.'

'Did it?' said the artist, 'could you move your head a bit to the right?' and added, 'grammercy. You a friend of His Majesty's, I suppose?'

Robert grew yet paler. It was a most awkward question. If he said he was it might arouse this madman to frenzy, and if he said that he wasn't it might equally rouse this madman to frenzy. . . . The whole thing was terrible, being alone with a madman like this. . . . He almost wished he'd never come . . . not quite, of course . . . he still remembered the vision of beauty he'd seen at the upstairs window. . . . He coughed again and said, 'Well – er – are you?'

'I?' said the artist, 'I'm one of his most intimate friends. We were discussing you only the other day. Ods bodkin – or is that Elizabethan? – you've got a difficult profile – grammercy.'

He seemed harmless enough, poor fellow, thought the artist – you could see at a glance that the poor chap was a bit wanting – gaping and staring like that all the time. . . quite young, too . . . very sad . . . poor fellow . . . and quite harmless.

Robert was just going to make some reply when the door opened and the artist's daughter entered.

Robert blushed to a dull beetroot shade and made signs intended to convey to her that he had got her letter and would rescue her from her father at once and take her to her aunt in Scotland. Then the artist turned round. The artist's daughter was staring at her would-be rescuer in amazement. She had to, of course, thought Robert, with her father watching. He'd better be a bit more careful, too.

'You've got a sitter, Daddy?' she said.

'Yes, dear,' he said, 'a gentleman of Charles the First's court.'

She went to her father's easel and looked at the sketch, whispering:

'What an extraordinary person, Daddy.'

'Yes, dear,' whispered her father, 'a bit potty, but absolutely harmless. I'm a bit vague as to where he comes from. He was brought here by a boy and will, I suppose, be fetched. He imagines that he's living in Charles the First's time. That's why he's dressed like that . . . they have to humour him . . . but harmless . . . quite harmless. I've not quite finished with him, but I want some more paper. Don't let him go till I come back, will you . . . humour him. . . he's quite harmless.'

He vanished into the next room.

Robert spoke in a hoarse whisper.

'You sent me that note, didn't you?'

She began the process of humouring him.

'Er – yes,' she replied fearfully.

'I'll rescue you,' he hissed, 'be ready. . . . As soon as he's finished drawing me. . . . We'll be at your aunt's in Scotland before morning.'

'One minute,' she said fearfully and joined her father in the inner room.

'Daddy,' she said, 'he's *absolutely* mad. He says that he's going to rescue me and take me to my aunt's in Scotland.'

'Oh, yes, I remember,' said the artist, 'that's one of his obsessions. They told me that. But he's harmless. Humour him. I simply must get that Charles I costume in four poses.'

She returned to the studio.

'You're ready to come?' said Robert.

'Er – yes,' she said.

'How shall we escape?'

'Oh – er – quite easily,' she said, watching him guardedly and backing towards the door.

'You trust me?' said Robert ardently.

'Er – yes,' she said.

The artist returned.

'One more,' he said, 'sitting there, please, and holding out one arm – thus – gadzooks – prithee—'

He opened a door in his bureau and stood stooping over it, his back to Robert. The opportunity of thus catching the oppressor of his beloved bending was too much for Robert. He leapt upon his back calling out to the girl.

'Get your things on – quick . . . I'll tie him up.'

'Good heavens!' said the artist, 'the blighter's turned dangerous.'

The artist was stronger than he looked and he soon had Robert neatly trussed. Then he turned to Gloria.

'A boy brought him,' he said, 'go and see if you can find him outside.'

But there were no boys outside.

The Outlaws, who had watched events through the French window till now, were hurrying homewards to establish alibis.

Yet on the way they called at the house of the little girl with the auburn curls. They had undertaken a respon-

ROBERT BLUSHED AND MADE SIGNS INTENDED TO
CONVEY TO HER THAT HE HAD GOT HER LETTER AND
WOULD RESCUE HER.

sibility to her and they meant to see it through. She was
not sitting on the doorstep so, summoning courage by
degrees, they knocked at the door. A woman opened it.
Inside the kitchen sat a man eating a pork-pie at a
table. The little girl was nursing a doll by the fire.

'WHAT AN EXTRAORDINARY PERSON, DADDY,'
WHISPERED THE GIRL.

The Outlaws entered sheepishly. William was spokesman.

'This your father?' he said to the little girl.

'Yes,' said the little girl.

'Well, we've sort of got him work,' said William, 'what I mean to say is that someone went to be drawed for him in these things an' we're goin' to try jolly hard to get the money from the man what drawed it tomorrow, an' – an' we'll give it him an'—'

The man laid down his knife and fork, swallowed a large mouthful of pork-pie unmasticated, and said:

'Wot cher mean?'

'Well,' explained William, 'she told us 'bout you bein' out of work—'

'*Me* out of work,' said the man indignantly.

'Oh, they are such *stupid* boys,' burst out the little girl. 'I was havin' a nice little game all to myself pretendin' to be a little girl in a book wiv a daddy out of work an' they came interferin' – an' then I was pretendin' to be a little girl in a book wiv a daddy what was ill an' they came again *interferin'*—'

'Weren't you ill?' stammered William.

'Me?' roared the man, 'never been ill in my life.'

'W-weren't you out of work?' said William.

'*Me!*' roared the man again, 'never been out of work in my life.'

'They kept *interferin'* with my games—' said the little girl.

'You interfere with 'er games again—' said the man threateningly, 'an' I'll—'

Bewildered, the Outlaws crept away.

CHAPTER 9

WILLIAM'S BUSY DAY

WILLIAM and the Outlaws strode along the road engaged in a lusty but inharmonious outburst of Community singing. It was the first real day of spring. The buds were bursting, the birds were singing (more harmoniously than the Outlaws) and there was a fresh invigorating breeze. The Outlaws were going fishing. They held over their shoulders their home-made rods and they carried jam-jars with string handles. They were going to fish the stream in the valley. The jam-jars were to receive the minnows and other small water creatures which they might catch; but the Outlaws, despite all the lessons of experience were still hopeful of catching one day a trout or even a salmon in the stream. They were quite certain, though they had never seen any, that mighty water beasts haunted the place.

'Under the big stones,' said William, 'why, I bet there's all sorts of things. There's room for great big fish right under the stones.'

'Well, once we turned 'em over an' there weren't any,' Douglas the literal reminded him.

William's faith, however, was not to be lightly shaken.

'Oh, they sort of dart about,' he explained vaguely, 'by the time you've turned up one stone to see if they're there they've darted off to the next an' when you turn over the next they've darted back to the first without you seein' 'em, but they're there all the time really. I bet they are. An' I bet I catch a great big whopper – a salmon or somethin' – this afternoon.'

'Huh!' said Ginger, 'I'll give you sixpence if you catch a salmon.'

'A' right,' said William hopefully, 'an' don't you forget. Don't start pretendin' you said tuppence same as you did about me seein' the water rat.'

This started a heated argument which lasted till they reached what was known locally as the cave.

The cave lay just outside the village and was believed by some people to be natural and by others to be part of old excavations.

The Outlaws believed it to be the present haunt of smugglers. They believed that smugglers held nightly meetings there. The fact of its distance from the sea did not shake their faith in this theory. As William said, 'I bet they have their meetin's here 'cause folk won't suspect 'em of bein' here. Folks keep on the lookout for 'em by the sea an' they trick 'em by comin' out here an' havin' their meetin's here where nobody's on the lookout for 'em.'

For the hundredth time they explored the cave, hoping to find some proof of the smugglers' visits in the shape of a forgotten bottle of rum or one of the lurid handkerchiefs which they knew to be the correct smuggler's headgear, or even a piece of paper containing a note of the smugglers' latest exploit or a map of the district. For the hundredth time they searched in vain and ended by gazing up at a small slit in the rock just above their heads. They had noticed it before but had not given it serious consideration. Now William gazed at it frowningly and said, 'I bet I could get through that and I bet that it leads down a passage an' that,' his imagination as ever running away with him, 'an' that at the end of a passage there's a big place where they hold their meetin's an' I bet they're there now – *all* of 'em – holdin' a meetin'.'

He stood on tiptoe and put his ear to the aperture. 'Yes,' he said, 'I b'lieve I can hear 'em talkin'.'

'Oh, come on,' said Douglas, who was not of an imaginative turn of mind. 'I want to catch some minnows an' I bet there aren't any smugglers there, anyway.'

William was annoyed by this interruption, but, arguing strenuously, proving the presence of smugglers in the cave to his own entire satisfaction, he led his band out of the cave and on to the high road again.

The subject of smugglers soon languished. They were passing a large barrack-like house which had been in the process of building for the best part of a year. It was finished at last. Curtains now hung at the windows and there were signs of habitation – a line of clothes flapping in the breeze in the back garden and the fleeting glimpse of a woman at one of the windows. A very high wall surrounded the garden.

'Wonder what it is,' said Henry speculatively, 'looks to me like a prison.'

'P'raps it's a lunatic asylum,' said Ginger, 'why's it got a high wall round it like that if it's not a lunatic asylum?'

Discussing the matter animatedly they wandered on to the stream.

'Now catch your salmon,' challenged Ginger.

'All right. I bet I will,' said William doggedly.

For a short time they fished in silence.

Then William gave a cry of triumph. His hook had caught something beneath one of the big stones.

'There!' he said, 'I've got one. I *told* you so.'

'Bet it's not a salmon,' said Ginger but with a certain excitement in his voice.

'I bet it is,' said William, 'if it's not a salmon I – I—' with a sudden burst of inspiration, 'I'll go through that hole in the cave – so there!'

He tugged harder.

His 'catch' came out.

It was an old boot.

They escorted him back to the cave. The hole looked far too small for one of William's solid bulk. They stood below and stared at it speculatively.

'You've *got* to,' said Ginger, 'you said you would.'

'Oh, all right,' said William with a swagger which was far from expressing his real feelings, 'I bet I can easy get through that little hole an' I bet I'll find a big place full of smugglers or smuggled stuff inside. Give me a shove . . . that's it. . . . *Oo*,' irritably, 'don't shove so *hard* . . . You nearly pushed my head off my neck . . . Go on – go on. . . . Oo, I say, I'm getting through quite easy . . . it's all dark . . . it's a sort of passage. . . .' William had miraculously scraped himself through the small aperture. Two large boots was all of him which was now visible to the Outlaws. Those, too, disappeared, as William began to crawl down the passage. It was mercifully a little wider after the actual opening. His voice reached them faintly.

'It's all dark . . . it's like a little tunnel . . . I'm going right to the end to see what's there . . . well, anyway if that wasn't a salmon I bet there *are* salmons there and I bet I'll catch one too one of these days, and—'

His voice died away in the distance. They waited rather anxiously. . . . They heard nothing and saw nothing more. William seemed to have been completely swallowed up by the rock.

William slowly and painfully (for the aperture was so small that occasionally it grazed his back and head) travelled along what was little more than a fissure in the rock. The spirit of adventure was high in him. He was longing to come upon a cave full of swarthy men with coloured handkerchiefs tied round their heads and gold ear-rings, quaffing goblets of smuggled rum or unloading bales of smuggled silk. Occasionally he stopped and listened for the sound of deep-throated oaths or whispers or smugglers' songs. Once or twice he was almost sure he heard them. He crawled on and on and on and into a curtain of undergrowth and out into a field.

He stopped and looked around him. He was in the field behind the cave. The curtain of undergrowth completely concealed the little hole from which he had emerged. He was partly relieved and partly disappointed. It was rather nice to be out in the open air again (the tunnel had had a very earthy taste); on the other hand he had hoped for more adventures than it had afforded. But he consoled himself by telling himself that they might still exist. He'd explore that passage more thoroughly some other time – there might be a passage opening off it leading to the smugglers' cave – and meantime it had given him quite a satisfactory thrill. He'd never really thought he could get through that little hole. And it had given him a secret. The knowledge that that little tunnel led out into the field was very thrilling.

He looked around him again. Within a few yards from him was the wall surrounding the house about which they had just been making surmises. Was it a prison, or an asylum or – possibly a Bolshevist head-quarters? William looked at it curiously. He longed to know.

He noticed a small door in the wall standing open. He went up to it and peeped inside. It gave on to a paved yard which was empty. The temptation was too strong for William. Very cautiously he entered. Still he couldn't see anyone about. A door – a kitchen door apparently – stood open. Still very cautiously William approached. He decided to say that he'd lost his way should anyone accost him. He was dimly aware that his appearance after his passage through the bowels of the earth was not such as to inspire confidence. Yet his curiosity and the suggestion of adventure which their surmises had thrown over the house was an irresistible magnet.

Within the open door was a kitchen where a boy, about William's size and height and not unlike William, stood at a table wearing blue overalls and polishing silver.

They stared at each other. Then William said, 'Hello.'

The boy was evidently ready to be friendly. He replied 'Hello.'

Again they stared at each other in silence. This time it was the boy who broke the silence.

'What've you come for?' he said in a tone of weary boredom. 'You the butcher's boy or the baker's boy or somethin'? Only came in this mornin' so I don' know who's what yet. P'raps you're the milk boy?'

'No, I'm not,' said William.

'Beggin'?' said the boy.

'No,' said William.

But the boy's tone was friendly so William cautiously entered the kitchen and began to watch him. The boy was cleaning silver with a paste which he made by the highly interesting process of spitting into a powder. William watched, absorbed. He longed to assist.

'You live here?' he said ingratiatingly to the boy.

'Naw,' said the boy laconically. 'House-boy. Only came today,' and added dispassionately, 'Rotten place.'

'Is it a prison?' said William with interest.

The boy seemed to resent the question.

'Prison yourself,' he said with spirit.

'A lunatic asylum, then?' said William.

This seemed to sting the boy yet further.

'Garn,' he said pugnaciously. 'Oo're yer callin' a lunatic asylum?'

'I din' mean *you*,' said William pacifically. 'P'raps it's a place where they make plots.'

The boy relapsed into boredom. 'I dunno what they make,' he said. 'Only came this mornin'. *They've* gorn off to 'is *aunt* but the other one – *she's* still here, you bet, a-ringin' an' a-ringin' an' a-ringin' at her bell, an' givin' no one no peace nowheres.' He warmed to his theme. 'I wouldn've come if I'd knowed. House-maid went off yesterday wivout notice. *She'd* 'ad as much as she wanted an' only the ole cook – well *I'm* not used to places wiv only a ole cook 'sides myself an' *her* upstairs a-ringin' an' a-ringin' at her bell an' givin' no one no peace nowheres an' the other two off to their aunt's. No place fit to call a place *I* don't call it.' He spat viciously into his powder. 'Yus, an' anyone can have my job.'

'Can I?' said William eagerly.

During the last few minutes a longing to make paste by spitting into a powder and then to clean silver with it had grown in William's soul till it was a consuming passion.

The boy looked at him in surprise and suspicion, not sure whether the question was intended as an insult.

'What *you* doin' an' where *you* come from?' he demanded aggressively.

'Been fishin',' said William, 'an' I jolly nearly caught a salmon.'

The boy looked out of the window. It was still the first real day of spring.

'Crumbs!' he said enviously, '*fishin'*.' He gazed with distaste at his work, 'an' me muckin' about with this 'ere.'

'Well,' suggested William simply, 'you go out an' fish an' I'll go on muckin' about with that.'

The boy stared at him again first in pure amazement and finally with speculation.

'Yus,' he said at last, 'an' you pinch my screw. Not *much*!'

'No, I won't,' said William with great emphasis. 'I won't. Honest I won't. I'll give it you. I don't want it. I only want,' again he gazed enviously at the boy's engaging pastime, 'I only want to clean silver same as you're doin'.'

'Then there's the car to clean with the 'ose-pipe.'

William's eyes gleamed.

'I bet I can do that,' he said, 'an' what after that?'

'Dunno,' said the boy, 'that's all they told me. The ole cook'll tell you what to do next. I specks,' optimistically, 'she won't notice you not bein' me with me only comin' this mornin' an' her run off her feet what with *her* ringin' her bell all the time an' givin' no one no peace an' *them* bein' away. Anyway,' he ended defiantly, 'I don't care if she does. It ain't the sort of place *I've* bin used to an' for two pins I'd tell 'em so.'

He took a length of string from his pocket, a pin from a pincushion which hung by the fireplace, a jam jar from a cupboard, then looked uncertainly at William.

'I c'n find a stick down there by the stream,' he said, 'an' I won't stay long. I bet I'll be back before that ole cook comes down from *her* an' – well, you put these here on an' try 'n look like me an' – I won't be long.'

He slipped off his overalls and disappeared into the sunshine. William heard him run across the paved yard and close the door cautiously behind him. Then evidently he felt safe. There came the sound of his whistling as he ran across the field.

William put on the overalls and gave himself up to his enthralling task. It was every bit as thrilling as he'd thought it would be. He spat and mixed and rubbed and spat and mixed and rubbed in blissful absorption. . . . He got the powder all over his face and hair and hands and overalls. Then he heard the sound of someone coming downstairs. He bent his head low over his work. Out of the corner of his eye he saw a large hot-looking woman enter, wearing an apron and a print dress.

'Gosh!' she exclaimed as though in despair. 'Gosh! of all the *places!*'

At that minute a bell rang loudly and with a groan she turned and went from the room again. William went on with his task of cleaning the silver. The novelty of the process was wearing off and he was beginning to feel rather tired of it. He amused himself by tracing patterns upon the surface of the silver with the paste he had manufactured. He took a lot of trouble making a funny face upon the teapot which fortunately had a plain surface.

Then the large woman came down again. She entered the kitchen groaning and saying 'Oh, Lor!' and she was summoned upstairs again at once by an imperious peal of the bell. After a few minutes she came down again, still groaning and saying, 'Oh, Lor! . . . First she wants hot milk an' then she wants cold milk an' then she wants beef tea an' then the Lord only knows what she wants . . . first one thing an' then another – I've fair had enough of it an' *them* goin' off to their aunt's an' that Ellen 'oppin' it an' *you* not much help to a body, are you?' she asked sarcastically. Then she looked at his face and screamed. 'My gosh! . . . What's 'appened to you?'

'Me?' said William blankly.

'Yes. Your face' as gone an' changed since jus' a few minutes ago. What's 'appened to it?'

'Nothin',' said William.

'Well, it's my nerves, then,' she said shrilly. 'I'm

startin' seein' things wrong. An' no wonder. . . . Well, I've 'ad enough of it, I 'ave, an' I'm goin' 'ome . . . *now* . . . first that Ellen 'oppin' it an' then *them* goin' off an' then *'er* badgerin' the life out of me. An' then your face changin' before me very eyes. Me nervous system's wore out, that's what it is, an' I've 'ad enough of it. When people's faces start changin' under me very eyes it shows I needs a change an' I'm goin' to 'ave one. That Ellen ain't the only one what can 'op it. *'Er* an' 'er bell ringing – an' – an' *you* an' your face-changin'! 'Taint no place for a respectable woman. *You* can 'ave a taste of waitin' on 'er an' you can tell *them* I've gone an' why – you an' your face!'

During this tirade she had divested herself of her apron and clothed herself in her coat and hat. She stood now and looked at William for a minute in scornful silence. Then her glance wandered to his operations.

'Ugh!' she said in disgust, 'you nasty little messer, you! Call yourself a house-boy – changin' your face every minute. What d'you think you are? A blinkin' cornelian? An' messin' about like that. What d'you think you're doin'? Distemperin' the silver or cleanin' it?'

At this moment came another irascible peal at the bell.

'Listen!' said the fat woman. ''Ark at 'er! Well, I'm

orf. I'm fair finished, I am. An' you can go or stay *has* you please! Serve 'em right to come 'ome an' find us *hall* gone. Serve 'er right if you went up to 'er an' did a bit of face changin' at 'er just to scare 'er same as you did me. Do 'er good. Drat 'er – an' all of you.'

She went out of the kitchen and slammed the back door. Then she went out of the paved yard and slammed the door. Then she went across the field and out of the field into the road and slammed the gate.

William stood and looked about him. A bell rang again with vicious intensity and he realised with mingled excitement and apprehension that he and the mysterious ringer were the only occupants of the house. The ringing went on and on and on.

William stood beneath the bell-dial and watched the blue disc waggle about with dispassionate interest. The little blue disc was labelled 'Miss Pilliter'. Then he bethought himself of his next duty. It was cleaning the car with the hose. His spirits rose at the prospect.

The bell was still ringing wildly, furiously, hysterically, but its ringing did not trouble William. He went out into the yard to find the car. It was in the garage and just near it was a hose pipe.

William, much thrilled by this discovery, began to experiment with the hose pipe. He found a tap by which it could be turned off and on, by which it could

be made to play fiercely or languidly. William experi-
mented with this for some time. It was even more
fascinating than the silver cleaning. There was a small
leak near the nozzle which formed a little fountain.
William cleaned the car by playing on to it wildly
and at random, making enthralling water snakes and
serpents by writhing the pipe to and fro. He deluged
the car for about a quarter of an hour in a state of pure
ecstasy. . . . The bell could still be heard ringing in the
house, but William heeded it not. He was engrossed
heart and mind and soul in his manipulation of the
hose pipe. At the end of the quarter of an hour he laid
down the pipe and went to examine the car. He had
performed his task rather too thoroughly. Not only
was the car dripping outside; it was also dripping
inside. There were pools of water on the floor at
the back and in the front. There were pools on all the
seats. Too late William realised that he should have
tempered thoroughness with discretion. Still, he
thought optimistically, it would dry in time. His gaze
wandered round. It might be a good plan to clean the
walls of the garage while he was about it. They looked
pretty dirty.

He turned the hose on to them. That was almost
more fascinating than cleaning the car. The water
bounced back at you from the wall unexpectedly and
delightfully. He could sluice it round and round the

wall in patterns. He could make a mammoth fountain of it by pointing it straight at the ceiling. After some minutes of this enthralling occupation he turned his attention to the tap which regulated the flow and began to experiment with that. Laying the hose pipe flat on the floor he turned the tap in one direction till the flow was a mere trickle, then turned it in the other till it was a torrent. The torrent was more thrilling than the trickle but it was also more unmanageable. So he tried to turn the tap down again and found that he couldn't. It had stuck. He wrestled with it, but in vain. The torrent continued to discharge itself with unabated violence.

William was slightly dismayed by the discovery. He looked round for a hammer or some other implement to apply to the recalcitrant tap, but saw none. He decided to go back to the kitchen and look for one there. He dripped his way across to the kitchen and there looked about him. The bell was still ringing violently. The blue disc was still wobbling hysterically. It occurred to William suddenly that as sole staff of the house it was perhaps his duty to answer the bell. So he dripped his way upstairs. The blue disc had been marked 6. Outside the door marked six he stopped a minute, then opened the door and entered. A woman wearing an expression of suffering and a very purple dress lay moaning on the sofa. The continued ringing of the bell was explained by a large book which she had propped up against it in such a way as to keep the button pressed.

She opened her eyes and looked balefully at William.

'I've been ringing that bell,' she said viciously, 'for a whole hour without anyone coming to answer it. I've had three separate fits of hysterics. I feel so ill that I can't speak. I shall claim damages from Dr Morlan. Never, *never*, NEVER have I been treated like this before. Here I come – a quivering victim of nerves, *riddled* by neurasthenia – come here to be nursed back to health and strength by Dr Morlan, and first of all off he goes to some aunt or other, then off goes the housemaid. And I shall report that cook to Dr Morlan the minute he returns, the *minute* he returns. I'll sue her for damages. I'll sue the whole lot of you for damages; I'm going to have hysterics again.'

She had them, and William watched with calm interest and enjoyment. It was even more diverting than the silver cleaning and the hose pipe. When she'd finished she sat up and wiped her eyes.

'Why don't you *do* something?' she said irritably to William.

'All right – what?' said William obligingly, but rather sorry that the entertainment had come to an end.

'Fetch the cook,' snapped the lady, 'ask her how

she *dare* ignore my bell for hours and *hours* and HOURS. Tell her I'm going to sue her for damages. Tell her—'

'She's gone,' said William.

'*Gone!*' screamed the lady. 'Gone where?'

'Gone off,' said William; 'she said she was fair finished an' went off.'

'When's she coming back? I'm in a most critical state of health. All this neglect and confusion will be the *death* of my nervous system. When's she coming back?'

'Never,' said William. 'She's gone off for good. She said *her* nervous system was wore out an' went off – for good.'

'Her nervous system indeed,' said the lady, stung by the cook's presumption in having a nervous system. 'What's anyone's nervous system compared with mine? Who's in charge of the staff, then?'

'Me,' said William simply. 'I'm all there is left of it.'

He was rewarded by an even finer display of hysterics than the one before. He sat and watched this one, too, with critical enjoyment as one might watch a firework display or an exhibition of conjuring. His attitude seemed to irritate her. She recovered suddenly and launched into another tirade.

'Here I come,' she said, 'as paying guest to be nursed back to health and strength from a state of neurasthenic prostration, and find myself left to the mercies of a common house-boy, a nasty, common, low, little rapscallion like you – find myself literally *murdered* by neglect, but I'll sue you for damages, the whole *lot* of you – the doctor and the housemaid and the cook and you – you nasty little – *monkey* . . . and I'll have you all hanged for murder.'

She burst into tears again and William continued to watch her, not at all stung by her reflections on his personal appearance and social standing. He was hoping that the sobbing would lead to another fit of hysterics. It didn't, however. She dried her tears suddenly and sat up.

'It's more than an hour and a half,' she said pathetically, 'since I had any nourishment at all. The effect on my nervous system will be serious. My nerves are in such a condition that I must have nourishment every hour, every hour at least. Go and get me a glass of milk at once, boy.'

William obligingly went downstairs and looked for some milk. He couldn't find any. At last he came upon a bowl of some milky-looking liquid. Much relieved he filled a glass with it and took it upstairs to the golden-haired lady. She received it with a suffering expression and closing her eyes took a dainty sip. Then her suffering expression changed to one of fury and she flung the glass of liquid at William's head. It missed

William's head and emptied itself over a Venus de Milo by the door, the glass, miraculously unbroken, encaging the beauty's head and shoulders. William watched this phenomenon with delight.

'You little fiend!' screamed the lady, 'it's *starch*!'

'Starch,' said William. 'Fancy! An' it looked jus' like milk. But I say, it's funny about that glass stayin' on the stachoo like that. I bet you couldn't have done that if you'd tried!'

The lady had returned to her expression of patient suffering. She spoke with closed eyes and in a voice so faint that William could hardly hear it.

'I must have some nourishment at once. I've had nothing – *nothing* – since my breakfast at nine and now it's nearly eleven. And for my breakfast I only had a few eggs. Go and make me some cocoa at once . . . at once.'

William went downstairs again and looked for some cocoa. He found a cupboard with various tins and in one tin he found a brown powder which might quite well be cocoa, though there was no label on it. Ever hopeful, he mixed some with water in a cup and took it up to the lady. Again she assumed her suffering expression, closed her eyes and sipped it daintily. Again her suffering expression changed to one of fury, again she flung the cup at William and again she missed him. This time the cup hit a bust of William

Shakespeare. Though the impact broke the cup the bottom of it rested hat-wise at a rakish angle upon the immortal bard's head, giving him a rather debauched appearance while the dark liquid streamed down his smug countenance.

'It's knife powder,' screamed the lady hysterically. 'Oh, you murderous little *brute*. It's knife powder! This will be the death of me. I'll never get over this as long as I live – never, *never*, NEVER!'

William stood expectant, awaiting the inevitable attack of hysterics. But it did not come. The lady's eyes had wandered to the window and there they stayed, growing wider and wider and rounder and rounder and wider, while her mouth slowly opened to its fullest extent. She pointed with a trembling hand.

'Look!' she said. 'The river's flooding.'

William looked. The part of the garden which could be seen from the window was completely under water. Then – and not till then – did William remember the hose pipe which he had left playing at full force in the back yard. He gazed in silent horror.

'I always *said* so,' panted the lady hysterically, 'I *said* so. I said so to Dr Morlan. I said "I couldn't live in a house in a valley. There'd be floods and my nerves couldn't stand them," and he said that the river couldn't possibly flood this house and it can and I might have known he was lying and oh my poor nerves, what shall I do, what *shall* I do?'

William gazed around the room as if in search of inspiration. He met the gaze of Venus de Milo soaked in milk and leering through her enclosing glass; he met the gaze of William Shakespeare soaked in water and knife powder and wearing his broken cup jauntily. Neither afforded him inspiration.

'It rises as I watch it – inch by inch,' shrilled the lady, '*inch* by *inch*! It's terrible . . . we're marooned . . . Oh, it's horrible. There isn't even a life belt in the house.'

William was conscious of a great relief at her explanation of the spreading sheet of water. It would for the present at any rate divert guilt from him.

'Yes,' he agreed looking out with her upon the water-covered garden. 'That's what I bet it is – it's the river rising.'

'Why didn't you *tell* me?' she screamed, 'you must have known. Why, now I come to think of it, you were dripping wet when you first came into the room.'

'Well,' said William with a burst of inspiration, 'I din' want to give you a sudden shock – what I thought it might give you tellin' you you was macarooned—'

'Oh, don't *talk*,' she said. 'Go down at once and see if you can find any hope of rescue.'

William went downstairs again. He waded out to the hose pipe and wrestled again with the tap beneath

the gushing water. In vain. He waded into a neighbouring shed and found three or four panic-stricken
hens. He captured two and took them up to the lady's
room, flinging them in carelessly.

'Rescued 'em,' he said with quiet pride, and then
went down for the others. The mingled sounds of the
squeaking and terrified flight of hens and the lady's
screams pursued him down the stairs. He caught the
other two hens and brought them up, too, carelessly
flinging them in to join the chaos. Then he went down
for further investigations. In another shed he found a
puppy who had climbed into a box to escape the water
and there was engaged in trying to catch a spider on
the wall. William rescued the puppy, and took it
upstairs to join the lady's menagerie.

'Rescued this, too,' he said as he deposited it inside.

It promptly began to chase the hens. There ensued
a scene of wild confusion as the hens, with piercing
squawks, flew over chairs and tables, pursued by the
puppy.

Even the lady seemed to feel that hysterics would
have no chance of competing with this uproar, so she
began to chase the puppy. William returned to the
deluge in which he was beginning to find an irresistible
fascination. He had read a story not long ago in which
a flood figured largely and in which the hero had
rescued children and animals from the passing torrent

and had taken them to a place of safety at the top of a house. In William's mind the law of association was a strong one. As he gazed upon the surging stream he became the rescuer hero of the story and began to look round for something else to rescue. There appeared to be no more livestock to be rescued from the sheds. He waded down to the road, which also was now partially under water, and looked up and down. A small pig had wandered out of a neighbouring farm and was standing contemplating the flooded road with interest and surprise. The hero rescuer of William's story had rescued a pig. Without a moment's hesitation William waded up to the pig, seized it firmly round the middle before it could escape, and staggered through the deluge with it and into the house. Though small it showed more resistance than William had expected. It wriggled and squeaked and kicked in all directions. Panting, William staggered upstairs with it. He flung open the door and deposited the pig on the threshold.

'Here's somethin' else I've rescued,' he said proudly.

The lady was showing unexpected capabilities in dealing with the situation. She had taken the china out of the china cabinet and had put the hens into it. They were staring through the glass doors in stupid amazement and one of them had just complicated matters by laying an egg.

The lady was just disputing the possession of a table runner with the spirited puppy who thought she was having a game with it. The puppy had already completely dismembered a hassock, a mat and two cushions. Traces of them lay about the room. Venus and Shakespeare, still wearing their rakish head adornments, were gazing at the scene through runnels of starch and liquid knife-powder. Miss Polliter received the new refugee in a business-like fashion. She had evidently finally decided that this was no occasion for the display of nervous systems. She seemed, in fact, exhilarated and stimulated.

'Put him down here,' she said. 'That's quite right, my boy. Go and rescue anything else you can. This is a noble work, indeed.'

The puppy charged the pig and the pig charged the china cabinet. There came the sound of the breaking of glass. The egg rolled out and the puppy fell upon it with wild delight. The hens began to fly about the room in panic again.

William hastily shut the door and went downstairs to continue his work of rescuing. He had by this time almost persuaded himself that the flood was of natural origin and that he was performing heroic deeds of valour in rescuing its victims. Again he looked up and down the road. He felt that he had done his duty by the animal creation and he would have welcomed a rescuable human being. Suddenly he saw two infants from the Infants School coming hand in hand down the road. They stared in amazement at the flood that barred their progress. Then with a touching faith in their power over the forces of nature and an innate love of paddling, they walked serenely into the midst of the stream. When they reached the middle, however, panic overcame them. The smaller one sat down and roared and the

'HERE'S SOMETHIN' ELSE I'VE RESCUED,' SAID WILLIAM, PROUDLY.

larger one stood on tip-toe and screamed. William at once plunged into the stream and 'rescued' them. They were stalwart infants but he managed to get one tucked under each arm and carried them roaring lustily and dripping copiously up to Miss Polliter's

'PUT HIM DOWN HERE,' MISS POLLITER SAID. 'THIS IS A
NOBLE WORK, INDEED.'

room. Again Miss Polliter had restored as if by magic
a certain amount of order. She had cooped up the hens
by an ingenious arrangement of the fireguard and she
had put the pig in the coal-scuttle, leaving him an air-
hole through which he was determinedly squeezing his
snout as if in the hope of ultimately squeezing the rest
of him. The puppy had dealt thoroughly with the table

runner while Miss Polliter was engaged on the hens and pig, and was now seeing whether he could pull down window curtains or not.

William deposited his dripping, roaring infants.

'Some more I've rescued,' he said succinctly.

Miss Polliter turned to him a face which was bright with interest and enterprise.

'Splendid, dear boy,' she said happily, 'splendid. . . . I'll soon have them warmed and dried – or wait – is the flood rising?'

William said it was.

'Well, then, the best thing would be to go to the very top of the house where we shall be safer than here!'

Determinedly she picked up the infants, went out on to the landing and mounted the attic stairs. William followed holding the puppy who managed during the journey to tear off and (presumably – as they were never seen again) swallow his pocket flap and three buttons from his coat. Then Miss Polliter returned for the pig and William followed with a hen. The pig was very recalcitrant and Miss Polliter said 'Naughty,' to him quite sternly once or twice. Then they returned for the other hens. One hen escaped and in the intoxication of sudden liberty flew squawking loudly out of a skylight.

In the attic bedroom where Miss Polliter now assembled her little company of refugees she lit the gas fire and started her great task of organisation.

'I'll dry these dear children first,' she said. 'Now go down, dear boy, and see if there is anyone else in need of your aid.'

William went downstairs slowly. Something of his rapture and excitement was leaving him. Cold reality was placing its icy grip upon his heart. He began to wonder what would happen to him when they discovered the nature and cause of his 'flood,' and whether the state to which the refugees were reducing the house would also be laid to his charge. He waded out to the hose pipe and had another fruitless struggle with the tap. Then he looked despondently up and down the road. The 'flood' was spreading visibly, but there was no one in sight. He returned slowly and thoughtfully to Miss Polliter.

Miss Polliter looked brisk and happy. She had apparently forgotten both her nervous system and its need of perpetual nourishment. She was having a game with the infants who were now partially dried and crowing with delight. She had managed to drive the hens into a corner of the room and had secured them there by a chest of drawers. She had tied the pig by a piece of string to the wash-hand-stand and it was now lying down quite placidly, engaged in eating the carpet. One hen had escaped from its 'coop' and was running round a table pursued by or pursuing (it was impossible to say which) the puppy. Miss Polliter was playing pat-a-cake with the drying infants and seemed to be enjoying it as much as the infants. She greeted William gaily.

'Don't look so sad, dear boy,' she said. 'I think that even though the river continues to rise all night we shall be safe here – quite safe here – and I daresay you can find something for these dear children to eat when they get hungry. I don't need anything. I'm quite all right. I can easily go without anything till morning. Now do one more thing for me, dear boy. Go down to my room on the lower floor and see the time. Dr Morlan said that he would be home by six.'

Still more slowly, still more thoughtfully, William descended to her room on the lower floor and saw the time. It was five minutes to six. Dr Morlan might arrive then at any minute. William considered the situation from every angle. To depart now as unostentatiously as possible seemed to him a far, far better thing than to wait and face Dr Morlan's wrath. The hose pipe was damaged, the garden was flooded. Miss Polliter's room was like a battlefield after a battle, strange infants and a pig were disporting themselves about the house, a destructive puppy had wreaked its will upon every cushion and curtain and chair within reach (it had found that it could pull down window curtains).

William very quietly slipped out of the front door and crept down the drive. The flood seemed to be concentrating itself upon the back of the house. The front was still more or less dry. William crept across the field to the stile that led to the main road. Here his progress was barred by a group of three who stood talking by the stile. There was a tall pompous-looking man with a beard, a small woman and an elderly man.

'Oh, yes, we've quite settled in now,' the tall, pompous-looking man was saying. 'We've got a resident patient with us – a Miss Polliter who is a chronic nervous case. We are rather uneasy at having to leave her all today with only the cook and house-boy. Unfortunately our housemaid left us suddenly yesterday but we trust that things will have gone all right. An aunt of mine was reported to be seriously ill and we had to hurry to her to be in time but unfortunately – ahem – I mean fortunately – we found that she had taken a turn for the better so we returned as soon as we could.'

'Of course,' said the woman, 'we'd have been back *ever* so much earlier if it hadn't been for that affair at the cave.'

'Oh, yes,' said the doctor, 'very tragic affair, very tragic indeed. Some poor boy . . . there were a lot of people there trying to recover the body and they wanted to have a doctor in the unlikely case of the boy being still alive when they got him out. I assured them that it was very unlikely that he would be alive and that I had to get back to my own patient. . . and it would only be a matter of a few minutes to send for me. . . . The poor mother was distraught.'

'What had happened?' said the other man.

'Some rash child had crawled into an opening in the rock and had not come out. He must have been suffocated. His friends waited for over an hour before they notified the parents and I am afraid that it is too late now. They have repeatedly called to him but there is no response. As I told them, there are frequently poisonous gases in the fissures of the rock and the poor child must have succumbed to them. So far all attempts to recover the body have been unsuccessful. They have just sent for men with pickaxes.'

William's heart was sinking lower and lower. Crumbs! He'd quite forgotten the cave part of it. Crumbs! He'd quite forgotten that he'd left the Outlaws in the cave waiting for him. The house-boy and the cook and the silver cleaning and the hose pipe and the flood and Miss Polliter and the hens and the pig and the puppy and the infants had completely driven the cave and the Outlaws out of his head. Crumbs, wouldn't everybody be mad!

For William had learnt by experience that with a strange perversity parents who had mourned their children as lost or dead are generally for some reason best known to themselves intensely irritated to find that they have been alive and well and near them all the time. William had little hopes of being received by his parents with the joy and affection that should be given to one miraculously restored to them from the fissures of the rock. And just as he stood pondering his next step the doctor turned and saw him. He stared at him for a few minutes, then said, 'Do you want me, my boy? Anything wrong? You're the new house-boy, aren't you?'

William realised that he was still wearing the overalls which the house-boy had given him. He gaped at the doctor and blinked nervously, wondering whether it wouldn't be wiser to be the new house-boy as the doctor evidently thought he was. The doctor turned to his wife.

'Er – it is the new house-boy, dear, isn't it?' he said.

'I *think* so,' said his wife doubtfully. 'He only came this morning, you know, and Cook engaged him, and I hardly had time to look at him, but I think he is – Yes, he's wearing our overalls. What's your name, boy?'

William was on the point of saying 'William Brown', then stopped himself. He mustn't be William Brown. William Brown was presumably lost in the bowels of the earth. And he didn't know the house-boy's name. So he gaped again and said:

'I don't know.'

There came a gleam into the doctor's eye.

'What do you mean, my boy?' he said. 'Do you mean that you've lost your memory?'

'Yes,' said William, relieved at the simplicity of the explanation, and the fact that it relieved him of all further responsibility. 'Yes, I've lost my memory.'

'Do you mean you don't remember anything?' said the doctor sharply.

'Yes,' said William happily, 'I don' remember anythin'.'

'Not where you live or anything?'

'No,' said William very firmly, 'not where I live nor anything.'

The other man, feeling evidently that he could contribute little illumination to the problem, moved on, leaving the doctor and his wife staring at William. They held a whispered consultation. Then the doctor turned to William and said suddenly:

'Frank Simpkins . . . does that suggest anything to you?'

'No,' said William with perfect truth.

'Doesn't know his own name,' whispered the doctor, then again sharply:

'Acacia Cottage . . . does that convey anything to you?'

'No,' said William again with perfect truth.

The doctor turned to his wife.

'No memory of his name or home,' he commented. 'I've always wanted to study a case of this sort at close quarters. Now, my good boy, come back home with me.'

But William didn't want to go back home with him. He didn't want to return to the house which still bore traces of his recent habitation and where his 'flood' presumably still raged. He was just contemplating precipitate flight when a woman came hurrying along the road. The doctor's wife seemed to recognise her. She whispered to the doctor. The doctor turned to William.

'You know this woman, my boy, don't you?'

'No,' said William, 'I've never seen her before.'

The doctor looked pleased. 'Doesn't remember his own mother,' he said to his wife: 'quite an interesting case.'

The woman approached them aggressively. The doctor stepped in front of William.

'Come after my boy,' she said. 'Sayin' 'is hours ended at five an' then keepin' 'im till now! I'll 'ave the lor on you, I will. Where is 'e?'

'Prepare yourself, my good woman,' said the doctor, 'for a slight shock. Your son has temporarily – only temporarily, we trust – lost his memory.'

She screamed.

'What've you bin doin' of to 'im?' she said indignantly, ''e 'adn't lorst it when 'e left 'ome this mornin'. Where is 'e, anyway?'

Silently the doctor stepped on to one side, revealing William.

'Here he is,' he said pompously.

''Im?' she shrilled. 'Never seed 'im before.'

They stared at each other for some seconds in silence. Then William saw the real house-boy coming along the road and spoke with the hopelessness of one who surrenders himself to Fate to do its worst with.

'Here he is.'

The real original house-boy was stepping blithely down the road, an extemporised rod over his shoulder, swinging precariously a jar full of minnows. He was evidently ignorant of the flight of time. He saw William first and called out cheerfully:

'I say, I've not been long, have I? Is it all right?'

Then he saw the others and the smile dropped from his face. His mother darted to him protectively.

'Oh, my pore, blessed child,' she said, 'what have they bin a-doin' to you – keepin' you hours an' hours after your time an' losin' your pore memory an' you your pore widowed mother's only child. . . . Come home with your mother, then, an' she'll take care of you and we'll have the lor on them, we will.'

The boy looked from one to another bewildered, then realising from his mother's tones that he had been badly treated he burst into tears and was led away by his consoling parent.

The doctor and his wife turned to William for an explanation. Their expressions showed considerably less friendliness than they had shown before. William looked about him desperately. Even escape seemed impossible. He felt that he would have welcomed any interruption. When, however, he saw Miss Polliter running towards them down the field he felt that he would have chosen some other interruption than that.

'Oh, there you are!' panted Miss Polliter. 'Such *dreadful* things have happened. Oh, there's the dear boy. I don't know what we should have done without him . . . rescuing children and animals at the risk, I'm sure, of his own dear life. I must give you just a little present.' She handed him a half-crown which William pocketed gratefully.

'But, my dear Miss Polliter,' said the doctor, deeply concerned, 'you should be resting in your room. You should never run like that in your state of nervous exhaustion . . . never.'

'Oh, I'm quite well now,' said Miss Polliter.

'Well?' said the doctor amazed and horrified at the idea.

'HERE IS YOUR SON,' SAID THE DOCTOR POMPOUSLY.

"IM?' SHRIEKED THE WOMAN, 'NEVER SEED 'IM BEFORE.'

'Oh, yes,' said Miss Polliter, 'I feel ever so well. The flood's cured me.'

'The flood?' said the doctor still more amazed and still more horrified.

'Oh yes. The river's risen and the whole place is flooded out,' said Miss Polliter excitedly. 'It's a most stimulating experience altogether. We've saved a lot of animals and two children.'

The doctor was holding his head.

'Good heavens!' he said. 'Good heavens! Good heavens!'

At that moment two more women descended upon the group. They were the mothers of the infants. They had searched through the village for their missing offspring and at last an eye-witness had described their deliberate kidnapping and imprisonment in the doctor's house. They were demanding the return of their children. They were threatening legal proceedings. They were calling the doctor a murderer and a kidnapper, a vivisectioner, a Hun and a Bolshevist.

The doctor and the doctor's wife and Miss Polliter and the two mothers all began to talk at once. William, seizing his opportunity, crept away. He crept down the road towards the cave.

At the bend in the road he turned. The doctor and the doctor's wife and the two mothers and Miss Polliter, still all talking excitedly at the same time, began to make their way slowly up the hill to the doctor's house.

He looked in the other direction. There was a large crowd surrounding the cave; men were just coming along the road from the other direction with pickaxes to dig his dead body from the rock.

He went forward very reluctantly and slowly.

He went forward because he had a horrible suspicion that the doctor would soon have discovered the extent and the cause of the 'flood' and would soon be pursuing him lusting for vengeance.

He went forward reluctantly and slowly because he did not foresee an enthusiastic welcome from his bereaved parents.

Ginger saw him first. Ginger gave a piercing yell and pointed down the road towards William's reluctant form.

'There – he *is*!' he shouted. 'He's not dead.'

They all turned and gaped at him open-mouthed.

William presented a strange figure. He seemed at first sight chiefly compounded of the two elements, earth and water.

He turned as if to flee but the figure of the doctor could be seen running down the road from his house after him; following the doctor were the doctor's wife, the infants' mothers with the infants and Miss Polliter. Even at that distance he could see that the doctor's face was purple with fury. Miss Polliter still looked bright and stimulated.

So William advanced slowly towards his gaping rescuers. 'Here I am,' he said. 'I – I've got out all right.'

He fingered the half-crown in his pocket as if it were an amulet against disaster.

He felt that he would soon need an amulet against disaster.

'Oh, where have you been?' sobbed his mother, 'where *have* you been?'

'I got in a flood,' said William, 'an' then I lost my memory.' He looked round at the doctor who was running towards them and added with a mixture of fatalistic resignation and bitterness, 'Oh, well, he'll tell you about it. I bet you'll b'lieve him sooner than me an' I bet he'll make a different tale of it to what I would.'

And he did.

But Miss Polliter (who left the doctor's charge, cured, to his great disgust, the next day) persisted to her dying day that the river had flooded and that the hose pipe had nothing to do with it.

And she sent William a pound note the next week in an envelope marked 'For a brave boy'.

And, as William remarked bitterly, he jolly well deserved it. . . .

CHAPTER 10

WILLIAM IS HYPNOTISED

IT seemed to William and his friends the Outlaws as if school had been comparatively peaceful till Bertie appeared upon the scene. Bertie was the headmaster's nephew who had come to the school for a term only (which to some of his associates seemed long enough – if not too long) and stayed with his uncle. Unfortunately he was in William's form.

Everybody except William and his form agreed that Bertie was charming. He had a beautiful smile and beautiful manners. Old ladies were often heard to declare that he must have a beautiful soul. He would recite beautiful poetry for hours on end without stopping. He had a beautiful conscience. It was his beautiful conscience that annoyed the Outlaws most. His beautiful conscience was always making him tell his uncle anything that he thought his uncle ought to know. And the things which he thought his uncle ought to know were just the things which the Outlaws thought his uncle ought not to know. For instance, Bertie thought that his uncle ought to know that the

Outlaws were keeping white mice in their desks, while the Outlaws on the other hand did not consider it at all necessary for his uncle to know this. Again, Bertie's beautiful conscience forced him to tell his uncle that it was the Outlaws who had stitched up the sleeves of his gown so securely that he had to go about for a whole morning without it, and this again the Outlaws did not consider it necessary for his uncle to know. Bertie thought that his uncle ought to know that it was the Outlaws who, when a committee meeting was being held at the school, had changed the position of all the neatly printed little notices, 'To the Committee room', so that the committee, after wandering desolately round and round the corridor, found themselves ultimately in the bootroom in the basement. All these things Bertie conscientiously reported to his uncle, and his uncle visited the full force of his wrath upon the Outlaws.

The uncle, as a matter of fact, did not quite approve of Bertie's beautiful conscience, but he could not resist the temptation to get a bit of his own back on the Outlaws. He'd suffered in (comparative) silence from the Outlaws for so long. He'd always found it so difficult ever to lay the crimes for which he was certain that the Outlaws were responsible at the Outlaws' door, that it was impossible to resist the circumstantial evidence laid ready to his hand day by day by the conscientious Bertie. The result of all this was that the advent of Bertie coincided with a period of what the Outlaws regarded as unmerited persecution for the Outlaws themselves. Sometimes idly on the way home from school the Outlaws laid tentative plans of vengeance upon Bertie, but they never came to anything because the Outlaws tempered boldness with discretion. A mass attack upon the unctuous Bertie would be highly enjoyable, but the resultant interview with Bertie's uncle would be less so. The Outlaws cherished a deep respect for Bertie's uncle's right arm. They had come into pretty frequent contact with it, they were good judges of its strength and they knew that it was not to be unduly provoked.

'What it comes to,' said William indignantly as they walked home discussing the situation, 'what it comes to is that we simply can't do *anythin'* excitin', not while he's about, simply can't do *anythin'*. . . .'

'There was yesterday,' agreed Ginger discon-solately, 'when he went an' told old Markie that it was *me* what had put the hedgehog into Mr Hopkins' desk.'

A blissful smile dawned upon William's freckled countenance. 'It was funny, wasn't it?' he said simply, 'watchin' him put his hand into the desk without lookin' to get his ruler out an' then seein' his face. . . .'

Ginger gave a constrained smile. 'Yes,' he said, 'I

daresay it seems funny to you. It seemed funny to me yesterday but you din't have to go up to *him* about it this mornin'. An' that old Bertie grinnin' at me all over the place afterwards. . . .'

'Never mind,' said Henry consolingly, 'it's only for a few weeks now. He's goin' at the end of the term.'

'What worries me,' said William slowly, 'what worries me is lettin' him go at the end an' nothin' happenin' to him. I mean him goin' round makin' trouble all over the place like this an' then jus' goin' off at the end of the term an' *nothin'* happenin' to him.'

'Let's jus' be glad he's going off at all,' said Douglas philosophically, 'an' never mind nothin' happenin' to him. Let's jus' be glad that things'll stop happenin' to *us*.'

''Sides,' said Henry, 'if we *did* do anythin' to him . . . you know what he is . . . he'd tell *him* an' then jus' go about grinnin' at us. You know what he is.'

'Yes,' said William sadly and thoughtfully, 'we know what he *is*, but – but it jus' seems a pity, that's all.'

It was the Vicar's wife who first suggested the pageant, but once suggested the idea took root firmly in the village. Mrs Bott of the Hall took it up and so did Mrs Lane and Mrs Franks and Mrs Robinson and all the rest of them.

Arrangements went on apace. The junior inhabitants of the village looked on with apathy. 'No children to be in it' had been pronounced very early on in the proceedings. The activities of the Outlaws may have had something to do with the distrust with which the senior element of the village regarded the junior.

William and the Outlaws treated the whole affair with superior contempt.

'A pageant!' said William scornfully. 'Huh! An ole *pageant*. Jus' dressin' up in silly clothes an' having a procession. Jus' a lot of silly ole grown ups. Huh! Well, I bet I could make a better pageant than that ole thing, if I tried. I *bet* I could. Well, *I* wun't be in it not if they asked me. I'm *glad* they've not asked me 'cause I wun't be in it not if they did.'

He was none the less disconcerted and secretly much annoyed to hear that despite the ban on children Bertie was to be in it. Bertie was to be Queen Elizabeth's page.

Queen Elizabeth was Mrs Bertram of The Limes. She was a newcomer to the village and her most striking characteristic was a likeness to the Virgin Queen as represented in her more famous portraits. She considered it a great social asset and was never tired of drawing attention to it. It was, as a matter of fact, Mrs Bertram who had first suggested the pageant to the Vicar's wife. And despite the reluctance of the committee and the ban they had placed on the younger generation, Mrs Bertram had insisted on having a boy page.

'We've – er – never found it wise,' objected the Vicar's wife mysteriously.

'But where I used to live,' said Mrs Bertram indignantly, 'we always had children in the pageants. Without exception. There's something so romantic and beautiful about children.' Mrs Bertram, it is perhaps unnecessary to add, had no children of her own.

The Vicar's wife cleared her throat and spoke again still mysteriously.

'Perhaps,' she said. 'Quite. But one or two occasions in this village have been spoilt – *wrecked* by the presence of certain children.'

'The children of this village,' said Mrs Franks still with something of the Vicar's wife's mysteriousness in her tone, 'seem, I don't know why, to bring bad luck to anything they take part in—'

Someone seemed to murmur the two words 'William Brown' in the background and then they all changed the subject.

But the next day Mrs Bertram met Bertie and fell in love with him at once. She found him 'adorable' and at the next pageant committee meeting she announced her firm intention of having him for her page.

'I *must*,' she said, 'I *must* have a page and he's a perfectly adorable boy. He'll look sweet in white satin.'

'Oh, *he's* all right,' said the Vicar's wife with relief, 'there couldn't be any harm in having *him*. It's—' again she dropped her voice and spoke darkly, mysteriously, 'it's some of the others.'

So it was decided that Bertie was to be Queen Elizabeth's page.

Bertie received the honour complacently. He, like Mrs Bertram, thought that he was eminently suitable for a page. Moreover, his position as the only boy in the village admitted to the pageant delighted him. While still retaining his charming manners towards the grown-ups he began to put on more and more side when with his contemporaries. He was enjoying his position of supremacy over the Outlaws. He had a pretty well-founded idea that William, despite his professed scorn, would have loved to be in the pageant. He smiled sweetly and meaningly at William in public and in private informed his uncle that it was William who had introduced the mouse into the drawing class and the handful of squibs into the anthracite stove. . . .

Bertie joined William in the playground where William and the Outlaws were playing leap-frog during 'break'.

'Hello, William,' he said pleasantly.

He always affected great friendliness of manner towards William and the Outlaws.

William, gathering together all his forces, took a mighty leap over both Ginger's and Douglas's back, landed on his nose, picked himself up, said 'Crumbs!' in a tone that expressed mingled pride in his exploit and concern for his nose and ignored equally Bertie's presence and greeting.

'You've heard about the pageant they're going to have in the village, haven't you?' went on Bertie, still with his most engaging smile.

William addressed his Outlaws still as though not seeing Bertie. 'Bet I can do three of you,' he said vaingloriously. 'Come on, Henry . . . you stand with Ginger and Douglas and I bet I'll do all three of you.'

'They decided not to have any children in at first,' went on Bertie suavely, 'but in the end they're to have just one for Queen's Elizabeth's page. Me.'

Ginger, Douglas and Henry crouched down. William went back, took a mighty run, a mighty leap and – landed on the top of Douglas and Henry. The wriggling mass of Outlaws disentangled themselves. William's nose, brought a second time in violent contact with the asphalt playground, began to bleed copiously. William held to it a grimy handkerchief already saturated in ink and mud and watched with interest the effect of the introduction of the fresh colour.

Douglas was persisting with great indignation that William had broken his neck and Henry was accusing Ginger of having completely altered the shape of his head by sitting on it violently on the asphalt. They abused each other with gusto and great impartiality.

'Sayin' you could jump three an' then bangin' down upon us like that . . . I tell you my neck's completely broke. I can feel it.'

'You couldn't go on livin' if your neck was broke.'

'Well, I prob'ly won't go on livin'. I feel almost as if I was dyin' now.'

'Well, you must've stretched out after I started – all of you. You didn't look as stretched out as all that before I started . . . and look at my nose . . . your neck can't be so bad 'cause it's not even bleedin'.'

'You don't know what it *feels* like havin' someone *sittin'* on your head. It's absolutely squashed up my ears somethin' terrible.'

'Jolly good thing. They stuck out enough before.'

Above the fracas came again Bertie's sweet and patient and gentlemanly little voice.

'I'm going to be Queen Elizabeth's page. I'm going to be the only boy in the pageant.'

'I'll try again,' said William, still holding his handkerchief to his bleeding nose. 'I bet I do it this time. I din' go back far enough that time before I started an' I bet if I go far enough back and you keep more squashed up together I can do all three of you.'

'No, thanks,' said Ginger holding his neck in both hands. 'I'm not goin' to be jumped on again with a broken neck.'

'Nor me,' said Henry tenderly caressing his ears, 'with squashed ears.'

A crowd of boys had gathered round.

Bertie again upraised his clear young voice.

'Don't you wish it was you going to be in the pageant instead of me, William?' he said.

William, his hair dishevelled, his collar burst open, his nose still bleeding, turned and surveyed him with slow scorn.

'Huh!' he said, 'you think you're goin' to be in the pageant, do you? Huh? Well, let *me* tell *you*, you're *not*. An' you think I'm not goin' to be, do you? Well, let *me* tell *you*, I *am*.'

It was a momentous announcement. There was a dead silence. Everybody gazed at William with surprise. Then Bertie giggled.

'You needn't be so mad at me, William,' he said. '*I* didn't tell uncle that you put the mouse in the drawing class.'

At that moment the bell rang.

*

No one had been more surprised by William's announcement than William himself. He had as a matter of fact felt a certain secret soreness at Bertie's inclusion in the pageant. Had William been asked to be a page in the pageant in the first instance his indignation and scorn would have known no bounds. But the fact that children were expressly excluded had filled him with as great an indignation as the enforced inclusion of him in any capacity would have caused him. And the further news that the ban had been raised in favour of Bertie – and Bertie alone – was regarded by William as an insult.

But until William saw the faces of his schoolmates, impressed despite themselves by his solemn prophecy, he had hardly realised what he had said. He had meant merely to reply crushingly to the obnoxious Bertie. He found that he had issued a challenge which he must justify or lose his prestige for ever. He spent the next two lessons (Geography and History) biting his pencil frowningly and wondering how on earth he could eject Bertie from the pageant and insert himself. He had a dark suspicion that even were he successful in ejecting Bertie he would be the last boy in the village to be chosen as page in his stead. He was so quiet during those lessons that the Geography and History masters, comparing notes afterwards, thought (without any great regret) that perhaps he was sickening for something.

On the way home with Ginger, Douglas and Henry he was still thoughtful. After a desultory conversation on the state of William's nose and Ginger's neck and Henry's ears and the question whether William could or could not have cleared them if he'd had a longer run and they'd been closer together, and a brief commentation on the dullness of the Geography and History lessons (William's failure to provide the usual diversions had been much resented by his class-mates), Henry suddenly said:

'I say, William, what you said, 'bout him not bein' in the pageant, you din' *mean* it, did you?'

Nothing on earth would ever induce William to retire from a position he had once taken up.

' 'Course I did!' said William.

'Well, how c'n you make him not be in it an' you in it?' challenged Douglas incredulously.

William took refuge in a 'Huh!' dark with meaning and hidden triumph, and added, yet more darkly and mysteriously, 'Jus' you wait an' see.'

Rather to William's consternation his prophecy spread round the school and opinion on the subject became sharply divided. William's followers supported William and Bertie's followers supported Bertie. For Bertie had a following and quite a large one. Any boy who lived as Bertie lived in close proximity to the

headmaster and suffered from such a beautiful conscience as Bertie's would have had a large following
among a certain kind of boy. Though only, as I said,
boys of a certain kind, they were very enthusiastic and
admiring followers. They delighted in jeering at
William from behind hedges and from the safe protection of their garden walls.

'Yah! Who thinks he's goin' to be in the pageant?
Yah! Who thinks he's goin' to be a page? YAH!'

On these occasions William, passing below,
assumed his famous expressionless expression and was
apparently deaf, dumb and blind so that the pleasure of
jeering at him was small indeed. William possessed the
art of retaining an utterly impassive, almost imbecile,
cast of features in face of all provocation. It had always
been one of his most potent weapons. Whenever the
jeerers ventured into open country it was quite
different. William then allowed his natural expressions
and actions free play. William's followers supported
him loyally. Their faith in him was unbounded.

' 'Course he's goin' to be in the pageant,' they said.
'Jus' you wait an' see.'

It was a common sight during that time to see a
follower of William's engaged in personal combat
with a follower of Bertie as the only means in their
power of deciding whether or no William would be in
the pageant in Bertie's place.

William's immediate circle – the Outlaws – though their official attitude was that there was no doubt at all that William would be in the pageant, and that Bertie would not, were in private apprehensive.

'I don' see how you're goin' to get into the ole pageant,' said Ginger despondently.

William, even before his Outlaws, preserved the attitude of the hero who trusts in his star.

''*Course* I am,' he said with his inimitable swagger, 'jus' you wait an' see.'

But in his heart William too felt apprehensive. The day of the pageant grew nearer. Bertie was attending rehearsals and behaving as beautifully as ever and there seemed no likelihood at all of his being ejected. For a few days William made frenzied efforts to establish himself in general public opinion as the sort of boy who would make a suitable page, but he soon gave them up. He himself found the process too wearing and no one else seemed to notice it. Wild plans of imprisoning Bertie and stealing his costume were dismissed as impossible. The day of the pageant drew nearer and nearer. William looked forward to it now solely as a day of humiliation. He regretted bitterly his rash prophecy, though in public he continued doggedly to support it with innumerable 'Huhs' and ''*Course* I ams'. The personal humiliation William minded less than the humiliation to his loyal followers who were fighting so many battles on his behalf.

The day of the pageant had arrived. The pageant was to pass along the village street and the boys of William's school, including William, were to be massed outside the school to cheer it on its way. The only member of the school who would not be present was Bertie who would be in the pageant as Queen Elizabeth's page. Bertie had gone home for the week-end to visit his parents and to fetch the page's suit which his mother had made for him. Bertie was enjoying his triumph over William. To make it yet more enjoyable he had told his uncle just before he went away that it was William who had uprooted the daffodils in his garden bed by night and planted rows of brussels sprouts in their stead, and William had had a painful interview with the Head on the subject that very morning. As it happened to be one of the few crimes committed in the neighbourhood for which in reality William was not responsible, he felt perhaps unduly bitter about it, forgetting, as one is apt to do on such occasions, how many crimes he had perpetrated successfully and without retribution.

He walked slowly along the road with Ginger and Henry and Douglas.

'*Well*,' commented Ginger with a deep sigh. There

was no need to ask what he meant. The day had come and William's public downfall seemed imminent and inevitable.

'Yes,' said Douglas bitterly. 'I dunno why you kept sayin' all the time that you *was* goin' to be in it.'

'Yes,' said Henry with spirit, 'why ever did you go an' *say* a silly thing like that for?'

'Oh, shut up!' groaned William, relinquishing his heroic pose and abandoning himself to his depression.

And just then they saw the figure of Bertie coming jauntily down the road towards them with a suitcase in one hand. He approached them with his beautiful smile.

'Hello!' he said. 'I've been home for the weekend. Got my page's clothes with me in the case. I'll have to be quick and change or I shan't be ready in time. You goin' to watch, I suppose?'

His meaning smile flickered at William as he spoke. William had assumed again his expressionless expression.

'S'pose we'll have to,' said Ginger with an air of boredom.

'I've had a jolly good time at home for the week-end,' went on Bertie who was evidently longing to confide in someone.

'An uncle took me to a sort of show,' he went on excitedly, 'an' I saw a hypnotiser – you know, a man what hypnotised people an' they did whatever he told them.'

'How'd he do it?' said William.

'He jus' looked at 'em an' moved his hands about an' then told them they were cats or dogs or rabbits till he told 'em to stop an' when they came to they didn't remember anythin' about it.'

William was silent for a minute then he said slowly: 'Bet you couldn't do it on me.'

'I bet I could if I tried,' said Bertie.

'All right,' said William. 'Go on, try.'

Bertie, after a moment's hesitation, put down his suitcase and made several passes with his hands before William's face.

'Now you're a cat,' he said without much conviction.

To the surprise of both Bertie and the watching Outlaws William promptly dropped on hands and knees and began to miaow loudly. Bertie's face beamed with pleasure.

'Now you're a dog,' he said.

William began to bark.

'Now you're a rabbit,' said Bertie almost drunk with delight and pride. William, not quite knowing what else to do, wrinkled his nose up and down.

'Now you can come unhypnotised.'

William stood up slowly and blinked. 'I don't

313

remember doin' anythin',' he said. 'I bet I din' do anythin'.'

'But you *did*,' squeaked Bertie excitedly, 'you *did*. You acted like a cat and a dog and a rabbit.' He appealed to Henry, Douglas and Ginger, 'didn't he?'

Henry and Douglas and Ginger, who were not quite sure yet what William wanted of them but were prepared blindly to support him in anything, merely nodded.

'*There!*' said Bertie triumphantly.

'I don't believe you,' said William, 'anyway, try again . . . try something harder – cats and dogs and rabbits are easy, I expect – try making me do somethin' I can't do ordin'ry. I can't turn cartwheels ordin'ry.'

The Outlaws gasped at this amazing untruth. But Bertie believed it. He was ready to believe anything. He was drunk with his success as a hypnotist. Again he made passes before William's face and again William assumed the languishing expression which he believed suitable to one hypnotised. 'Turn cartwheels,' ordered Bertie. William turned six perfect cartwheels one after the other.

'Now come unhypnotised,' said Bertie quickly, anxious to prove his success.

'You did turn cartwheels, didn't he?' to Douglas, Ginger and Henry.

Again Douglas, Ginger and Henry nodded non-committally.

''*Course* I didn't,' said William aggressively. 'I don' believe you. I *can't* turn cartwheels.'

'But you can when you're hypnotised,' said Bertie, 'you can do things when you're hypnotised that you can't do when you're not hypnotised. You can do anything you're told to when you're hypnotised. I'm a hypnotiser, I am,' he swaggered about, 'I can make anyone do anythin' I like, I can.'

'I remember readin' about hypnotism in a book once,' said William slowly, 'it said that anyone could hypnotise people standin' jus' near them, but that only a very good hypnotiser could make someone do somethin' where he couldn't see them.'

'I could,' boasted Bertie, 'I bet I could. I'm a good hypnotiser, I am.'

'I don't b'lieve you did me at all,' said William calmly. 'I don' remember anythin'.'

'But you *don't* remember when you're hypnotised,' explained Bertie impatiently, 'that's all the point of it . . . you don't remember.'

'Then how'm I to know you *did* hypnotise me?' said William simply.

'*They* saw,' said Bertie, pointing to his witnesses. 'I *did* hypnotise him, didn't I?'

The witnesses, still not quite sure what their

leader's tactics were, again nodded non-committally.

'I don't b'lieve you, any of you,' said William defiantly, 'you're pullin' my leg – all of you. He din't hypnotise me. I *din't* carry on like a rabbit, or any of those things he said.'

Bertie stamped, almost in tears.

'You did. . . you *did*.'

It was evident that more than anything in the world at that moment he longed to convince William of his hypnotic powers.

'In this book I read,' went on William, 'it said that only very good hypnotisers could make anyone do anything with a suitcase. It said that those two were the hardest things that only very good hypnotisers could do – makin' anyone do something when they can't see 'em doin' it, an' makin' anyone do somethin' with a suitcase. . . . But we've not got a suitcase here,' he glanced contemptuously at the case that contained Bertie's page's costume. 'That's too small to be a suitcase. It wun't do.'

'It *is* a suitcase and it would do,' said Bertie, 'it *would* do and I bet I could make you do something with it.'

'I bet you couldn't,' said William. 'I don't believe you're a hypnotiser at all. Tell you what,' slowly, 'I'll believe you if—'

'Yes?' said Bertie eagerly.

'If you c'n make me do the two hardest things –
make me do somethin' with this suitcase an' make me
do somethin' where you can't see me doin' it. . . . Tell
you what—' as though a sudden idea had just struck
him.

'Yes?'

'I'll b'lieve you if you can make me take this suitcase down the road, an' in at our gate an' round to the
back of our house an' back again here – an' tell me to
do somethin' – any thin' – to prove to me that I've
done it.'

' 'Course I can do that,' said Bertie boastingly. 'I
can do that easy 's easy.'

'Well, do it then,' challenged William.

Bertie again made passes before his face and
William composed his features again to that utter
imbecility that was meant to imply the hypnotised
state.

'Take the suitcase,' ordered Bertie, 'and take it
down the road and round your house an' back again
here an' do somethin' – anythin' – to show yourself
that you've been hypnotised.'

Still wearing his expression of imbecility, William
picked up the suitcase and walked down the road. The
watchers saw him go down his drive and disappear
behind his house. After a short interval he reappeared,
still with the suitcase and still with his imbecile

expression, though, a close observer might have noticed, rather breathless, came again along the drive up the road and joined the four watchers. He held something in his clasped hand. Bertie's face was a proud beam of triumph.

'There, you've *done* it,' he shouted gleefully. 'Now, come unhypnotised.'

William assumed his normal expression and blinked.

'I didn't do it,' he said. 'I told you, you couldn't make me do it.'

'But you *did* it,' screamed Bertie.

William slowly unclasped his hand and looked down at something he held in his palm.

'Crumbs!' he ejaculated as though deeply impressed, 'here's Jumble's ball what he was playing with this mornin' in the garden. I *knew* it was in the garden. So I *must*'ve jus' been there.'

'So you *know* I'm a hypnotiser now,' said Bertie with a swagger.

'Yes, I do,' said William, 'I know that you're a hypnotiser now.'

But at that moment the church clock struck two and Bertie suddenly remembered that as well as being a hypnotiser he was Queen Elizabeth's page.

'Crumbs!' he said seizing his suitcase, 'I must go and change or I'll be late.' He smiled maliciously at

STILL WEARING HIS EXPRESSION OF IMBECILITY, WILLIAM
PICKED UP THE SUITCASE AND WALKED DOWN THE ROAD.

William. 'Hope you'll enjoy watchin' the procession,' he said as he ran off.

William, Ginger and Douglas and Henry stood and watched him.

Then William turned and, followed by the others, went quickly homewards.

Bertie stood in his bedroom surveying the contents of his suitcase. He found them amazing. They seemed to comprise not a page's costume but a much worn and tattered Red Indian costume. Still – he knew that his mother had made the costume in accordance with Mrs Bertram's directions. Perhaps Elizabeth's page wore this curious costume. Perhaps he didn't dress like other pages. Anyway his mother and Mrs Bertram ought to know. They'd arranged it between them. And there didn't seem to be anything else in the case. He turned it upside down. No . . . only this. This must be right. Anyway, the only thing to do was to put it on. It must be all right really. He put it on . . . fringed trousers and coat of a sort of khaki and a feathered head dress. He looked at it doubtfully in the mirror. Yes, it did look funny, but he supposed it must be all right . . . really he supposed that they must have made it from pictures of the real thing . . . it must be the sort of dress that Elizabeth's page really wore. . . . Funny . . . very funny . . . he'd never looked at it before and his mother had made it without trying it on, but if he hadn't *known* that it was a page's costume made by his mother according to directions sent to her by Mrs Bertram, he'd have thought it was a Red Indian costume. It was just like a Red Indian costume. But he was late already. He hurried down to the Vicarage where the actors in the pageant were to assemble.

Mrs Bertram had been having hysterics on and off ever since she got up. Mrs Bertram was 'highly strung'. (Other people sometimes found a less flattering name for it.) Mrs Bertram often hinted to her friends that the very fact of her likeness to Queen Elizabeth was a strain on the nervous system which less heroic natures would have found unendurable. Everything seemed to have gone wrong with her since she began to dress for the pageant. Her dress was wrong, for one thing. She was sure that it was fuller than it ought to be. It took six or seven people to calm her about her dress. Then her hair was wrong. It wouldn't go right. The hairdresser came to do it and she tore it down again and had another fit of hysterics. The six or seven people managed with great difficulty to calm her again and get her hair up though she said that there was a fate against her and that she was going to sue the hairdresser for damages and that she'd never looked so hideous before in her life. The Vicar's wife with the kindest intention and merely in order to calm her, assured her that she had, and this brought on yet another attack. Then, fearing that the six or seven comforters were going to desert her, she said that her shoes were wrong. She said that they were the wrong shape and that they were too big. When her six or seven comforters had proved that they were not too big she had another fit of hysterics and said they were too small. The whole cast was needed to calm her over the shoes and she said finally that she supposed she'd have to wear them and that she hoped she'd never again be called upon to suffer as she'd suffered that day and that people who weren't highly strung had no idea how terribly she suffered and that she got no sympathy and she knew she looked a sight and that if this was how she was going to be treated she'd never be in another pageant as long as she lived. Then she suddenly began to suffer about her page. She'd told him to be here an hour before time and he wasn't and she wouldn't act without a page. She didn't care what anyone said. She *wouldn't* act without a page. It was an insult to expect her to. Her comforters assured her that Bertie would be in time. Bertie had never been known to be late for anything. Then she began to suffer about Bertie's stockings. She'd said particularly to his mother that he must have good white silk stockings to go with his white satin suit and shoes and she was sure that he'd have common ones. If he came in common white silk stockings she wouldn't act in the pageant. She *wouldn't* act with a page with common white silk stockings. It would be an insult to expect her to. . . .

It was just a quarter past two and he hadn't come and she'd *told* him to be there by half-past one, and if he didn't come she wouldn't be in the pageant at all. She wouldn't stir a foot, and she'd sue them all for damages. She sat down on a chair with her back to the door and had another fit of hysterics. The whole cast had gathered round her. They were looking rather anxious. It was time to start on the procession and her page had not turned up and they saw that nothing on earth would persuade Gloriana to set off without him. She was still suffering terribly.

'I – I'll just send up to his uncle's, shall I?' Sir Walter Raleigh was suggesting when the door opened and Bertie stood upon the threshold dressed in the full panoply of a Red Indian. He smiled very sweetly at them all.

'I'm so sorry I'm so late,' he said. 'Am I all right?'

'Is that you, child?' said the Virgin Queen in a hoarse, suffering voice without turning her head.

'Yes,' said Bertie. 'I'm so sorry I'm late.'

The others were watching him, paralysed with horror.

'Have you got on *common* silk stockings?' said Elizabeth wearily, still without turning her head. 'I'm *worn* out body and soul by all this worry and anxiety and responsibility . . . have you got on *common* silk stockings, boy?'

Bertie looked down at his khaki frilled trousers.

'No,' he said brightly. 'No, I haven't got on common silk stockings at all.'

Elizabeth was evidently still too worn out in body and soul to turn her head. She appealed to the others.

'Has he got on common silk stockings?' she asked.

She was met by silence. The others were still gazing at Bertie in paralysed horror.

Slowly Mrs Bertram turned round. She saw Bertie dressed as a Red Indian. Her face changed to a mask of fury. She uttered a piercing scream.

'You wretch!' she said, 'you hateful, *hateful* boy!'

Then with a spirit worthy of the Virgin Queen herself she flung herself upon the unfortunate Bertie and boxed his ears. . . .

The cast of the pageant was in despair. Bertie, battered and bewildered, had fled howling homewards and Mrs Bertram was suffering more terribly even than she had suffered before. She was engaged in gliding from one fit of hysterics into another. In the intervals she informed them that nothing would induce her to take part in the pageant without a page and that it was an insult to ask her to and that they couldn't get a page now and that she'd sue the boy's mother for damages and that she'd sue them all for damages and that she'd never get over this as long as she lived. They stood around her offering sal volatile and smelling salts and eau de Cologne and sympathy and consolation. They coaxed and soothed and pleaded all to no avail. Mrs Bertram continued to suffer. A mild and well-meaning suggestion from Sir Walter Raleigh that she should lend her clothes to someone else who didn't mind going without a page threw her into such a state that Sir Walter Raleigh crept into the next room so that the sight of him might not continue to increase her sufferings.

'All right,' he remarked despondently to the Vicar's favourite aspidistra, 'she *can* sue me for damages and write to the papers about me' (these had been two of her milder threats). '*I* don't care.'

Then when the chaos and despair and suffering were at their height there came a loud knock at the door. The Vicar's wife went to open it. In the doorway stood a boy with a bullet head, fair bristly hair and very plain features. It was Ginger. His expression was a good imitation of William's most expressionless one.

'I DON'T LIKE HIS FACE,' MRS BERTRAM PRONOUNCED
FINALLY, 'BUT THE SUIT'S ALL RIGHT. LET HIM COME.'

WILLIAM HID HIS ELATION BENEATH HIS IMPASSIVE
STARE.

'Please do you want a page?' he said stolidly,
'' 'cause I know a boy what's got a page's suit what
wun't mind comin' an' bein' a page for you.'

There was a moment's tense silence, then someone
said eagerly:

'Where is he? Would it take long to fetch him? Could he put it on quickly?'

'He's here,' said Ginger, 'an' he's got it on.'

He put both his fingers into his mouth and emitted an ear-splitting whistle.

Another boy, wearing a white satin suit, emerged from the shadow of the doorway, and entered the room. It was William. He wore his imbecile expression as a protection against awkward questions. They gazed at him open-mouthed. Mrs Bertram abruptly ceased suffering. In the background the Vicar's wife was heard to groan: 'It's that boy . . . it's that awful William Brown.'

But there was no time for asking questions. Already the procession would be late. Mrs Bertram cast one piercing glance at him from head to foot. The others watched her breathlessly. His stockings were of quite good silk and his suit was perfect.

'I don't like his face,' she pronounced finally, 'but the suit's all right. Let him come.'

The route of the procession of the pageant was thickly lined. Near the school was a massed crowd of boys among which stood Bertie looking bewildered and infuriated. Next to him stood Ginger who was explaining the situation to him patiently for the twentieth time.

'You see, Bertie, you're such a good hypnotist . . .
you hypnotised him so that he didn't know what he
was doin'. You told him to go round with that case an'
do somethin' to show himself that he'd been round . . .
well, you'd hypnotised him so well that he did two
things 'stead of only one. He got the ball *an*' he
changed the things in the case. He ran upstairs an'
changed them for somethin' of his own . . . while he
was hypnotised an' din't know what he was doin'. He
was only doin' somethin' to show that he'd taken it
round same as you said, but he din' know what he was
doin' 'cause he was hypnotised. Well, when he came to
himself an' found that white satin suit where his Red
Indian things used to be (Douglas's fetchin' that
Red Indian suit back from your house now) he din't
know what to do. He din't know where it'd come from
'cause he'd been hypnotised when he put it there an'
when he heard the pageant wanted a page he thought
he'd try 'n help them by puttin' on the white satin suit
that he didn't know where it had come from 'cause of
bein' hypnotised an' go over jus' to see if he could help
them 'cause he'd heard that they wanted a page an' he
din't know where the white suit had come from 'cause
of bein' hypnotised when he put it there . . .'

But a sudden hush fell. The procession was
approaching. The central figure of the procession
was Mrs Bertram as Queen Elizabeth. Behind her

walked William as the page. Behind William walked his dog Jumble – as unpolished-looking a dog as was William a boy. Jumble had joined the procession as it passed William's gate and had firmly resisted all attempts at ejection. William's appearance had been the subject of many unfavourable comments as he passed along the route behind Mrs Bertram.

'*Most* unsuitable . . .' had been the kindest.

'To think of choosing *that* boy when they must have had the choice of all the boys in the village.'

'I'd heard that they were going to have Bertie. . . . I must say I think they'd have been wiser to have a boy of that type.'

'There's nothing in the least – *romantic* or mediaeval about his face.'

'When I think of him chasing my cat yesterday . . .'

'He's so *plain*.'

'And that *awful* dog.'

But when he reached the place where the school was massed a mighty roar of applause burst forth. The air rang with cheers and with 'Good ole Williams'.

William was not quite proof against it. The expressionlessness of his expression flickered and broke up for just a second. He grinned and blushed like any *jeune première*.

Then, hastily composing his features again to imbecility, he passed on. . . .

JUST
WILLIAM

RICHMAL CROMPTON

WITH A FOREWORD BY SUE TOWNSEND

'He's mad,' said Mr Brown with conviction. 'Mad. It's the only explanation.'

There's only one William Brown – better known as Just William. Whether he's trying to arrange a marriage for his sister or taking a job as a bootboy as step one in his grand plan to run away, William manages to cause chaos wherever he goes.

MORE
WILLIAM

RICHMAL CROMPTON

WITH A FOREWORD BY MARTIN JARVIS

'Me?' said William in righteous indignation. 'Me? I'm helpin'!'

When Aunt Lucy tells William that 'a busy day is a happy day', William does his best to keep himself very busy indeed. Not everyone appreciates his efforts to cheer up Christmas Day – and when a conjuring trick with an egg goes badly wrong, William finds himself in more trouble than ever!

WILLIAM
AGAIN

RICHMAL CROMPTON

WITH A FOREWORD BY LOUISE RENNISON

'Me?' said William in horror. 'I've not done any-thing.'

Totally bankrupt, William and Ginger can't even buy sweets. But then William has a brilliant idea – they could sell Ginger's twin cousins as slaves! Before long, the irrepressible William is in serious trouble – again . . .

WILLIAM
THE FOURTH

RICHMAL CROMPTON

WITH A FOREWORD BY FRANK COTTRELL BOYCE

'He's – he's more like a nightmare than a boy.'

Whether he's occupying a bear suit that's slightly too small for him, cloaked in mystery as a fortune-teller or attired in the flowing robes of a Fairy Queen, William is unmistakably himself: trouble in human form. Only Great-Aunt Jane manages to take William on at his own game – and win!

STILL WILLIAM

RICHMAL CROMPTON

WITH A FOREWORD BY TONY ROBINSON

'If all girls are like that –' said William. 'Well, when you think of all the hundreds of girls there must be in the world – well, it makes you feel sick.'

William's natural desire to do the right thing leads him into serious trouble, as usual, and when blackmail and kidnapping are involved, it's no surprise. Even when he turns over a new leaf, the consequences are dire. But it's his new neighbour Violet Elizabeth Bott who really causes chaos – and no one will believe that it's not William's fault . . .

A selected list of titles available from Macmillan Children's Books

The prices shown below are correct at the time of going to press. However, Macmillan Publishers reserves the right to show new retail prices on covers, which may differ from those previously advertised.

Richmal Crompton

Just William	978-0-330-53534-2	£5.99
More William	978-0-330-53535-9	£5.99
William Again	978-0-330-54518-1	£5.99
William the Fourth	978-0-330-54517-4	£5.99
Still William	978-0-330-54470-2	£5.99
William the Conqueror	978-0-330-54519-8	£5.99
William in Trouble	978-0-330-54471-9	£5.99
William the Good	978-0-330-54525-9	£5.99
William at War	978-0-330-54520-4	£5.99

All Pan Macmillan titles can be ordered from our website, www.panmacmillan.com, or from your local bookshop and are also available by post from:

Bookpost, PO Box 29, Douglas, Isle of Man IM99 1BQ

Credit cards accepted. For details:
Telephone: 01624 677237
Fax: 01624 670923
Email: bookshop@enterprise.net
www.bookpost.co.uk

Free postage and packing in the United Kingdom